Cassie Scot

~~Para~~Normal Detective

by Christine Amsden

Twilight Times Books
Kingsport Tennessee

Cassie Scot: ~~Para~~Normal Detective

This is a work of fiction. All concepts, characters and events portrayed in this book are used fictitiously and any resemblance to real people or events is purely coincidental.

Paladin Timeless Books, an imprint of
Twilight Times Books
P O Box 3340
Kingsport TN 37664
http://twilighttimesbooks.com/

First Edition, May 2013

Library of Congress Control Number: 2013939161

ISBN: 978-1-60619-275-7

Cover art by Ural Akyuz

Printed in the United States of America.

Acknowledgments

I would like to give special thanks to all those who struggled through early drafts of this book. Your insights helped bring Cassie to life.

Linda Amsden
Stephen Amsden
Krys Bradley
Leah Cypess
Vylar Kaftan
Crystal Layne Futrell
Anaea Lay
Austin Morgan
Kat Otis

I

My parents think the longer the name, the more powerful the sorcerer, so they named me Cassandra Morgan Ursula Margaret Scot. You can call me Cassie.

I've been called a lot of things in my life: normal, ordinary, and even a disappointment. After the Harry Potter books came out, a couple of people called me a squib. Since I haven't read them, I have to assume it's a compliment.

Personally, I prefer normal, which is why the sign on my office door reads: Cassie Scot, Normal Detective.

You have to understand that around here, when your last name is Scot, people are easily confused. Not only are my parents powerful practitioners, but I have six talented brothers and sisters. Plus, my family hasn't always been known for its subtlety. When weird stuff happens around here, the people who are willing to believe in magic are prone to suspect the Scots.

The day I opened for business I got a call from an old woman who swore her cat was possessed by the devil. She also swore she'd read my web site, which clearly stated the types of work I did and did not do. Exorcisms were on the *No* list, and while I hadn't specified pet exorcisms, I would have thought it was implicit.

After that auspicious beginning, things went downhill. It seemed people weren't entirely convinced an associates' degree and six months as a deputy with the local sheriff's department was quite enough to fly solo. I did receive three calls from people asking me to cast spells to look for lost items, two from people in search of love potions, and two from a pair of neighbors who each wanted me to curse the other. I thought I'd hit bottom, when a ten-year-old boy wandered into my office one afternoon and asked me to help him summon Cthulhu.

It was a near thing, but I managed to rein in my sarcasm long enough to explain the difference between the real world and horror worlds created by early 20th century authors. He seemed more or less convinced until my brother, Nicolas, came in and started juggling fireballs. Kind of walked all over my point there. He's a terrible showoff; thinks it helps him with women. For some reason, it does.

Sheriff David Adams, my old boss, stopped by once every couple of weeks to "check in on me" and offer me my old job back, but I always turned him down. It's not that I disliked working for him. In fact, he was a great boss and a good person, albeit in a little over his head. Eagle Rock, Missouri and the surrounding areas have more than their fair share of strange and unexplained cases. I would even say that I took the job hoping to use my better-than-average knowledge of the paranormal to help protect the innocent, but in the end, those cases only served to remind me that despite my magical connections, I, too, was in over my head.

So I quit. I got my private license, rented an office, and installed a frosted-glass door like in the old movies, then I furnished it with the sort of busted up furniture that costs an arm and a leg to make look just right. The old wooden filing cabinets behind the desk and the office chairs in front came from estate sales, but I finished the desk myself. It was a beautiful piece of lacquered mahogany before my hammer and screwdriver got through with it. I did that just after the cat exorcism call. It was rather therapeutic.

By the door stood an old wooden hat and coat rack, while a nearby table held a coffee maker, compliments of my father. I don't actually drink coffee, but Dad told me to have some for my customers, so I brewed a pot every morning while I waited for my tea to steep.

It was June seventh, a Monday. I'd spent six months in that office, going in to work at eight o'clock, breaking for lunch at noon, then going home at five. That day started like all the others. I updated my Facebook page to say that I was at work and feeling happy, though that last was a lie. I checked a few of my favorite blogs, posted a couple of comments that I'm sure were witty and insightful (though I suspect no one read them), and twittered that I'd just posted the comments to the blogs. After that, I picked up my kindle and buried myself in some mystery novel I'd already solved by page thirty seven.

When the door opened, I was sure it would be Sheriff Adams, in for his bi-weekly chat. As the months wore on with no sign of a client, it was becoming harder to politely turn him away. In recent weeks, my replies had become more blunt, bordering on rude. I'd really hoped he wouldn't come around that day, on my half year anniversary, but just in case he did, I had come up with a story about a statewide convention I was sure would help me find work. The convention part was true–the certainty less so.

All I can say is, it was a good thing my parents were rich.

I lowered my kindle and raised my eyes to the door. The words, "Hi, Sheriff," started to spill from my mouth when I realized it wasn't the sheriff at all. It was Frank Lloyd, from Lloyd and Lyons, a man I knew more by name and reputation than anything else. My boyfriend had a summer internship with his firm, and a good friend of mine worked there as a receptionist. Lloyd and Lyons specialized in family law, especially divorces, and the gist of the reputation was that if your marriage was over, you'd better get to Frank Lloyd before your soon-to-be-ex did.

He looked impressive. His head nearly touched the top of the door frame, while his broad shoulders aimed for the sides. He wore an expensive dark gray suit that had been tailored to fit his athletic frame. His face was long and handsome, featuring deep, dark eyes and a wide, curving mouth that formed into a friendly smile. It was the sort of face that commanded trust.

Lightning flashed outside, brightening the room for the space of a few seconds, and I couldn't help but smile. All the best stories started in a thunderstorm, didn't they? I had no idea what the day would bring, but one thing was for certain–Frank Lloyd was not there to ask me to exorcise his cat.

He laid a long, black umbrella carefully against the wall near my coat rack, and strode confidently inside. "Hello, Ms. Scot."

"Cassie, please." I wound my way out from behind my desk and offered him my hand. He took it, his grip firm and self-assured.

"Cassie, I'm Frank Lloyd." He released my hand but held my gaze as if he could take the measure of me by looking through them to my soul. Some practitioners can do that, actually, but I've never met one.

"Yes, I know." I did not lower my eyes. Something told me that would be a sign of weakness. "What can I do for you?"

"I've got a small job for you, if you have the time." It was very diplomatic of him to say it like that, since I'm sure he knew I had plenty of time.

"What's the job?"

"Serving a subpoena,"

Ok, so it wasn't sexy, but it was a job, and it had nothing whatsoever to do with magic–or so I thought. In any case, at that precise moment, I couldn't have been more excited if he'd dropped some line out of a movie about someone trying to kill him.

"I can do that," I said in a calm, measured tone. "Who am I serving?"

Frank broke eye contact and stepped around me to the desk, where he laid his black briefcase down and opened it. On top of a large sheaf of papers lay a plain white envelope with the name, "Belinda Hewitt" written on it in a long, slanted handwriting.

Hewitt was another name that many people in town associated with magic, though few were diplomatic where the Hewitts were concerned. Even my mom called them witches, and she normally wouldn't call a woman a sorceress. (She thinks it's sexist.)

Belinda was a gifted herbalist and an expert potion maker. A gift is, well, it's a special power tied to the soul in such a way that it can be performed almost without thought, and it has a strong influence over the bearer's personality. Most sorcerers possess a gift, as well some seemingly ordinary people, though in the latter case you can usually find magic in their family tree. Belinda's gift was growing things, but to say she had a green thumb would be like saying a diva could sing. Belinda could grow things, anything, anywhere, and under conditions that would starve farmers out of business.

She sold a lot of her plants and herbs to local practitioners, though my parents refused to buy from her because of the other thing she liked to do–brew potions, especially love potions. At any given time, she would have two or three men under the influence of powerful love potions that made them hopelessly devoted to her. She would play with them for a few months or a few years, depending upon how interesting they were, and then cast them aside. She'd torn families apart.

It was mind magic. My dad liked to say that magic itself is never black; only the uses to which it is put, but mind magic is already tinted a deep, dark gray.

As far as I knew, though, Belinda had never been married, so I wasn't sure what Frank Lloyd would want with her.

"Belinda Hewitt?" I raised an eyebrow at Frank in question.

"My firm is filing a class action lawsuit against her on behalf of a number of men who feel her love potions have caused them irreparable harm."

"Gutsy move." I approved. I whole-heartedly approved, but going head to head against a practitioner could be dangerous, to say the least. For the most part, they did what they wanted to do and suffered no interference, not from other practitioners and certainly not from the law.

I wasn't entirely sure what Belinda would do to me if I showed up on her doorstep with a subpoena. Probably, nothing, since she'd have to answer to my parents for anything she did to me. That may even have been why Frank chose me, but I wasn't too proud to take advantage of my connections when it suited me, as long as the job itself was normal.

"Belinda is going to curse you for this," I said as I took the envelope from Frank.

He just smiled. "I appreciate your concern, but it's about time the sorcerers living in our community learn they are not above the law."

What a beautiful sentiment. I used to think that way, back when I'd first dreamed of becoming a cop. Fat chance, though. The sorcerers in our community owned this town, whatever most of the regular folks thought. Everyone else was tolerated, and that included me.

For a minute, I wondered if I should try to talk him out of it. As much as I loved the idea of putting an evil witch in her place, Belinda wasn't someone to mess with. That either meant he didn't believe in magic, didn't understand it, or he had an ace up his sleeve.

I lifted my eyes to his and saw the confident, calculating expression there. He was still sizing me up, and in that moment I took the measure of him as well. He wasn't insanely successful because he walked into anything blindly.

"You have an ace," I said. It wasn't a question.

Frank just smiled.

"I'll run this over to Belinda's this morning," I said. "I'll give you a call when it's done."

Frank reached into his pocket and pulled out a business card. "If this works out, we may have some more work for you."

I took the card from him, letting a genuine smile touch my lips. Lightning struck again and thunder rumbled. "Thank you."

He packed up his briefcase and left without another word.

2

MOST OF THE MAGICAL PRACTITIONERS IN THE AREA PREFERRED TO LIVE outside of town, and Belinda was no exception. Her two-story home was within easy walking distance of Table Rock Lake. Since my parents hated her, I had never been to her home, but I knew the house doubled as a shop, and many of her potions were for sale, including some weaker love potions.

It should have been an easy job, since Belinda's shop was open for business Sunday through Thursday from nine to one. As I headed to her place, the rain even eased to a drizzle, and a hopeful ray of sunshine peered out between a couple of dark clouds.

For someone who liked to use rich men, the house itself was relatively modest. It had a red brick facade in front and white vinyl siding along the sides and back. There wasn't much noteworthy about it, but perhaps that was because the eyes immediately moved to the surrounding grounds.

The front yard didn't seem to have a single blade of regular grass, or any weeds for that matter. Instead, marbled walkways wound around beds of flowers, bushes, trees, and other plant life. The house stood on a full acre and from what I could see, she could have charged admission. Whatever else she was, Belinda possessed a true gift.

I parked my powder blue Jaguar in the long, circular drive behind a red pickup truck that earned only a passing glance. I grabbed the leather folder I had used to keep the subpoena flat and dry, and made my way to the front door, which was also the entrance to her shop. A black and orange sign hung from the door, proclaiming in no uncertain terms that the store was CLOSED. Beneath the sign, her clearly posted hours indicated she should have been open for business at nine o'clock. I glanced at my watch, which read nine thirty.

Frowning, I rang the doorbell. I heard it chiming through the house, but there were no echoing footsteps or movement of any kind. I rang it again several times before backing away from the porch.

Something felt wrong. Sure, she could have just gone off to the grocery store, and gotten hung up on the way back, but that didn't explain why several hanging vines on her porch were starting to wilt.

I took another look behind me at the red pickup, really seeing it for the first time. It couldn't have been Belinda's. Granted, I didn't know for sure what she drove, and she might need a truck for hauling landscaping materials, but given her tendency to lure wealthy or powerful men into her web, I suspected she would only drive new vehicles. This one was at least five years old and had a dent in the fender, as if it had once been in an accident. That dent, more than anything else, told me the truck wouldn't fit with her neatly ordered existence. It might have belonged to a customer, of course, but if the shop was closed, then where had the customer gone?

There was an unattached two-car garage a little further down the driveway, so I took a quick walk that way to see whether Belinda had a car parked inside. It didn't tell me as much as I'd hoped. There was a car parked inside—a fairly new red Jeep Cherokee with a personalized license plate reading "LUV U," but beside it was a spot for another vehicle. She could be out, or she could just have one car, but it didn't shed any light on who owned the pickup truck.

My natural curiosity tempted me to explore the grounds and the back of the house, but good sense told me the place would be warded. I didn't like it, but I didn't have much choice in the matter. I would have to wait. I reasoned that if Belinda had gone out during business hours, she would have to come back soon.

But as I walked back to my car, I couldn't help noticing the hanging plants again. I shivered, dug the cell phone out of my purse, and dialed the sheriff's number. I ignored the tiny twinge of guilt telling me I was taking advantage of our friendship, reasoning that I had a hunch, and my hunches were usually good.

"Sheriff here," said the deep male voice on the other end of the line.

"Hi, it's Cassie."

"Cassie, I was just thinking of stopping by. When are you coming back to work?"

"Not today." I allowed myself a moment of pride. "I have a job."

"Really?" He didn't sound enthusiastic. "What do you need?"

"I found an abandoned car out by the lake," I said. "I've got a weird feeling about it, and wondered if you'd run the plates."

"All right. I'm in the middle of a dozen things, but give me the number and I'll get back to you as soon as I can." It was a mark of his esteem for me that he didn't even question the request. I only prayed he didn't have his hopes up about my returning to work for him.

After rattling off the number and disconnecting the call, I moved my car to the other side of the circle drive so I wouldn't impede anyone trying to get in. Then I put it in park and cast about for something to do. I hadn't brought my Kindle because I had expected this to be a twenty minute job, so I pulled out my cell phone and sent random text messages to my friends. Every so often, I would get one back, but most of the others had things to do.

My mind began to wander, and I found the wilted plants became the central focus of my daydreams. Somewhere out there, I imagined Belinda hurt or dead. Something wasn't right, and while I didn't want to jump to conclusions, conclusions were busily jumping at me.

I checked my watch so often it didn't seem to move, but at some point it must have, because an hour came and went. No one came by her store, and no one returned to the truck, but I had no idea how much business Belinda usually got. Maybe she had so little business that she didn't bother opening the shop some days. I had an idea how that felt, and I had only been at it for six months.

I had nearly decided to give up when a car pulled into Belinda's driveway, but it wasn't hers. The metallic blue Prius looked familiar, but I didn't place it until Evan Blackwood stepped out, raked his fingers through thick, nearly black hair that touched his shoulders in waves, and started up the front path. He had spent a moment looking at the pickup truck parked right in front, but he hadn't seemed to notice me on the far side of the drive.

I hadn't seen Evan more than a handful of times since high school, which was something of a relief to my father, who has hated Evan's father for longer than I've been alive. We weren't exactly what you would call friends, at least not since junior high. I'm not quite sure what we were, actually, though we were best friends in grade school.

After that, things got complicated. From a shy, uncertain boy, Evan became an outwardly confident teen with a bit of a dark side. More than a bit, depending upon who you asked.

He looked like a man on a mission as he strode up the porch steps and took a long look at the CLOSED sign. I opened my mouth, ready to shout out to him what little I knew for sure–that Belinda wasn't home–but something held me back. What was Evan doing there? The obvious answer, that he needed some plants or herbs, didn't fit because I knew for a fact that Henry Wolf, the man to whom Evan was apprenticed, refused to buy from Belinda for the same reasons my parents did. I even thought Evan's father had issues with the woman, though that might have simply been a rumor I picked up somewhere.

A sick possibility twisted my stomach–perhaps Belinda had him under one of her spells. True, he was about half her age, but it wouldn't be the first time she had gone after a much younger man, especially one as dangerously attractive as Evan. Plus, he was among the most powerful sorcerers in town, one of those who could get away with anything and knew it, and Belinda would find that compelling.

When Evan rang the bell, I decided to announce my presence. I stuck my head out the car window and called, "She's not home."

I must have caught him by surprise, because as he jumped, so did two rocking chairs, a swing, and the wilting plants. With a startled gasp, I drew my head back inside the car. It's not a good idea to sneak up on a sorcerer, especially one with a strong gift like telekinesis. I didn't think he would consciously hurt me, but accidents happened. With six powerful brothers and sisters, I knew that better than anyone.

"Hi, Cassie. It's been a long time." Evan tucked his hands into his jeans pockets and strode down the driveway to my car. He had given up wearing all black, choosing instead blue jeans and a dark green t-shirt that suited his complexion far better than the black ever had. Not that I had ever told him, but I thought black made him look more washed out than dangerous.

He looked good. And tall. He'd grown in the last three years, so that by the time he reached my car, he practically towered over me, giving him, impossibly, an air of even greater strength than before.

"Hi, Evan," I said with forced casualness. "You locked yourself away with Mr. Wolf and haven't come down to see the rest of us mere mortals."

"He's a slave driver, but he's brilliant." He leaned against the side of my car, the image of practiced nonchalance.

"What are you doing here?" I asked, though I wasn't sure I wanted to know the answer. I wished he would look at me. You can tell if someone is the victim of a love potion if you can get a good look at the whites of their eyes–they'll look a little pink. He wasn't avoiding my gaze, precisely, but he did seem preoccupied with the red pickup truck.

"I'm just here for some herbs." It was such an obvious lie, I couldn't believe he bothered to tell it.

"Come on, Evan. Mr. Wolf doesn't buy from Belinda."

He glared at me, and it occurred to me that not too many people would have called him on the lie. "She's the only herbalist within three hundred miles to get mandrakes this year."

Another lie, but this time, I let it go. I didn't fear him, the way many others did, but if he didn't want to talk, I couldn't force an answer from him.

"So, how long have you been waiting here?" Evan asked.

"About an hour. I was just about to give up, actually. This was supposed to be a quick job."

"Yes." He ran his fingers through his hair. "I didn't think you'd still be here."

"You knew I'd be here?"

"I told Frank to hire you."

"You did?" I had no idea whether to feel flattered or embarrassed. On the one hand, I didn't want to feel like some kind of charity case, but on the other hand, I needed the business, and it was nice of Evan to think of me. I hadn't even known he knew about my business.

"Of course I did," Evan said, as if it were obvious. He shifted slightly, and looked down at me, finally holding my gaze long enough for me to see that the whites of his eyes didn't contain a hint of pink, although by then I had pretty much dismissed the love potion theory.

"I admit," Evan continued, studying my face, "I was surprised to find out you'd quit the sheriff's department, but I always knew you'd do well at whatever you tried."

I turned my face away, so he wouldn't see the slight flush creep across my cheeks. I wouldn't admit it to him, but it had been a long time since anyone had paid me a real compliment, and there was something about his matter-of-fact tone that told me he meant it.

"How do you know Frank?" I asked.

"I'm helping him with his lawsuit."

"Really?" I didn't know which surprised me more: that he was helping with a lawsuit at all, when doing so might require him to share knowledge, something sorcerers avoided at all costs. Or that he was helping with this lawsuit, involving love potions. Rumor had it, he had cast a few himself once upon a time, and surely this would revive those rumors.

"Master Wolf told me to do some community service as a senior project, so I volunteered as an expert witness."

"You're an expert on love potions?" I meant to tease him, but somehow the words sounded all wrong as soon as I said them. My mind flashed back to a day when we were fourteen, and I asked him if the rumors were true. Afterward, he didn't speak to me for six months.

"I don't brew them, if that's what you mean."

"Of course not. I'm sorry. I shouldn't have said it."

For a minute, he didn't say anything, then he took a deep breath and reached through the driver's side window to take my hand in his. Though casual and almost unconscious, the touch sparked something in me that reminded me of the silly crush I'd had on him in high school. It had been entirely one-sided, since he had never noticed me as a woman, and ill-advised for even more reasons than that, not the least of which was our families' mutual enmity. Still, like dozens of other silly girls, I felt the attraction. To the danger? To his looks? To the power? I don't know. I'd like to think, in my case, it was to the boy he had been before all that, and who, deep down, I thought was still the real him.

"I'm not an oversensitive fourteen-year-old anymore," Evan said. "It's okay."

"Good." I pulled my hand away from his, and reminded myself that I didn't have silly crushes any longer. I had a boyfriend, after all.

Evan tucked his hands back into his pockets, and looked at the red pickup one more time. "You know, if Belinda hasn't shown up all morning, there's probably no point waiting around for her. You should go home."

It wasn't quite a command, but it came close. He knew who owned the red truck, I decided, and he had business here he didn't want me to see. Since I didn't see any hope of carrying out my business in the near future, I agreed to leave without much fuss, even if my curiosity gnawed at me.

"I'll stop by to see you sometime soon," Evan said. "We should catch up."

"Yeah," I said, barely aware of my rote response. "That would be great."

As I pulled the car out of the driveway, my cell phone rang. I answered it before turning onto Lakeshore Drive.

"Hi Cassie," Sheriff Adams said from the other end of the line. "I ran that check you asked for. Car belongs to Nancy Hastings."

"Really?" Nancy Hastings was Evan's cousin, and only sixteen or seventeen.

"She's a minor," Sheriff Adams said, "but we don't have any reports about her. Do you think there's a problem?"

"Maybe, but her car probably just broke down." I didn't believe it, not with Evan there, and acting so strangely, but if his family didn't want the sheriff's help, I wasn't going to involve him.

But my own personal curiosity refused to be assuaged, so as soon as I got off the phone, I found a place to turn around and headed back to Belinda's house. If Evan had been any other sorcerer, I might not have dared, but I thought I could handle him. He wasn't safe, as my father used to constantly remind me, but I understood him, to a point. He wouldn't hurt me.

He didn't hear me approach, which made sense when I saw him sitting on Belinda's front porch, surrounded by black candles, and lost in some kind of spell. Judging by the wicks, the candles had not been burning for long, but how long he might be there was anybody's guess. Spells could take anywhere from a few seconds to a few days to cast. Evan's position, his posture, and the black candles made it look to me as though he was attempting to break through whatever magical protections Belinda had on her house.

A gentle breeze began playing with my hair, tying it into tiny knots. The same breeze blew out the candles surrounding Evan, and very slowly, his posture shifted.

"How long have you been standing there?" he asked, and I couldn't tell, from his tone, whether or not he was upset.

"A few minutes."

"I should have known you wouldn't leave. You're too curious for your own good, you know that?"

"So my parents keep telling me. Evan, why are you trying to break into Belinda's house?"

"I don't want you involved with this," he said.

"I am involved. I used to work for the sheriff and even if I don't anymore, there are some things I can't ignore." I paused before adding. "Like breaking and entering."

"Are you threatening to call the sheriff on me?" Evan arched his eyebrows in a manner I can only call arrogant. He had perfected the look years ago, and it reminded me that he, too, was part of the untouchable elite that had helped drive me out of law enforcement.

"Of course not," I said, knowing I sounded petulant, but not caring. "It wouldn't do any good. It never does."

"Is that why you left the sheriff's department?" He had always been too perceptive, especially where I was concerned.

"Just forget it."

He narrowed his eyes, looking like he wanted to say something else, but I waved him off.

"I need to clean up here." Evan gave me an inquisitive look, as if he thought he needed permission to use magic in front of me.

"It's okay." I was used to watching the people around me perform magic; that wasn't the part that bothered me.

With an almost casual wave of his arm, all the candles flew into the air and threw themselves into the backseat of his car.

"I know that's your cousin's truck," I said.

His eyes searched my face. "How do you know that?"

"Does it matter?"

"My aunt and uncle were hoping to handle this quietly, in case someone decided to take advantage of the situation. I don't know what happened to her, but I don't want the wrong person to find her before I do."

"I had the sheriff run a license plate check," I said. "I asked him when I first got here, because it didn't look right, but when he told me who it was a few minutes ago, I did try to convince him to let it go."

"Okay, nothing to be done about it now." He ran his fingers through his hair again, and looked at the door.

"Can I help, since I'm here? You know I won't say anything."

"I trust you, but I don't want you hurt. I don't know what's going on here, but Nancy never went home last night, and when I started looking for her this morning, I couldn't even find her with a hair sample. Anything but blood can be fooled, but not without... skill." I had the impression he meant to say something else, more along the lines of power, but I didn't push.

"I can help," I said. "If magic isn't working, you need an investigator."

"Cassie–"

"I'm going with you or I'm calling the sheriff. Which is it going to be?" I was mostly bluffing, but I also found myself curious to know what he would actually do if I did call in the mundane authorities, as some of the practitioners liked to call them.

Evan closed his eyes tightly, and when he opened them again, he fastened his crystal blue eyes on me in a manner I had seen him use countless times to intimidate, though never with me. "I could stun you and lock you in your car. Is that what you want?"

I knew he'd done something similar to Marshall Burks in the ninth grade, leaving the boy on the school bus all night. Most people agreed that he'd had it coming for stealing a smaller boy's lunch money, but since Evan hadn't been speaking to me at the time, I hadn't felt like cutting him any slack. Besides, I thought the incident, along with many others, had more to do with him wanting to prove his own power. Well, he could pull that act on other people if he had to, but I refused to let him intimidate me.

"If you really think there's danger here," I said, "wouldn't I be in worse shape locked in a car, completely helpless?"

His eyes darkened, but he nodded, stiffly. "Fine, but stay quiet for a while. I'm not quite done with the protections."

I stepped onto the porch, but did not interrupt his spell casting. The magical world is full of all kinds of dangers. There are magical creatures, negative energies, unfriendly spells, and of course, other magic users. Sorcerers tend to be the worst. There is nothing so evil in the world as what humans can do to one another, or so Dad always said.

The point is, it's unwise to simply burst into a magic user's house. There would undoubtedly be wards, spells, traps, and protective plants. I had a feeling his earlier spell had disarmed most of the wards, but there were still the plants. Even wilted, the ivy wouldn't take kindly to trespassers.

After a minute or so, I felt a spray of dust on my face. It coincided with a small, almost unremarkable popping noise.

"All clear," Evan said.

I coughed and brushed the dust out of my hair.

He offered me his hand. "Just in case I missed something."

He made it sound like a request, but it wasn't. I took his hand, and with Evan slightly ahead, we stepped over the threshold.

Nothing happened.

"Hmm," Evan said. "That's not a good sign. Not even a tingle."

I'd never experienced what he was referring to, but I understood that sorcerers are weaker when crossing a threshold uninvited. Some magical creatures, such as vampires, can't cross a threshold at all.

Most of the first floor of Belinda's house was given over to a shop with shelves, bottles of potions, magical herbs, and a few new-age trinkets, some of which work. We breezed through it on our way in, and made a careful search of the rest of the house.

I would describe Belinda's decorating style as elegant. She chose rich colors and patterns that commanded attention and proclaimed wealth. She seemed to love knick-knacks. Her collection of crystal and porcelain flooded shelves, curios, and the tops of tables.

An efficient three-year-old could have destroyed the place in five minutes. Ten, with supervision. Belinda didn't have so much as a niece or nephew to pay her a visit.

We didn't speak as we looked through the formal living room, dining room, kitchen, and laundry room. There was no sign of Belinda. No sign of a struggle, either, but that didn't put me at ease. I was still very aware of the fact that I was trespassing in a witch's home.

Upstairs was more of the same. Belinda had three bedrooms: one for her, one for guests, and one that she had turned into an office. We looked in bathrooms and in closets, but nobody was home.

When we went back downstairs, I noticed a door leading to a screened-in back porch and started to turn the handle when my hand froze on the doorknob. My whole body stiffened, and my mouth went dry, so it took me several tries to alert Evan to what I'd seen.

"I found her," I finally managed, in barely a whisper.

Nancy Hastings, Evan's sixteen-year-old cousin, lay in a pool of her own blood, eyes vacant and staring. Her hair had been a rich, luminous brown but was now matted with blood. It looked as if her throat had been torn out.

"No!" The cry tore from his throat and before I had a chance to stop him, Evan was inside the room and leaning over the body, looking for any sign of life, and probably destroying any trace evidence the police might have collected. But I couldn't blame him. I would have reacted precisely the same way, if it had been my family. As it was, I had to wipe away tears before I could get to my phone and call the sheriff. The need for secrecy had passed.

"Sheriff's department, this is Jane Conway."

"Jane, it's Cassie. You need to get out to Belinda Hewitt's house right away. There's been a murder." I hung up before she could ask for more details.

Slowly, Evan rose to his feet and made his way back into the house with me. He had smeared the blood and left footprints on the floor, but somehow none of it had ended up on him. Or if it had, then he had some way of removing it.

"The police are on their way," I said, not sure if he would be upset with me for calling. Probably not. He looked too shocked to care.

"Yeah." He leaned against a wall and closed his eyes.

"You should call your uncle."

"Can I borrow your phone?" Evan asked. "Master Wolf doesn't believe in phones."

"Sure." I handed him the phone without analyzing his reasons for needing it, then I went out the front door to give him some privacy and wait for the sheriff. Brushing the fine layer of dust from the front steps–all that remained of the wilting plants–I sat down with my head in my hands.

Evan joined me a few minutes later, sat beside me without bothering about the dust, and silently handed me back my phone.

"I'm so sorry," I said.

He didn't say anything for a long time. Not that I expected him to. Really, what was there to say?

"I want to know what happened to her," Evan said. "Do you need a job?"

The request caught me off guard, and even though I wanted to take the job, for Evan and for the girl, I hesitated. I had a feeling this would become the type of paranormal investigation that had caused me to leave the sheriff's department. Also, the kind that had made me want to work there in the first place.

"It looked like a vampire attack to me," I said.

"It did, but some friends of Nancy told me they last saw her around noon yesterday, and that she had left to get some herbs before Belinda's store closed at one. I don't know why she would have stayed all afternoon, let alone after dark."

He took one of my hands in his, the way he had done earlier. He used to do those sorts of things in high school. Oh, never to me, but to other girls, the ones he ended up dating. Most of the rumors surrounding him suggested he wove his love spells with those casual touches. I didn't believe it, but I did yank my hand away, feeling as if it had been burned.

"Now that you mention it," I said, "there's another problem with the vampire idea. The porch should be within the threshold. A werewolf might have done something like that, but it's not the full moon, and again, it was daytime."

Evan stiffened. "Scott would have known if any of his wolves were hunting humans, anyway."

I had almost forgotten that one of Evan's best friends was a werewolf, yet another rebellious move, and obviously, one he had not outgrown.

In the distance, I heard the scream of approaching sirens.

"The sheriff will do everything he can to try to figure this out," I said, still uncomfortable at the idea of taking on a supernatural case. "Why do you think you need me?"

"Because there are things the sheriff doesn't know, and I can't tell him. For example, if it was a vampire attack, it will be tough to tell because she was protected. She won't turn."

Secrets and lies, I thought. But he had a point, and as much as I hated the idea of getting involved with anything supernatural, I knew I couldn't let a friend down, not even one as uncertain as Evan. Besides, a young girl had been murdered, and I couldn't let that go. When I closed my eyes, I could still see the blood and the silent scream on her young face.

"All right, I'll do it."

He offered me his hand and I shook it, somewhat tentatively, though he didn't hesitate. When he released my hand, the first car had arrived on the scene.

"So you're saying he broke into the house?" Sheriff Adams asked me an hour or so later, after I had already gone over the story with two of his deputies. It was noon, which meant I would miss my usual lunch date with my friends, but given what I had seen that morning, I didn't think I wanted to talk to any of them anyway.

"So did I," I said. "Are you going to charge us with breaking and entering?"

"Would it do any good?" he asked.

There wasn't a prison in the world that could hold Evan, but I didn't say so. I just gave the sheriff a blank look, and noticed that he had more hair than the last time I had seen him. Strange, since his hairline hadn't moved in the ten years he had been in town.

"If the girl was missing," Sheriff Adams continued, "you should have told me. And you say Belinda hasn't been home all morning?"

"That's right. I was supposed to serve her a subpoena." It was still in my car, but at this point I had serious doubts about my ability to deliver it. I didn't see how Belinda fit into any of this, but the fact that she was missing and I'd found a dead body on her back porch made finding her my top priority.

"And what time did Evan show up?"

"Ten thirty. Look, I've already been over this with Jeff and Ryan. I know the drill – that asking the same question in different ways might shake loose an important detail–but is there any way we can finish tomorrow?" I already felt worn out, though the day was barely half over, and somehow I would have to find a way to sleep with images of Nancy Hastings haunting me. I had never handled a murder before. Small towns like Eagle Rock don't have the kinds of murder rates the larger cities do.

The Sheriff sighed, slapped his notebook shut, and nodded. His face looked drawn and weary, and there was something a little off in his tone. Something I couldn't put my finger on. "I want you in my office bright and early tomorrow, though, all right?"

"I'll be there."

"Listen." The sheriff lowered his voice. "Right now, I'm mostly worried about you. Do you trust him?"

I glanced over my shoulder at Evan, who maintained a mask of cool composure that I was sure hid a world of hurt and anger over his cousin's fate. It reminded me of the day, in eighth grade, when he had explained his discovery that showing emotions was perceived as a weakness. I wanted to disagree with him, but I couldn't argue with results. After that, he only opened up to me, and then, only sometimes.

"Trust Evan? I don't know. I mean, it depends upon what you want to trust him with. He'll do just about anything to protect his family." We had that in common, as a matter of fact.

"There are rumors about him."

"There are rumors about me, too."

"Not the same kind." Sheriff Adams studied my face. "I don't pretend to understand the power game in this town, but by all accounts, he's winning it. He acts like nothing can touch him. Practically dared me to try to lock him up, almost like he wanted to prove it wouldn't work."

That sounded like something Evan would do, and I suspected the sheriff had pegged his motives correctly. I didn't say so, though. I just shrugged.

"He also said you're going to look into this murder for him. Can I trust him with you?"

"Yes." That much, I knew.

"All right. Listen, let me know what you find out and we'll do the same. There's no reason to duplicate one another's efforts on this."

"Okay." We both knew I wasn't being entirely truthful, but the sheriff had long-since accepted that I couldn't tell him everything, and most of the time he allowed me to use my own discretion.

"What's your dad going to think about you working for a Blackwood?" Sheriff Adams asked.

I didn't have a good answer for him, but I thought about Evan as I drove back to town, not so much to work out my father's feelings, which had more to do with Evan's father, but to work out my own.

3

Evan and I became best friends in the first grade. In elementary school he was a shy, uncertain boy who needed a friend, and I found myself drawn to that, as well as to his willingness to listen to me. I could even talk to him about magic, and for a long time, he was the only person outside my family who knew about my deficiencies. I let the rest think what they would; there was a certain power in that.

I never felt like I had to compete with him, and even though I knew he had magic of his own, I never saw it except in minor ways, silly tricks that even I could do.

He didn't use magic at school. That sort of public display was typically frowned upon, even in the Eagle Rock schools, where most of the students and teachers were aware of the rumors, speculation, and evidence not easily explained away. That's not to say they knew much of anything for certain. Heck, the most powerful families kept enough secrets from one another that even they could not come to a consensus on exactly how or why magic worked. Sometimes, I didn't know if warning kids away from using magic at school had more to do with keeping the information from the regular townsfolk, or from one another.

Whatever the reason for it, Evan took the admonishment to heart. Whereas my brother, Nicolas, showed off in ways that intentionally made him seem more like a clown or stage magician than anything else, Evan kept that aspect of himself shut up inside. He let people push him around for years, never striking back. I suppose it couldn't have lasted forever, especially when he found himself faced with the surge in magic that often comes with adolescence.

We were in seventh grade when Paul Ellerson, backed by two cronies, found him on the playground at recess one fall day. He and I had been talking, but we stopped when we saw the threesome approach, instantly wary. They didn't usually mess with me, except to offer insults I could more or less brush off. I won't go so far as to say they didn't affect me, but I always had friends and family to back me.

Evan had it much worse, partly because he took the insults more to heart, and partly because the boys sometimes got physical with him. Somehow, the teachers never saw.

"Look," Paul said, "it's the freak and his girlfriend."

I rolled my eyes and started to move away, taking Evan's hand to guide him with me.

"Isn't that sweet?" Paul said. "They're holding hands."

I dropped his hand, but kept walking away, trusting Evan to follow. This tactic often worked, but not on that fateful day. Paul's cronies blocked my escape, and when I turned around, Paul grabbed me by the hair and twisted, hard. It was the first time they had ever gotten physical with me, and it had me pretty scared, but I didn't have time to work myself into a real panic.

There was no warning. If there had been, I couldn't have been certain the attack was an accident, unplanned and instinctive. One second, Paul had me by the hair, and the next he was gone. I never even saw Paul's dramatic flight through the air, but I heard the ominous crack as he hit the tree, and when I did look, I saw him slumped against the trunk, eyes closed, red-gold leaves fluttering around his head where a trickle of blood ran down his cheek.

I had seen magical accidents before, but they had never involved Evan, who I had somehow come to think of as safe. He may have talked about magic, but I didn't see it, which gave me the illusion that he was like me. But he wasn't like me, and at that moment, the fact hit me as hard as Paul had hit the tree.

I tore my eyes away from Paul, directing them instead at Evan, who looked different. It might simply have been the product of my shattered illusions, but I never forgot the remorseless expression on his face.

His eyes, colder than an ice storm, took in Paul's accomplices, who stood with their mouths hanging open. Beyond us, a girl screamed, but I barely registered her reaction or the rush of teachers to the scene.

"Don't mess with my friends," Evan said. Then, as if to emphasize the point, Evan waved his hand, almost casually, and the two cronies toppled backwards.

They weren't really hurt, but then again, Evan had been in control when he knocked them over. Paul ended up in a coma for two months, and I'm not sure he was ever the same. I know Evan wasn't.

ꙮ

Despite my earlier resolve that I didn't want to talk to any of my friends, I found myself steering my car back into town, toward Kaitlin's Diner. Technically it was the Main Street Cafe, but my best friend, Kaitlin, had been working there since she was sixteen, and would probably inherit the place from her mom someday. I even thought Kaitlin's Diner had a better ring to it, but nobody agreed, least of all Kaitlin, who desperately wanted to find a way out of waitressing. Trouble was, she kept waiting around for a fairy tale.

Kaitlin and I used to be on the cheerleading squad together in high school, back in the days when anything seemed possible in love and life. We spent glorious afternoons pretending to be something special as a way to cover our own inadequacies. At least, that's what Kaitlin said once. I'm sure she wasn't talking about me.

Since small town gossip travels faster than the speed of sound, Kaitlin already knew about the murder by the time I arrived. So, apparently, did the other dozen or so customers milling around on a Monday afternoon, because they didn't even try to hide their attempts to overhear our conversation when Kaitlin sat down in a booth across from me and asked for details.

"Don't you have to work?" I asked.

"I'm on break. Lunch rush is over." She tucked a stray lock of red-gold hair behind her ear and leaned forward. "So come on, spill."

"I can't say much."

"You never can." Kaitlin was one of those in town who eagerly, almost desperately, believed in magic, but living on the outside, she didn't know much about it. It wasn't as if the fact of my family's sorcery was a secret, the obscurity was all in the details. How powerful? What, exactly, could they do? And how does the magic work? Therein lay the secrets.

As someone who lived between the two worlds, it was always a bit odd to me to see the range of disbelief in a town where so many practitioners dwelt. Some refused to believe at all, using faith in God or science like a shield. Others, like Kaitlin, eagerly believed any rumor, true or not. Most, though, lived somewhere in the middle, acknowledging the strangeness, but from a distance, as if it couldn't touch them if they didn't try to meet it head on. For the most part, they were right.

"What are people saying?" I asked.

"That Belinda Hewitt killed Nancy Hastings."

I cringed. "We don't know who killed her."

"But it was magic, wasn't it? People are also saying Evan Blackwood was there, swearing vengeance."

"She was his cousin."

"And Belinda is missing?" Kaitlin tried to make this sound very significant. "I wonder if he's torturing her."

Before I had a chance to defend Evan, the diner bell jingled and the man himself strode inside, angling straight for me. Kaitlin, sitting with her back to the door, didn't notice.

"Where do you think he's been all these years, anyway?" Kaitlin rushed on. "People are saying he learned black magic, and now that he's back, he'll take over the town."

Evan paused, no more than a couple feet from our booth, an odd expression that looked like a cross between a laugh and a grimace on his face. A few nearby customers hurriedly dropped money on the table and left the diner.

"I suppose I could," Evan said, deliberately drawing out the words, "but what would I do with it?"

Kaitlin's face went pale, but she did not turn to look.

"You shouldn't listen to rumors so much," I said. Not that she'd listen. I'd said so before.

"I'm sorry," Kaitlin whispered.

"He's not going to hurt you," I said, motioning for Evan to sit beside me. "And he couldn't take over the town if he wanted to. He was teasing."

He arched an eyebrow and shrugged, but accepted the invitation to sit beside me.

"What are you doing here?" I asked.

"Looking for you." He turned to Kaitlin, who was studiously avoiding his eyes. "Can I have a minute with Cassie?"

"Sure." She scurried out of the booth and practically ran for the double doors leading into the kitchen.

"You could have been nicer," I said, watching the doors swing shut.

"Me? I just walked in to discover my role in a dastardly plot to take over the town."

"She's just repeating what she's heard, and besides, you've never exactly denied any of the rumors. What did you expect to happen?"

"I don't know." He sighed. "I'll make things right with your friend."

"Don't do it for me."

"I need to be with my family this afternoon," Evan said, in clear dismissal of the subject, "but I wanted to talk to you first."

I nodded. "We need to find Belinda."

"That's what I thought, too. Can you meet me at her place tonight after dinner, maybe around seven?"

"Yeah, I'll be there."

"Great." He gave my hand a little squeeze before sliding back out of the booth and leaving the diner. My hand tingled where he had touched it, and as I stared at the spot, I remembered the love spell rumors, despite my best efforts to avoid the irksome thoughts. Hadn't I just told Kaitlin not to listen to rumors?

I glanced at my watch. It wasn't particularly close to dinner time, but since I might be up late, I decided to head home anyway. After I talked to Kaitlin.

4

My parents live in a modern-day castle. It looks like a cliché, complete with four towers and a drawbridge that swings out like a door. My dad often jokes about putting in a moat and getting a moat monster, but all that is just his personal flair. I assure you that the castle-home gets hot and cold running water, telephone, and electricity. No cable, but only because the phone company offered them a better deal on DSL and a satellite dish.

Inside, my mom's sense of style takes over, at least on the ground floor. She likes a more modern feel. The living room is furnished in black leather, the walls painted some shade of morning sunshine. She went with black and white for the kitchen, a sort of checkered pattern with occasional splashes of bright red.

My father got to do the second-floor library. It's got shelves stretching so high that he had to install one of those wheeled ladders to reach the topmost levels. A fireplace, nearly big enough to stand in, interrupts the shelves' progress along one of the walls. Nine high-backed armchairs, one for every member of the family, make a cozy formation in the center.

All in all, the styles clashed badly, but it was home.

When I arrived, drained and still a little shell shocked from the day's horrors, the entire family was gathered in the kitchen, where Mom was brewing some kind of potion in a cauldron on the stove. It seemed a little odd that everyone was gathered in one room before dinnertime, but I knew if I stopped to investigate, I would never get to my room and the solitude I craved.

I tried to sneak past the kitchen unseen, but six-year-old Adam spotted me and practically screamed my name. He dropped whatever snack he'd been munching on, and ran to wrap bony arms and legs around my waist.

I ruffled his light brown hair affectionately. "It's nice to see you too. Can't I just slip off to my room to get out of these shoes?"

"No!" Adam said. He smiled at me, which isn't fair, since his gift is charisma. It's not like mind control. You can say no to him, but it makes you feel very, very bad inside, like you just kicked a puppy. I don't envy my parents having to raise him. "Aunt Sherry's here!"

My mom had mentioned something about her sister coming to visit this week, but I had forgotten. Realizing my defeat, I let Adam take my hand and usher me into the kitchen, where I had missed the extra face in the crowd. Aunt Sherry was mom's identical twin sister, although they looked more like mother and daughter. My mom took daily potions that gave her the appearance of a twenty-something, and the older I got, the more she and I looked like twins. We had the same auburn hair, blue eyes, delicate facial features, and gently rounded curves.

"Nice to see you again, Cassandra," Aunt Sherry said.

"Cassie," I corrected, automatically. "How are you? How's Jason?"

It wasn't an entirely idle question. My cousin, Jason, was a vampire hunter, and while I hadn't seen him in years, I had been thinking about him earlier that day. If I learned for sure that we had a vampire in town, I would need to call a hunter.

"I worry about him," Aunt Sherry said. "He's all I have and he hasn't exactly chosen a safe calling. I don't even know where he is most of the time."

Mom turned away from the stove and pushed a lock of hair behind her ear. She gave me a strained sort of smile, like she was juggling too many things and couldn't handle it all. "Sherry reminded me that Christina needs her vampire vaccine, and Adam needs a booster."

"I'm not drinking that!" Adam made a sick face that made Christina giggle. She made her own face and shook her head back and forth.

"You will drink it," Dad said, firmly. Adam smiled sweetly at him, and Dad looked away. "That's not going to work. It's for your own good."

"What's it for?" Elena, the nine-year-old, asked in her usual ethereal whisper. She doesn't speak much, and when she does it's hard to hear. I think I was the only one who heard her, because Dad and Nicolas started in on a discussion about baseball, and Mom opened the oven door to pull out some rolls.

Elena deflated, and started to go back into her usual far-off place where, I assume, dead people dwell. Her gift is to talk to them, but some days I'm not sure gift is the right word for it. She seems to spend more time talking to the dead than the living.

"It's to stop the venom," I said to Elena, taking her hand and drawing her back into the world. "The venom is what turns a person into a vampire."

Elena nodded. "Yes, that's what grandpa said, too."

"He was a smart man." I worry about Elena. She's more stuck in the middle than any of the others, and no one seems to have the time and patience to draw her out.

"Dinner in thirty minutes," Mom said. "Elena, Juliana, set the table. Isaac, take the trash out. Adam, go wash your hands. Nicolas, you're on dish duty tonight. Isaac–no! Just pick the trash bag up with your hands and walk it to the trash bin."

Isaac had his eyes closed and, I assume, was working a spell to try to levitate the trash. He opened his eyes and scowled. "I was just practicing. Besides, it's not fair. Cassie doesn't have a job."

"Cassandra just got home from work and hasn't even had the chance to set her purse down," Mom said. I let her call me Cassandra. I lost that fight a long time ago.

"Pfft," Isaac said. "What work? She just surfs the net and reads trashy romance novels all day."

I froze, my mind flashing back to the young girl and the pool of blood. Isaac teased me all the time, more so than any of the others, and most of the time I took it in stride, but when I closed my eyes and still couldn't shut out the vision of death, I lashed out almost at random, swinging my purse and catching him in the back of his head.

"Ouch!"

"Cassandra!" Mom scolded in a tone she hadn't used with me in years.

"I'm sorry, I just—I had a bad day. I'd better go."

As I walked away, I heard Isaac muttering the words to a curse, so I stopped by the dining room table to remove a fresh snapdragon, a protection from most curses, from the vase in the center. I made sure Isaac saw it before I headed upstairs to my bedroom.

I suppose I should have been nicer to Isaac. He's the only one of my siblings, aside from me, who was born without a gift. Oh, he's got plenty of magic, but his lack of a special gift left him with a serious inferiority complex. He liked to take it out on me, because he thought he could, but there really wasn't anything he knew how to do to me that I didn't know how to block. At least, not yet. In a few years, if we didn't work out our issues, I could have some serious problems.

My bedroom was the entirety of the north tower, a place I liked to call my fortress of solitude. It was a circular room with a single window that looked out over the lake, providing a breathtaking view. From that height, I could imagine I existed above the world, rather than in it.

I hadn't decided if I preferred Mom's modern style or Dad's extreme retro, so I chose black. Everything from the walls to the bedding was a dark monochrome. I thought of it as my blank slate. The only color in the room was in my drawers and closet. I'm sure there's some deep, psychological reason that I did that–paint the walls black and myself in living color–but I'm not sure what it is.

I took a full thirty minutes to compose myself before going back downstairs to the noise and the chaos. You would think that, as the oldest of seven, I would thrive on it, but the best I can say is that I'm used to it. I always retreated to my fortress when I needed to.

Back in school, I used to retreat to my fortress when the others were taking their after school magic lessons. I sat through them for a few years, especially when Nicolas started learning, always desperately hoping to find an ounce of repressed talent, or maybe uncover a gift, but nothing manifested.

My parents' bedroom lay directly beneath mine, which was significant only because I could sometimes hear them talking through the vents. They had said some interesting things, unaware that I was listening. The entire family knew they'd had seven children, each of us spaced three years apart, because seven and three are powerful magical numbers that protected the family from evil magic.

What they didn't know was that Mom, and to a lesser extent Dad, weren't sure if I counted as one of the seven. I had heard them discussing it shortly after Christina's birth, when I was eighteen.

That summer, I had sat in on magic lessons again. I told my parents I just wanted to know what was out there, and how to protect myself from it, especially using herbs and potions that require knowledge more so than power, but in the dark of the night, in my fortress of solitude, I tried once more to call forth repressed magic. I no longer tried nightly, but every once in a while, when I got in a mood, I still made my futile attempts.

ꕥ

Dinner at the Scot house was mandatory family time. We ate in the dining room around a modern, straight-legged rectangular table with an espresso finish. The two leaves were not optional features for a family of nine, but even with both leaves in place, the large dining room did not feel at all cramped. Nine upholstered chairs in white (I'm sure magic was involved in keeping them that color) normally surrounded the table, but that night, they'd brought in the spare for Aunt Sherry.

There were always fresh flowers on the center of the table, such as the snapdragons, and they usually became the focus of a dinnertime lesson. That night was no exception.

"Elena, Adam, what are these called?" Dad asked, pointing to the flowers.

"Snapdragons," Adam said, without hesitation. Elena echoed him a second later, and in a much softer voice.

"Sap-gons," Christina ventured.

"That's right," Dad said. "Now, why does Cassandra have one tucked behind her ear?"

"Cause Isaac tried to curse her," Adam said.

Dad shot Issac an evil look, but did not publicly reprimand him. A few years ago, he probably would have, but I had convinced him that I needed to be able to stand up for myself, or no one would ever respect me.

Aunt Sherry leaned over and whispered, "Have you tried nettle? It sends the curse right back."

"Yeah," I said. "Too bad we don't have any right now. I may have to pick some up in town tomorrow."

"Isaac, stop!" Mom shouted. I wasn't sure what Isaac had been doing to earn a reprimand, though I could take a guess, but at that moment, no one was looking at Isaac. We were too busy gaping at Mom's deeply flushed cheeks. Suddenly, the snapdragons in the middle of the table burst into flames.

"Uh oh," Christina said.

Now, small accidental fires in the Scot household weren't all that unusual. Both my father and brother, Nicolas, were gifted fire starters, but Nicolas hadn't lost control in years, and Mom hadn't set a fire like that since she had been pregnant with him.

My fork clattered to my plate as I realized the truth. Mom wasn't a fire starter. Her gift was an eidetic memory, but she has been known to channel the gifts of her children during pregnancy.

Apparently, she had decided that I did not count.

Nicolas and Dad both rushed to put out the fire, but Dad got there first. With a quick wave of his hand, the flames were gone, but the room still felt hot to me.

Smoke curled around Mom's ears. "I, um, was going to say something tonight about-" She stopped and looked at us each in turn, though I think only Nicolas and I understood what was going on. Her gaze lingered on me, but I had no idea what she was trying to tell me with her eyes.

"Mommy had accident," Christina said, clearly oblivious.

"What's going on?" Juliana, my fifteen-year-old sister, asked.

"I'm pregnant," Mom said. "Due in December. I was just looking for the right time to tell everyone."

My mouth felt dry, and I wasn't hungry anymore. Congratulations were the furthest thing from my mind.

"You're going to have another baby?" Isaac said. "But didn't you say we were protected because there's seven of us?"

The weight and import of an overheard three-year-old conversation thudded into my head, and I couldn't be in that room anymore.

"I need to go," I said, standing. "I've got to finish a job."

"What job?" Mom asked. "Cassandra, come back."

Damn. I hadn't wanted to mention the job in front of my parents, not with a Blackwood involved. "It's not important—just delivering a subpoena but it's not done."

"It is important," Mom said. "It's your first customer. Why didn't you say something?"

"I don't get it. What's wrong with Mom?" Adam asked. "Cassie, sit down, please. We're eating dinner."

"No, Adam." In my mind, a puppy whimpered, but I ignored it.

"Cassandra," Dad said, "it doesn't have to be now, does it?"

"It was nice to see you again, Aunt Sherry," I managed to say as I fled from the room.

5

As I made my way back to Belinda's house, I tried to calm down and gain some perspective. A new baby wasn't the end of the world. There were a hundred reasons they could have decided to have another baby that had nothing to do with me. Maybe Mom just wanted another one. Maybe they had decided that three by three would be a more powerful protection for the family. It could even have been an accident, since neither scientific nor magical protections were one hundred percent effective.

Even if, worst case, she had decided I did not count as part of the protective seven, it wouldn't change much. I would still be a part of the family in all the ways I normally was. Magically speaking, I had always been an outsider.

I also realized I'd been rude, so I called the house to apologize. Dad answered the phone with his usual formal greeting. "Scot residence."

"Dad, it's me. I need to talk to Mom."

"Good girl," Dad said in a hushed voice. Then, more loudly, "Sheila, Cassandra is on the phone."

After a brief shuffle, Mom took the phone from him. "Is everything all right?"

"It's great, but I just realized I'd forgotten to say congratulations before I left. So, um, that's why I called. Congratulations."

"Thanks," Mom said, though her voice still sounded tense. "Did you finish your job?"

"Not yet. I may be out late."

"Well, take your time, but we need to talk when you get home."

That didn't sound good. "What about?" I asked.

"Not over the phone," Mom said. "Just find me when you get in tonight, all right?"

"Okay."

"Bye." Mom disconnected before I had a chance to question her further. I stared at the phone for a moment before shoving it back into my purse.

A minute or two later, Belinda's house came into view, looking still and empty in the darkening twilight. The police had gone, leaving behind yellow tape as the only evidence of their presence, and of the gruesome scene I had stumbled upon earlier that day.

Evan was already there, or at least his car was, so I parked my car behind his, and headed for the house. Getting inside took no time at all the second time around, despite the more obvious barricade of the police line, but I paused inside her shop, listening carefully for movement, and wondering if I knew what I was doing. I did need to find Belinda, and searching her house seemed like the most logical place to begin, but it worried me that I no longer had the same qualms about breaking into her house that had plagued me earlier in the day.

I heard someone upstairs, either in the guest bedroom or Belinda's study, so I carefully moved through the house, feeling my way in the dim illumination until I found the staircase and made my way up. I found Evan in the study, leafing through a thick scrapbook.

"Hi, Cassie," Evan said. "I heard you pull into the driveway."

"Have you found anything?" I asked.

"She's very clean. No blood, no nails, and no hair. I didn't even find a hairbrush."

"You didn't?" That struck me as odd. "What about a toothbrush?"

"No."

"I wonder if she packed up and left."

Evan shrugged. "It's possible, but I'm short on magical ideas to figure it out."

"Then let's try some non-magical ones. What's in the scrapbook?"

Evan glanced at me, uncertainty evident in his eyes. It was an expression I hadn't seen on him in years. "She seems to have kept careful records of her conquests over the years."

"Really?" I admit it, that piqued my interest, and not just in a professional way. "Can I see?"

"You won't like it."

"Why?" I entered the room fully and walked the short distance to the oversized desk, leaning over Evan to get a look at what had him rattled. He could have kept me from seeing, but he didn't.

He didn't move, either. To see the book, I had to lean over him, close enough to feel the heat of his body against mine. For an instant, I wondered if that had been such a good idea, but then the picture staring up at me from the scrapbook shoved away all other concerns.

"Isn't that your dad?" I asked.

Evan nodded. Then he turned the page, and I gasped, taking a step back, because the picture staring up at me from the next page was my dad.

"Looks like she was playing with both of them about twenty-four years ago," Evan said.

"Think that's why they hate each other? I never actually asked." I had been curious, but mentioning a Blackwood to my father was never a good idea.

"I did," Evan said, "but I didn't get much of an answer."

There was an awkward silence for a minute or two, but then I shook it off. What did it matter, really, if our fathers had both run afoul of the same witch a quarter century ago, even if they hadn't mentioned it? Knowing my father, he was probably too embarrassed to admit to such a thing. In the meantime, we had far more important things to worry about.

"Who else is in there? Is it recent?"

"Pretty recent," Evan said.

"Do you mind if I take a look?"

Evan stood and offered me the chair, but he didn't leave the room while I scanned the records of over two decades worth of conquests. It made me feel as if I were under a magnifying glass, but I didn't ask him to leave.

Belinda had gotten around, no question about that. She had records of at least a hundred men, some local, some out of town. She tended to have two to three men at any given time, and her tastes varied widely. She would see older men, younger men, tall or short, small or large. They tended to be rich or powerful, but that wasn't always true, either. She would make notations, sometimes indicating that a man made her laugh or was good in bed–with details that made my face burn. At least Evan couldn't see my reaction, and I didn't turn to see his.

When I finally reached the end of the book, I knew at once that something was wrong. "This ended six months ago."

"Maybe she updates it yearly," Evan suggested.

"Maybe, but I don't think so. She's too meticulous." I tapped the last page of the book, a profile of a wealthy man from Springfield. "I've heard tumors that she's dating at least two people in Eagle Rock, but neither of them are mentioned here. I suppose she might also update the scrapbook after she breaks things off, but it doesn't feel right. Where did you find this book, anyway?"

"It was sitting out."

"That doesn't seem likely, either," I said. "She's spent her life playing dangerous games with powerful people. Do you think she'd leave the evidence sitting right out here on her desk?"

"Everyone knew," Evan said.

I flipped back to the beginning of the scrapbook, and pointed to the picture of Evan's father. "Does everyone know this?" To emphasize the point, I flipped to the next page and pointed to the picture of my own father. "Or this?"

"Good point."

"Did you search the rest of the study?" I asked, looking at the perfectly organized workspace.

"Not yet."

I did the job, meticulously opening every drawer, looking through every notebook, and glancing at the titles of the books on her shelf, most of which contained potion recipes. My parents had similar books at home.

Finally, I shook my head. The motion caused the snapdragon behind my ear, which I'd nearly forgotten, to fall to the ground. Evan picked it up before I had a chance, whisking it into his hand with a tendril of magic.

"Expecting trouble?" he asked, a teasing note in his voice.

I appreciated his attempt to lighten the mood, but somehow a witty and lighthearted reply got stuck in my throat. All I could see was that snapdragon, pitiful protection though it was against anyone older than about twelve, and wonder if it would soon be all that stood between me and the world.

Now what had brought that on? Yes, my parents were having another baby, but that didn't make me any less a part of the family. They would always stand between me and any real magical threats.

Yet my brain had real trouble convincing my heart of that fact. I just couldn't shake the feeling that something was about to happen, something big.

Evan brushed my hair back so he could replace the flower behind my ear. "It's a good idea. You can never be too careful."

"Oh yeah, because this is going to help if I get into any real trouble. Tell me the truth, does it do anything for you?"

He smiled, playfully. "It brings out the blue of your eyes."

"Ha!"

"Hey, what's wrong? Last I checked, you weren't exactly short on protection."

I didn't know how to explain my fears, so I shrugged them off. "Maybe I don't want to have to be protected anymore."

"I see." But I could tell he knew that wasn't it.

"Let's go check the store," I said.

ꕥ

Belinda's collection of potions was extensive and many of her customers believed in the power of her brews. They were probably crap, especially those offering up money and wishes, because if she really could brew them, why would she need to sell them? Others, such as those offering weight loss or hair regrowth, might have been legitimate–I had no real way of knowing.

Then my eyes fell on a tiny vial with the word "MAGIC" on the label. I picked it up and turned it over to read the details: "Tap into magical energies you never knew were there. You'll be able to cast spells and brew potions. Curse your neighbors and find true love. $15.95"

"Impossible," I muttered. Surely, if such a thing could be, my parents would have fed it to me years ago.

"That stuff is crap," Evan said.

I jumped. I had almost forgotten he was there. He stood by a bulletin board, where he had been staring at pictures of Belinda, her friends, and her family. "Belinda mostly knows how to brew love potions, and even then she keeps the strongest ones to herself...the ones that truly ensnare the mind and heart."

I replaced the vial of MAGIC, with just a tiny twinge of regret, and moved on to Belinda's love potions. She had one full shelf dedicated to love, decorated with pink hearts and red roses. A lot of these potions were in the form of perfumes, creams, shampoos, and most especially–chocolates. The bottom third of the shelf was dedicated to boxes of chocolate candy in different flavors and potencies.

While a strong love potion will ensnare the mind and the heart, most of the weaker love potions are what you might call suggestive magic. They could cause you to feel affection, adoration, or arousal, but they typically left the higher brain functions intact.

At random, I picked up a bottle of perfume from the top shelf and read: "Induces powerful lust. Spray on your intended and make sure you are the first person they see. Lasts about an hour."

The thing you have to understand about any magic is that there are good ways to use it, and bad ways to use it. The concept of black magic is a hotly debated topic among sorcerers. Even death, in self defense, is a shade of gray. As I stood there, reading the functions of the various love potions, I thought of all the innocent and harmful ways they could be used. A couple in a committed relationship might have a lot of fun with a spray of lust. On the other hand, using it on an unwilling victim...

I shuddered as I replaced the bottle and accidentally knocked one of the neighboring bottles of perfume to the ground. It shattered, splashing perfume all over my open-toed sandals.

"Crap."

"What happened?" Evan asked, his voice hard and alert. I could hear him moving closer.

"Stop! I don't want to see you right now."

"Which potion was that?" Evan asked, still in that hard-edged voice of command.

I pointed to the row of similar bottles on the top shelf. "Lust."

One of the little bottles floated away from the shelf, but I did not turn around to see what Evan was doing with it. Instead, I started looking through my purse for a pack of tissues to clean the mess off my feet.

"Cassie, I have some bad news for you."

"Worse, you mean?"

"This potion doesn't take affect until you actually look at someone. Your hour starts then."

"Crap. I don't suppose there's an antidote?"

"Sure,, but it will take me about three days to brew, once the moon is full."

"Okay." I considered my options as I wiped the mess off my foot and started gathering the tiny shards of glass. "Well, I guess I could-" I stopped, I had nothing to put at the end of that sentence. I kind of hoped Evan would have a suggestion, but to my surprise, he started laughing at me. "This isn't funny."

"Come on, it is a little funny."

Maybe it would be funny in a few days, if I didn't die of embarrassment first. "I suppose I could call my boyfriend." I didn't want to explain any of this to him, and though I trusted him, I didn't really want him to become the object of my uncontrolled lust for an hour. I just didn't know what else to do.

"Who are you seeing?" Evan asked, all traces of amusement gone.

"Braden," I said.

"Who?"

"Braden Walker. He was a year ahead of us in school. He was on the football team."

"Oh. I think I remember him." Evan paused for a long moment. "You know you could do better, right?"

"It's none of your business." I had to fight the urge to glare at him when I said that. He barely knew Braden, so what made him think he could make any judgments? Besides, I didn't know why he thought

I could do better, when I had done very little dating in high school. I hadn't known if my family name scared people off, or if there was something fundamentally wrong with me, but Braden had at least restored my confidence that the latter was not true.

"Listen," Evan said. "I need to do another spell. It'll just be a few minutes. We'll figure something out after, just don't look at me until I'm done."

"I get that." I sounded more annoyed at the admonition than I should have, because his quip about Braden still stung.

Within seconds, I smelled candles and incense, and heard Evan muttering under his breath. I found a trash can by a nearby desk, and tossed the damp tissues inside. Then I spotted a black day planner on top of the desk. It was the sort of thing that ancient relatives used to buy me for school, but I never used. Belinda seemed to have liked it, though. Nearly every page through the end of July was covered in notes and reminders.

Over the weekend, she wrote, she had rented a cabin in the woods by the lake. She should have been back, though, because in about half an hour, she had a dinner date at Hodge Mill with Sheriff Adams. I blinked and re-read the name several times to be sure I had seen it correctly, but unfortunately, I had. My old boss and friend had been acting a little strangely that afternoon, but I hadn't guessed he might be under the influence of a love spell.

"Finished," Evan said. I heard him gathering up his supplies. "This isn't good. I suspected it this afternoon, but now I'm sure–there's no threshold on this home. Which either means Belinda has permanently moved, or else she's dead."

"Do you think she had something to do with your cousin's murder?" I asked.

"I don't know what to think. I can't come up with a reason she'd do it, but then again, where is she?"

"I found her day planner," I said, holding it up over my shoulder so Evan could see. "She was supposed to go to the lake this weekend, and she's got a date tonight at Hodge Mill. You'll never guess who it's with."

"Who?"

"The sheriff."

"Huh."

"I know it's a long shot, but I figure we should go to Hodge Mill and see if she shows up–or if the sheriff does. After that--"

"Cassie," Evan interrupted.

"Yeah?"

"How much do you trust me?"

"Er-Why?"

"Turn around," he said.

"Did you figure something out?" I said, my heart beating a little faster. "Some way to stop the potion?"

"Yes."

"But you said-" I never got a chance to finish, because just then, Evan moved into my field of vision and I turned to stare at him properly.

In all the years I had known him, I had somehow missed the fact that Evan has the most incredible blue eyes. They sparkle like diamonds when he laughs, and darken like the sea when he's angry. At that moment, I thought I could swim in those eyes. I had never spent much time looking at his lips before, but I suddenly became aware of just how kissable they were. I started towards him, my focus set on those beautiful, kissable lips.

I couldn't move. Something was forcing my body absolutely still.

"Sorry about that," Evan said, not sounding sorry at all. He swung a satchel over his shoulder and started out the door. I found myself following behind him, but I wasn't the one moving my legs. "Nothing to do but let it run its course. If you want to hate me in an hour, I'll understand."

Part of my brain worked out what was happening to me. That part was either shocked or angry or afraid, possibly all three at once. It pushed at the rest of my brain, the part that wanted Evan Blackwood in an entirely inappropriate way.

"Let me go," I said. "I can handle it."

I felt my legs loosen and I thought I had control of them again, but they didn't take me to my own car. Instead, they followed Evan to his.

I didn't get all the way there before my body froze again. Frustration warred with sense as I tried to free myself from both the full body lock and the mind-altering affects of the potion. "Oh, come on, would one kiss hurt?"

Evan laughed. I didn't get what was so funny.

"Cassie, I can't leave you here like this, not when there's a killer out there somewhere. Going to Hodge Mill is a good idea, and the worst of the potion's effects should wear off by the time we get there. Do you think you can follow me in your car?"

Since the alternative apparently involved immobility, I planned to try. "I can do it."

"All right." But he didn't exactly release me. Instead, I felt a force at my back, urging me toward my car until I opened the door and slid behind the wheel. At about the same time, I heard his car door slam shut and the engine roar to life.

I still itched to go to him, to kiss him, and to touch him, but futility weighed heavily on my heart. He didn't want me. Not that it came as much of a surprise when he had dated nearly every girl in high school except me. We hadn't even managed to remain close friends past the ninth grade. I wished now that I had gone to more effort, even if he had been the one to put a lot of that distance between us. What had he said when I asked him about the love spells? *You're just like everyone else, accusing me of stuff because of my name. I thought you knew me.*

Did I know him? After that day, I was never sure again.

With regret weighing heavily on my heart, dampening my need, I put my car into gear and followed Evan into town.

6

I KISSED EVAN BLACKWOOD ONCE, WHEN WE WERE BOTH EIGHT YEARS OLD. It was the third grade, and that year we had one of the worst teachers ever, Mrs. Marsh. She sat us together, at the back of the classroom where we "wouldn't be a bad influence on the rest of the children."

That wasn't exactly new. In fact, we had met in first grade under similar circumstances. There were those in the community who feared and hated the old sorcery families, which may explain why some go out of their way to keep a low profile. Mrs. Marsh took it to the next level.

"I have bad news," she said one day. "Our class frog died last night. I'll give you two guesses who did it."

The rest of the class looked in our direction, while Evan and I looked at one another, utterly perplexed.

Another time, it was a haircut. One of the girls had apparently had a bad run-in with a pair of scissors, because it was jagged and cut to the length of a boy. She tried to wear a hat to cover it, but Mrs. Marsh would not allow it. When Mrs. Marsh saw the haircut she tsked and said, "Did you notice? Cassie's hair looks more beautiful than ever today." She let the implications hang.

I could go on, but I typically try to forget the third grade. It's safer that way. Mrs. Marsh quit teaching three years later, when Nicolas was in her class, and he set her hair on fire. When I think of Mrs. Marsh, the image I treasure is the one of her running down the hall, hair ablaze, screaming that she'd had enough.

One day, Mrs. Marsh read the students some classic fairy tale in which the prince and princess kissed at the end. Of course, I was expected to think it was gross, and I did, but I was also intrigued that so many grown ups did it, including my parents. At recess that day, I told Evan how gross I thought it was, and he agreed.

"So," I said, "you want to try it?"

"What?"

"Kissing? You know, just to see what it's like?"

Evan shrugged. "'kay."

We pursed our lips and pushed them forward until they brushed against one another. Then we hastily withdrew. It felt wet.

"Yuck," we said at the exact same time, wiping our mouths with the backs of our hands.

Most unfortunately, Mrs. Marsh saw us. "You'll be pregnant by the time you graduate high school. Mark my words."

Luckily, she's not a seer. She did call my parents, though, which resulted in a heated lecture and a demand that I cease any and all contact with Evan immediately. They even had the school switch me to a different class, ostensibly to get me away from Mrs. Marsh, but really to get me away from Evan. I never told them Evan's parents switched him to the same class.

I didn't hate Evan at the end of an hour, but I did wish I never had to see him again. Alas, there would be no such reprieve, since we had already agreed to meet at Hodge Mill, the nicest restaurant in town. They have linen tablecloths and napkins, and serve the freshest seafood you can get in a small town nowhere near a major highway in the middle of a landlocked state. It's surprisingly good. I don't know where they found their head chef, but he knows how to do amazing things with sauces and glazes that compensate for the quality of the fish.

When I pulled into the parking lot, Evan was leaning against his car, eying me warily, probably ready to manhandle me with more magic. I forestalled him by putting up a hand.

"Don't ever mention that again," I said.

"Mention what?" He gave me a look of such wide-eyed innocence that it put me instantly at ease.

"Is the sheriff here?" I glanced at my watch, surprised at the lateness of the hour. It was already almost eight o'clock. According to the day planner, Belinda and Sheriff Adams had agreed to meet at eight.

"Not yet, but we can get a table and wait for them."

"I already had dinner," I said.

"Then have some dessert."

I followed him inside, where the head waiter showed us to a table for two along the back wall, giving us a good view of the mostly empty dining room. I ordered the chocolate mousse, while Evan ordered the salmon, and then both of our eyes drifted to the door.

"My apprenticeship is almost over," Evan said, breaking the silence. "Master Wolf doesn't mess with mundane things like calendars, but he's hinting that there's not much left to teach me."

"Congratulations," I said, "So what are you going to do next?"

"I don't know, exactly." He looked me straight in the eyes, and I had trouble looking away. "I have some ideas."

I shivered, and managed to tear my eyes from his.

"Do you remember telling me about why you wanted to become a cop?" Evan asked.

"Not really, no." I searched my memories, but came up blank.

"You said you wanted to protect people who can't protect themselves. I always liked that idea."

I felt an irrational stab of jealousy, though I should have felt flattered that he had remembered those words. If he set his mind to it, and I hoped he would, he really could help a lot of people. I only wished I could have done the same.

Pushing down my feelings, I offered him an encouraging smile. "I'm glad I could inspire you. Although, if you didn't try so hard to make people afraid of you, they'd know you already did some of that back in school."

"I wasn't planning to advertise. The reputation works for me."

I rolled my eyes. "Tell that to Kaitlin. Who, by the way, I couldn't console until I went down the street to buy a crystal from a tourist shop and gave it to her for protection."

"They don't usually sell spelled crystals to the public."

"They sure don't." I narrowed my eyes at him. "But she's not in any real danger."

"Not from me. I told you, I'll make things right with her."

I nodded, deciding to drop the subject. He'd already promised, twice now–no point becoming a shrew about it.

"You know, Cassie," Evan said, slowly, "My reputation isn't entirely undeserved."

"I know."

"I'm not as nice as you think I am."

I didn't know what to say to that, but luckily, the waiter chose that moment to deliver our food. I thought I had a balanced picture of Evan, but admittedly, I didn't know him as well as I used to.

Evan spent the next few minutes outlining some of his ideas, though he had not decided on a specific course of action. Mr. Wolf thought he should join the magical unification effort–a national movement attempting to bring order and oversight to the magical world–but Evan didn't know how he felt about the concept, especially since so many attempts had failed in the past. Local governments were common, but not a wider network. Eagle Rock didn't even have a local government, only some mutual understandings that everyone gets left alone as long as certain lines aren't crossed. Murder is over the line. Revenge isn't.

Sheriff Adams didn't arrive until nearly eight fifteen. He started for a lone table, but paused when he saw us, and headed our way instead.

"I was supposed to meet Belinda here tonight," he said without being prompted.

I looked into his brown eyes, ringed with whites tinted pink. I had guessed as much since seeing the day planner, but hoped I would be proven wrong when I saw him. If Belinda had him under one of her spells, he would not be a reasonable investigator.

"How long have you been seeing her?" I asked.

"Just a couple of weeks. I've been trying to find her, of course. She's not answering her cell and her family hasn't seen her in days."

I wanted to mention the cabin by the lake, but didn't want him to know I had returned to Belinda's house, especially not now I knew she had him under her spell. At least I didn't have to suppose he knew anything about her disappearance. If he did, he never would have shown up at the restaurant like a love-sick puppy.

"I'm sorry, Sheriff," I said, "but I don't think she's coming."

He nodded, miserably. "I'm afraid she might be... that something might have happened to her."

I wished I could argue. "Why don't you head home? If she arrives in the next forty-five minutes, we'll call you."

"Thanks, Cassie. I'll see you tomorrow." And head hanging, he left the restaurant.

"How long do you think the love potion will last?" I asked Evan.

He watched the sheriff until the older man left. "It depends. A strong potion might last twenty-four to forty-eight hours, but if he keeps renewing it, then it could last longer. It would help if we knew how he's taking the potion. It works orally or topically, so it could be in chocolates, shampoo, perfumes..."

I thought about it for a minute, while Evan concentrated on his fish, but it didn't take me long to arrive at the answer. "She mixed it in with a hair regrowth potion. I noticed his hair was thicker, and the last time I saw him, he hadn't been with Belinda."

"Good thinking. I'll see what I can do."

After that, we lapsed into silence. I tend to be uncomfortable with silence, so I cast about for something to say, but I found I only had one thing on my mind. Finally, I broached the painful subject.

"How are your aunt and uncle holding up?"

He shook his head. "I went over there before I returned to Belinda's house. It's not good. They're out for blood."

I knew what that meant. No one would ever prosecute this case; the murderer wouldn't live long enough. It probably should have upset me, but it didn't, not as long as they found the right culprit before acting, and I would make sure of that.

If there's one thing you don't do in Eagle Rock, it's mess with a powerful family, and Nancy, while not the most powerful young practitioner in town, had dangerous connections. Which begged the question: Who in his right mind had hurt her? I had the feeling we were looking for someone or something not in its right mind.

7

It was nearly nine thirty by the time I got home, but I knew Mom would still be awake. She never went to bed before ten o'clock, not even when she was pregnant. In fact, she almost seemed more energetic during pregnancy. Maybe that's why she had wanted to do it one more time.

So it surprised me when Nicolas told me Mom had already gone to her bedroom. I headed up two flights of stairs, passed the younger kids' bedrooms, and gently knocked on the master bedroom door.

Dad opened the door a crack and peered around it at me. "Yes?"

"Mom said she wanted to talk to me."

"Not now, she's asleep."

"Oh." I backed away, and Dad retreated into the bedroom, but I didn't believe him.

I went up one more flight of stairs to my fortress of solitude, tossed my purse and shoes near the door, then put my ear to the vent to find out why they had lied. To my surprise, I heard Mom sobbing. Dad's words of comfort were too muffled for me to understand, but I felt bad about intruding.

"Maybe," I said to myself, "Mom's whole world doesn't revolve around me."

My bedroom door creaked open and Juliana's black cat, Sphinx, wandered in. He sat on his haunches and stared at me with gold eyes.

"If you want to talk to me, come on up," I told the cat.

It blinked and retreated. A minute later, my fifteen-year-old sister, Juliana, came in and flung herself across my bed, her dark brown hair spilling across the black sheets. She's the only girl in the family who did not get Mom's auburn tresses. She looks a lot like Dad, which is why many people who see us together aren't sure if we're sisters or not.

"Mom's upset," Juliana said.

"Yeah, I know." I really didn't want to talk about it.

"You were rude at dinner."

"Yeah, I know."

"You should apologize."

"I did, on the phone."

"Oh." Juliana sat up. "I got a job. I was going to say something at dinner, but it was kind of chaotic."

"Congratulations," I said, and eagerly latched onto the new topic. "Where?"

"At the hospital, candy striping."

"Oh," I said, without enthusiasm.

It's not that I wasn't happy for her. In a way, the job was perfect. Juliana was a gifted healer, and for as long as I can remember, healing people was all she wanted to do, but since when was life ever that simple?

Since true healers are rare and in high demand, her gift is one of the family's greatest secrets. Even the Mrs. Marshes of the world tend to reserve judgment of people like Juliana, especially if they or someone they know has a life-threatening illness.

The trouble is that Juliana isn't an endlessly renewable resource. She's more like a rechargeable battery. Healing drains her. Time and rest refresh her ability, but even a rechargeable battery has a finite lifetime. How finite? No one can say, but we don't like to take unnecessary chances.

Juliana, on the other hand, was fifteen, and like most girls her age, thought she was immortal. There was no doubt in my mind that she wanted to volunteer at the hospital so she could use her gift to heal people. If she got caught, things could be bad. If she burned out, they would be worse.

"Dad wasn't too happy for me," Juliana said. "I think he and Mom had a fight about it."

That explained why she hadn't wanted to speak to me, and why she'd been crying. No, her world didn't revolve around me.

"You would need to be careful, of course," I said. "If anyone found out..."

"I've heard it a hundred times from Mom and Dad," Juliana said with a scowl. "I don't need it from you, too."

I put my hands up. "Sorry. Big sister instincts taking over."

"They want me to start this week, but Dad hasn't said I can yet."

"Oh, well..." I hesitated, not sure what to say. The truth was, I didn't think he would change his mind, and I didn't even think he should, but I wasn't the decision-maker here, I was the big sister. So I lied. "I'm sure he'll come around."

I threw myself onto my bed, next to Juliana, and propped my head against a pillow.

"Can you talk to him for me?"

"Talk to him?" Maybe I shouldn't have lied. "What makes you think he'd listen to me? You said he's not even listening to Mom."

"Well, Mom may not be entirely on my side. She has this idea that I'm going to go around healing everyone until I burn out. Hey! Your toe is bleeding."

I looked down, and saw that she was right. One of the glass shards from the bottle of love potion had wedged itself in my big toe. I bent over and tried to pull it out, but it was too small and had worked its way in too far. I could feel it beneath the skin, just out of reach. "I'll have to get the tweezers. I'll be right back."

Before I had a chance to move, Juliana touched a finger to my toe. There was a warm, tingling sensation, and then my toe looked as if it had never been damaged at all. Even the blood and the shard of glass were wiped clean.

I sighed. "Juliana, you can't go around doing things like that or Dad will never see things your way. It was just a little piece of glass."

Juliana shrugged. "Exactly, it was just a little piece of glass. No big deal. I'm not even tired."

"It is a big deal. If you don't understand that, then I won't talk to Dad for you."

I expected her to argue, but she didn't. Instead, she went very quiet for nearly a minute, and then changed the subject completely. "I'm learning crystal gazing."

I wasn't sure what I was supposed to say about it. "Okay?"

"I was practicing after dinner. Saw you at Belinda's house with Evan."

The color drained from my face.

"I know why you had the glass in your foot."

Great. Just great. "Uh huh."

"So, you'll talk to Dad for me?" Juliana said. "It might make it easier for me not to mention to him that you were with Evan tonight. Or, you know, mention to your boyfriend that you dropped a love potion on your foot, and thought you'd die if you couldn't have Evan."

"Get out of my room." I pushed her until she rolled off the bed.

She laughed. I'm glad one of us found the situation funny. Just then, her laugh sounded to me like a cackle. "You'll talk to Dad though?"

"I'll think about it." Or, more precisely, I'd think of a way to keep her from following through on her blackmail.

"Better not think too long." Juliana stood up and headed for the door. "Dad's still up."

With no time to think, I had to weigh my potential humiliation against Juliana's ability to control herself when surrounded by hundreds of sick people, some of whom might die without her help. It wasn't a hard choice, really. I'd survive. I couldn't be as certain about Juliana, especially when she was prone to such rash behavior.

"Good night," I said.

Juliana stood in the doorway and gave me a look of utter astonishment. "Seriously? You're just going to let me leave?"

"Don't spy on me anymore," I added.

"Stop me!" Juliana left, slamming the door behind her.

I stared at the door for a long time after she left. In truth, her threats didn't have me that bothered. Given Dad's hatred of Evan, it could be awkward, but he was bound to find out about my taking a job for him sooner or later. Dad had never gone to extreme measures to keep us from being friends before, possibly as a form of reverse psychology, and I didn't see that changing now that I'd grown up. Braden could be a problem, depending upon how Juliana spun it, but we weren't exclusive, so he didn't have the right to get jealous. Not that I'd mind if he did.

No, the thing that really bothered me was the fact that Juliana might continue spying on me, and as far as I knew, there wasn't anything I could do to stop her.

Or maybe not. We did have a large library full of books on magic that might provide me with a better answer, such as the snapdragon to throw off a curse. At times, knowledge could be power.

I sighed and reached for a housecoat. It was going to be a long night.

8

I MIGHT AS WELL HAVE GONE STRAIGHT TO BED, BECAUSE FOUR HOURS AND dozens of books later, I had come up with nothing. There were plenty of ways to conceal oneself from magical spying, but they all involved magic–powerful magic. In fact, most of the sources I found made it out to be a base power struggle, in which the person with access to the most magic won. The most effective spells involved a full coven, and access to a node, such as the one under Table Rock Lake.

Around two in the morning, Nicolas wandered in to ask if he could help, and I called it quits for the night. The trouble was, sleep didn't come easily or well. I still couldn't get the image of Nancy Hastings out of my mind, and when I did slide into exhausted slumber, I kept waking myself up in fits of panic, imagining a tiny fireball taking my place in the family. Apparently, I hadn't managed to convince my subconscious that everything would be all right. I really needed to talk to Mom, but by the time I woke, she was already juggling three kids and two potions.

My morning meeting with the sheriff only lasted about fifteen minutes, and we spent most of that time sharing ideas and planning the next steps of the investigation. The sheriff, not wanting to believe anything bad of his precious Belinda, was sure the woman had been hurt by the same person who killed Nancy Hastings. I, on the other hand, had Belinda Hewitt's name at the top of my suspect list. If she remained alive and unhurt, then the reason we hadn't found her was because she knew better than to stick around.

The sheriff, therefore, had plans to talk to Nancy's family and friends to discover if she had any enemies. I decided to talk to Belinda's family and friends, but I also had a hunch about visiting the lakeside cabin where she had spent the weekend, probably with a lover. I didn't tell the sheriff about that part.

Experience told me it was best to bring protection when talking to Jasmine Hewitt, Belinda's mom, so I stopped by a small, local herbalist on the way to my office. I went with stinging nettle, which my Aunt Sherry had suggested the previous evening, because of its reflective property. To keep the poisonous plant from hurting me, it required some Queen Anne's Lace, which I also found at the shop. I made them into a little corsage that I tied to my ankle.

I had planned to contact Mrs. Hewitt by phone, thinking it would be safer than a face to face confrontation, but as ill-luck would have it, I spotted her coming out of McClellan's Antique Shop on the walk back to my office. She was an old woman, stooped and gray-haired, who had not aged well. Her skin looked like leather and her hair like a bird's nest, but her biggest problem was a perpetual scowl. Maybe she only wore it for me, but I doubted it.

"Good morning, Mrs. Hewitt," I said, politely.

"I don't think it is," she replied, right on form.

I ignored her rudeness. "It's a good thing I ran into you, actually. I was hoping you could help me get in touch with your daughter, Belinda."

"Why would I do that?"

I decided not to mention the dead body found in her daughter's home. "Because yesterday, I spent all afternoon outside her shop, hoping for a word, and she never showed up. I'm worried about her."

"Like hell you are. You think she killed that girl, but she didn't. She's not that stupid." It didn't escape my attention that Jasmine Hewitt had touted her daughter's intelligence as a defense, rather than any sort of kindness.

"I don't think she killed her, either," I said, only half lying. "But it's strange, and she's missing."

"Stay away from her, if you know what's good for you."

"Mrs, Hewitt," I said, leaving politeness behind, "you don't really want a repeat of the last time you tried to hurt me, do you?"

Something flashed in her eyes, probably remembering the incident that had nearly led to the fiery destruction of her house. "I really don't care. My daughter hasn't returned my calls in days, and right now I'm spoiling for a fight."

Since she had told me what I wanted to know, I returned to my polite approach, plastering a fake smile to my face. "Thank you, Mrs. Hewitt."

I stepped past her, but before I had walked another block, the nettle bound to my ankle began to vibrate, a sign that it had been activated. At the same time, I heard a howl of pain and rage from somewhere behind me, indicating that Mrs. Hewitt had gotten her curse right back. Not wanting to tempt fate, I broke into a run until I reached my office.

I couldn't believe the old witch had actually tried to curse me. Given what my parents would do if they found out, I had a feeling that behind her scowls, she was more worried about her daughter than she let on.

I only stayed in my office long enough to catch my breath and look up an address online. If Belinda's mother didn't know where she was, I didn't think I would get much more information out of more distant relatives or friends, so I headed to Brooks Lakeside Rentals, where Belinda had supposedly spent the weekend.

I drove out of town to the east, where most of the resorts and cabins staked their claim along the lake shore. It was a picture perfect day, not a cloud in the sky, and the tourists were out in force. There were many resorts along that road, but the cabin where Belinda had been staying was past all of them, in a more remote location.

I stopped by the resort's main office, where the proprietor sat in a rocking chair on the porch, sipping his morning coffee. He was an older man, and a long-time resident of Eagle Rock, though I couldn't recall his name until he introduced himself as Sam.

"As far as I know, Belinda's still here," Sam said when I told him what I needed.

"She is?" The news surprised me. Surely, it couldn't be that easy.

"She was supposed to check out Sunday morning, but she called and said she needed to extend her stay a couple of days."

"Can you tell me which cabin number?" I asked.

"Number three," he replied, and then gave me directions.

Cabin #3 lay in the quiet shade of half a dozen large trees. The small, single bedroom structure looked picturesque and still, but then again, so had Belinda's house, yesterday afternoon. I felt a vague sense of deja vu as I walked up the wooden steps to the small front porch and knocked on the door.

No one answered, but somehow, I wasn't surprised. Sighing, I decided to take a walk around the building, and then maybe head to the lake to see if Belinda was sunning herself on the shore.

As I rounded the cabin, I was hit by a foul stench that made the hair on my neck and arms prickle. In back, a large cedar deck spanned the length of the structure. It ran straight off the back of the house, leaving a space underneath, blocked off by wooden mesh. Except for one section that looked as if it had been ripped out. Wooden splinters littered the ground nearby.

With a terrible sense of foreboding, I approached the deck, reeling and nearly losing my breakfast as the stench grew stronger. I ducked my head under the deck, blinked a few times to adjust to the darkness, broken only by shafts of light slanting in through breaks in the wood, and spotted something to take my mind off the smell.

A body lay to my right, bent at an odd angle so the feet were behind the back. I couldn't see much with the poor illumination, and I couldn't even be sure that the corpse was Belinda's, but I could see the head was no longer attached to the body. It lay a few feet away, off to my left.

Backing away to escape both the sights and smells, I phoned in yet another murder.

❧

Half an hour later, the cabin was swarming with deputies. It turned out, the front door to the cabin was unlocked, so Jeff and Ryan went inside to gather evidence. I didn't see the inside, but I overheard them saying it looked like there had been a lot of blood at one point, because they found traces of it on the sofa and carpet, but someone had done their best to clean it.

The sheriff arrived shortly after everyone else, and I had never seen him looking so grim. Wordlessly, he went around back, and when he returned a few minutes later, he looked even worse.

"Is it Belinda?" I had to ask.

"I don't know," he said. "I think–I want you to take a look."

My stomach squirmed at the idea, but when he handed me a flashlight, I gave him a determined nod and headed back to the scene.

With the help of the flashlight, I could make out far more detail than before. The body definitely belonged to a woman. She had been wearing a tank top and shorts that would have left most of her skin exposed, had there not been so many insects crawling over it. As I panned the flashlight over the body, I could see half healed wounds on her wrists, thighs, and shoulders. They might have been bite marks, but it was tough to tell.

There was also a wooden stake protruding from her chest.

Swallowing hard, I panned my flashlight to the left. I saw dead, yellow eyes, like a feline's, staring at me through wild, platinum blond hair. It was Belinda, all right, except it hadn't been Belinda at all. She had become a vampire.

I quickly backed away, returning to the front of the cabin. The Sheriff followed.

"Well?" he asked.

I took a moment constructing my answer. It was perfectly obvious that she had been attacked by a vampire, and in fact, had turned into one herself, but I had to decide what I could and could not tell the sheriff. His position in the town gave him more access to truth than the average person, especially since he had a sharp wit and keen attention to detail, but he wasn't a sorcerer.

"Was it a vampire?" he prompted.

I nodded. By and large, vampires were not considered a secret and in fact, sorcerers had done everything they could to get the information out there. Keeping secrets in the magical world was a power game, and the only ones who gained power by lying about vampires were the monsters themselves. The recent craze of vampire romance had undermined a lot of efforts to get the truth out there, and some suspected the vampires themselves were responsible.

"She must have been attacked recently, judging from the bite marks. She turned. You can tell from the yellow, catlike eyes. They get that way when they hunt; when they're feeling the bloodlust."

I trailed off, wrinkling my brow in confusion. It just didn't make sense. For one thing, Belinda Hewitt was a witch whose mother should have given her the anti-venom potion when she was a small child. She shouldn't have been susceptible to the venom. She shouldn't have turned. Of course, it was possible Mrs. Hewitt didn't know about the potion. Sorcerers rarely shared information with one another, but I had always gotten the impression that the anti-venom potion was something most practitioners knew about.

I turned back to the sheriff, who seemed to be trying hard to keep it together. My heart went out to him. Even though he had been under the influence of a love potion, he believed he loved her, and the hurt he felt now was entirely real.

"I'm so sorry." The words were as inadequate as they had been when I'd spoken them to Evan the day before, but if there are others, I don't know them.

"What else can you tell me?" He seemed determined to get down to business, and I decided to let him.

"They said there was blood in the cabin," I said, thinking aloud. "Probably lots of it, though it had been cleaned. But that doesn't make any sense, either."

"Because a vampire would have drunk it all?"

"Yes," I lied. I couldn't tell the sheriff about the anti-venom potion, which was the real issue. It was one of those secrets I was expected to keep.

The potion is given to counteract vampire venom, so in the event of an attack, the person will not turn. The venom doesn't just create new vampires, however; it has three purposes: It creates vampires, acts as a drug to put the victim in thrall, and it coagulates the blood so the victim won't bleed out. This allows a vampire to feed without necessarily killing.

So I had a contradiction. If Belinda had been attacked in that cabin, the presence of a lot of blood suggested she had been protected from the venom. But she turned, proving she had not been.

"It looks like she's been dead for a few days," Sheriff Adams said.

I shook my head. "I doubt it. Sam said she called him two days ago. You can't always tell with vampires." Because they reverted to their natural level of decay upon death, meaning, more than likely, that Belinda had been turned several days ago.

I really needed to talk to my cousin, Jason. He was the family expert on all things vampire. He knew things the rest of us didn't, secrets held by the community of hunters.

"How strong are vampires?" the sheriff asked.

"Very strong, why?"

"Because I'm wondering, if she was so strong, who could have killed her?"

I must have gaped at him. He and I were clearly not operating on the same wavelength, if he was under the impression that whoever had staked Belinda had killed her. Love potion or no love potion, on this point, I had to set him straight.

"The vampire who turned her, killed her. Whoever staked her, and cut off her head, slayed a monster. It wasn't Belinda anymore."

The sheriff didn't look convinced.

"Belinda might have killed Nancy Hastings," I said, in an attempt to get through to him.

"Do you know how to kill a vampire?" Sheriff Adams asked.

"*I* don't. I may know someone who does, though."

"He wasn't around this weekend, was he?" the sheriff asked.

"No." Apparently, it was a good thing, too, or the sheriff might accuse the wrong man. I definitely needed to get him off the love potion, so he could start thinking clearly.

"Well, find out what you can, but I can't wait for him. We've got a lot of work to do, and I want to find the monster who did this. How do I do that?"

"Well," I said, "He won't be out during the daytime."

Sheriff Adams glanced up at the clear blue sky. "No sunlight, garlic, holy water, crosses?"

"Exactly," I said. "Bram Stoker pretty much got it right. The one thing you need to keep in mind, though, is that vampires are strong and fast. Unbelievably strong and fast." I hesitated, unwilling to tell him about the existence of hunters, but not sure how else to keep him from going after the vampire himself.

"What if we found them sleeping in their coffins?" Sheriff Adams asked.

"It takes a lot of strength to drive a piece of wood through a man's ribcage," I said. "If you can't do it, or if you miss the heart, you'll be dead in half a heartbeat."

"I just need to know what I have to do to find and kill this thing," Sheriff Adams said. "There has to be something. If not a wooden stake, then what about a wooden arrow? I'm good with a bow and I hear you're good too."

I was better than good. I'd won many competitions over the years, though it had been a few months since I'd practiced. "Even the best archer misses sometimes. And before you can even take that shot, you have to see him before he sees you–a vampire's eyes work very well in the dark."

The Sheriff scowled. "I can't just sit here and do nothing."

Unfortunately, I couldn't think of a single thing the sheriff could do without seeing Belinda clearly for who she had been. We needed to know who had stayed with her at that cabin, and who had seen her last. The sheriff wouldn't want to acknowledge that Belinda might have come to the cabin with another man.

"Just let me talk to my family and get back to you. Meanwhile, get some holy water and crosses, and get inside after dark. A threshold is really your best defense."

9

By the time I escaped the new crime scene, it was nearly eleven o'clock. I headed for home, even though doing so would make me late for my usual lunch date, again, because I wanted to ask how to get in touch with Jason and warn my family about the vampire attack.

If we had time, I also wanted to know what Mom had wanted to talk to me about the night before. After a sleepless night, I felt more anxious than ever about the possibilities. All of my reasonable ideas of the night before were gone, replaced with a strange certainty that it had something to do with the new baby.

I wasn't often home on weekday mornings. With school out and everyone home, all of the kids were busy with magic lessons. Nicolas had graduated from home school magic when he had graduated from high school, but all the rest, from Juliana to Christina, had a curriculum to follow.

When I walked in, Mom was on the floor with Christina, singing her a playful song about ivy to the tune of "Frere Jaques."

Here's an ivy, here's an ivy,
What's it for? What's it for?
Healing and protection, strength and binding.
Ivy is strong. And it's good

I groaned. It had been years since I'd had to listen to that.

"Don't be such a critic," Mom said. "It doesn't have to be poetic, it just has to work." She called over her shoulder. "Adam."

He ran in from the next room. "What?"

"What's ivy for?"

"Healing and protection. Strength and binding," he intoned.

"There's a bit more to it than that," I muttered.

"Well, she's three." Mom pulled a stray lock of hair behind her ear, and gathered Christina into her lap.

"Cassie! What are you doing home?" Adam asked, rushing forward to entwine bony limbs around my leg. "Will you play cars with me?"

"No, Adam," Mom said, "Cassie doesn't have time right now, and neither do you. You're supposed to be working on spell detection."

"I'm done!" Adam announced. "The black and red box were spelled. The orange and purple ones weren't."

"Oh." Mom sounded impressed. "Very good."

"So can I play with my cars?" Adam smiled at her. "Please?"

Mom glanced at her watch. "Thirty minutes."

"Yeah!" Adam ran off down the hall.

A few seconds later, Isaac came in, his brows furrowed in concentration, a soccer ball floating a few feet ahead of him. "I think I'm getting it," he said. The moment he spoke, the soccer ball fell to the floor and bounced across the room. He cursed, and ran after it.

"Language!" Mom called.

Juliana came in next, and gave me a reproachful look. I pretended not to notice. I wondered, briefly, whether she had followed through on her blackmail, but I had bigger problems.

"Listen," I said, trying to move things along, "I was kind of hoping for a private word with you and Dad."

Mom nodded. "Juliana, keep an eye on the kids. We'll be back in a few minutes."

I followed Mom up the stairs to the library, where Dad and Elena were practicing linking. Two sorcerers can be more powerful than one if they know how to combine their magic, but it was a skill that took years to perfect. It also took a bit more maturity than the typical nine-year-old possessed, but Elena wasn't like other girls her age.

Dad and Elena sat across from one another, legs crossed, hands resting against one another. Eventually, if they got good enough, they wouldn't even need to touch.

As soon as we walked in, Dad looked up and broke the connection. "Elena, Mom and I need a few minutes with Cassandra. Will you wait downstairs?"

"Okay." Elena stood and drifted out of the room, closing the door behind her.

As soon as she had gone, I turned to face Dad, but when I saw his face, my reasons for wanting to see him fled my mind. I had rarely seen Dad looking so angry, and all of that rage was directed at me. His ears were smoking.

"What is going on between you and Evan Blackwood?" Dad asked.

"Huh?" I looked from him to Mom, but her mask had fallen off. She now had the look of a deer caught in headlights.

"Juliana said you were with him last night," Dad said.

My mouth fell open. Whatever I had expected him to do when Juliana told him what she'd seen, this wasn't it. Or maybe he was upset because I'd taken the job. I knew he'd be upset about that, but I hadn't guessed it would send him into a rage.

"What is this about?" I asked, looking between them. "I've been friends with Evan for a long time."

"We thought you had a falling out," Mom said.

"Not exactly." Honestly, I didn't usually talk to them about Evan because of their irrational reactions whenever it came up. "Yesterday, he hired me to help him find out who killed his cousin. I told you I had a job."

"A job?" Dad said. "Is that what you're doing for him?"

"Juliana told us what she saw last night," Mom said.

"I don't suppose you were half as angry at her for spying on me?" I asked. "You're being ridiculous. I'm not a little girl anymore, and I'm trying to earn a living. And yes, Evan and I are friends. Not that it's any of your business."

"Friends?" Dad asked. "Is that what you're calling it?"

"What did Juliana tell you?" From their reactions, I wondered how much truth had been involved.

"Everything," Dad said, significantly. "She told me he sprayed you with love potion-"

"I dropped it on my foot," I corrected. "We were in Belinda's shop. It was swimming in them."

"Oh please," Dad said. "Use common sense. You do know what his gift is, don't you? He could have knocked a bottle off a shelf as easily as breathe, although I suppose with a bit of effort, even Isaac could drop a bottle off a shelf."

This conversation was going nowhere. I threw my hands in the air and spun on my heels. "I'm out of here. Let me know if you ever return to reality."

Mom stood by the door, as if guarding it. She didn't look inclined to let me leave, and in fact, her cheeks had started to grow dangerously red. Remembering her condition, I took a step back and tried to make my voice soothing. It was difficult. I was pretty angry. "Mom, calm down."

"Cassandra, we need to talk about this. It's important. There are things you don't understand."

"Oh yeah?" I asked. "I understand it's none of your business. I'm an adult. It wouldn't even be your business if we were sleeping together."

At that moment, my purse burst into flames. I screamed and threw it aside, but it had caught my shirt on fire as well. Instincts took over and I dropped to the floor, rolling to smother the flames.

Dad was there in an instant, suffocating the last of the fire, but the damage was already done.

"Oh, God, Cassandra, I'm so sorry!" Mom was there then, leaning over me with an anxious expression, all signs of anger gone.

I took inventory of the physical damage. It hurt like hell. The entire right side of my body was scorched from my hair to my hips. There were second degree burns on my shoulder, arms, and hand, and first degree burns running down the side of my torso. The remains of my purse lay a couple feet away, a smoldering ruin. I'd need to spend the afternoon replacing the contents. Worse, my hair had been scorched. Without a mirror handy, I had no idea how badly. Mom could probably regrow it, but I wasn't inclined to ask her for help.

The worst damage, though, was on the inside. Even though I knew it was an accident, the fact remained that my own mother had set me on fire in a moment of anger.

"I'll get Juliana," Mom said.

"No!"

They both stared at me, but I stood my ground. I didn't want to be taken care of, and I didn't want to be protected, especially not by a girl who had stabbed me in the back.

"I don't want that lying *witch* to touch me." I put extra emphasis on the word witch, because I knew it would drive Mom crazy. "What did she tell you happened, exactly?"

Dad's anger had been replaced with uncertainty. "She said you'd slept with him."

"I see." I started to rise to my feet.

"No, wait," Mom said. "I'll get some burn ointment. It's just next door in the lab." She left without waiting for me to respond.

"You didn't, did you?" The hardness on Dad's face melted away as the realization struck.

"No."

"I'm sorry. You know what Mom did–it was an accident. She lost control. She almost set Isaac on fire this morning. He managed a spectacular shield..."

Dad trailed off, but I filled in the rest for him. If I hadn't been such a disappointment, I could have protected myself, too.

"We were just worried about you."

"Why?" I asked. I just didn't get the level of anger. This wasn't about loss of innocence–I had trouble imagining they'd react that way if they heard I slept with Braden. "What is so bad about Evan, anyway? I know you hate his dad, but he's always been good to me."

Dad shook his head. "You don't know everything about him."

"Enlighten me."

Just then, Mom came rushing back in with a bottle of burn ointment. She had the cap unscrewed before she even reached me, then she started rubbing huge quantities of the pale green ointment into the burns. They tingled, and began to feel better right away. She rubbed the ointment into shoulders, side, arm, and hand, then asked if she had missed anything.

"No, that's it." I inspected my arms. The burn was already fading, though I knew it would take a couple more applications to get it all.

"Put this on before bed tonight, and first thing in the morning." Mom placed the bottle in my hand. "If that doesn't take care of it, let me know right away."

"Yeah, okay."

"I'm sorry," Mom said again.

I didn't say anything.

"Why did you need to talk to us?"

Since I still needed to have this conversation, I bit back my hurt feelings and told them about the vampire attack. They were both silent for a while, after I had finished.

"I wanted to call Jason," I said, "but I don't know how to get in touch with him."

"I'll give you his number," Mom said. "It's just so hard to believe... we haven't seen a vampire around here in a long time. I didn't think they would dare."

"One of them did." I stood, and prepared to leave. I didn't think I could stand anymore of their company. "I've got to get going. I'm already late for my lunch date. Oh, and I won't be home for dinner tonight. I have a date with Braden." I put special emphasis on the last sentence.

"Braden?" Mom's face brightened. "That's nice. He's good for you, right?"

"I guess."

There was a pause. "I love you," Dad said.

"Yeah."

"Cassandra," Mom began, then in a whisper, "Cassie."

She had never called me that before. I didn't want to, but I softened at the show of effort.

"I'm so sorry. I love you."

I swallowed. "I love you too, Mom."

I just wished I knew why they had been so angry.

10

When I was in the tenth grade, the Eagle Rock cheerleading squad made the state finals. We were incredibly excited when we heard the news, even when the coach told us we'd have to get on a bus at five in the morning to make it to Jefferson City in time to compete.

The day before the finals, I cut school to go to Springfield and get some gifts for the team. It was a spur of the moment decision. I'm not the sort of person who usually cuts class, but that day, I decided, was special. I talked an older teammate into driving me, and we browsed the shelves at the outlet mall until I found the perfect gifts–tiny gold crosses on woven gold chains. I found two similar crosses in the Catholic style (with a miniature Jesus) for the two Catholic girls on the squad, plus one for myself because I liked it better. For the agnostic in our group, I found a gold pendant in the shape of a teardrop.

On Saturday, bright and early, we boarded the bus, and I passed the necklaces out to everyone on the team. "For protection," I said. They took me seriously. It's the last name.

Here's what you have to understand about crosses and other religious symbols: They have power because we believe they do. The necklaces were just gold–24 karat. One of them wasn't even a cross, it was a teardrop. But we had faith in what those symbols represented. To each of us, I suppose, it was something subtly different: love, hope, salvation, redemption... What does it mean to you? That is it's power.

The night before our bus trip, a truck driver by the name of Jerry stayed up all night long, listening to loud music, and sipping energy drinks to stay awake. At around seven in the morning, he lost his fight with sleep and crossed the grassy median of Interstate 44 into the eastbound lanes.

There wasn't much of our bus left after the collision. Jerry and the bus driver were airlifted to a nearby hospital in critical condition (the bus driver later recovered; Jerry did not), but everyone else on the bus walked away with minor cuts and bruises.

That's the power of faith. We never made it to the state finals, but we made it home alive, and everyone agreed that was miracle enough for one day.

I stopped to phone Jason before leaving the house, picturing him as the awkward fifteen-year-old he had been the last time I had seen him. That had been eight years ago, and he must have changed a lot since then, because his voice, recorded on voice mail, did not fit my image.

"Hi, this is Jason Blane. I'm either dead or with a vampire. Leave a message, and I'll get back if I can."

What struck me about the recording was the calm certainty of it. He wasn't joking. I left a quick message, feeling rather unsettled.

Kaitlin's Diner was packed when I finally made it to lunch, half an hour late.

"There you are!" Kaitlin practically stampeded me at the door. "I tried to call you twice. Why didn't you answer?"

Because my cell phone had melted into the library floor. "Phone's broken," I said, not offering the details.

"Oh God, Cassie, what happened to you?" Kaitlin pulled forward a lock of singed hair.

"It's a long story." I wanted to tell Kaitlin about it, but not when any second, someone would call her over to refill their coke.

As if on cue, someone yelled, "Hey, miss!"

"Sorry," Kaitlin said, hurrying away, leaving me to seek out my friends, Angie and Madison, at our usual booth.

Among other things, Angie was a link to Lloyd and Lyons. She worked there as a receptionist. She also used to be on the cheerleading squad with Kaitlin and me, though our friendship had been a little off and on in high school. Her parents had religious issues with me, and sometimes, I thought she did as well.

Angie was picture perfect, from her sun-streaked brown hair to her straight, white teeth. She was tall and thin, willowy I think some call it. She did look a bit like a strong wind would bend her. That day she wore a sleeveless red turtleneck, which made her look taller and thinner than usual. Lunch, as always, was a garden salad with light Italian salad dressing. Some days, she took half of it home in a doggie bag, but I hoped, for her sake, that it was all public show. One day I would get a look in her closet and find a private stash of candy bars or potato chips.

Sitting next to Angie, Madison looked large, though the contrast itself wasn't fair. Madison is a little on the heavy side, but on her it's all curves. Kaitlin says she looks like the girl next door, but my nearest neighbor is an 85-year-old witch who never looked a thing like Madison, even when she was young. Madison had friendly, attractive features: long, dark hair, bright green eyes, and a cherubic smile, but the best thing about her was her voice. Because of her shyness, I had only heard her sing a few times, but each time stood out in my memory.

Madison and I weren't great friends in high school, but we had gradually become close since then, when she came home from college. She had just graduated in May, managing to earn her degree in only three years. She had gone into college with something like twenty-six credits, and then flown through her coursework. In the fall, she would be student teaching elementary school music, and in the meantime, she worked part-time at the bank her father managed.

When I joined them, they were both staring at my singed hair, their eyes wide with surprise, or curiosity, or disbelief. In Angie's case, definitely disbelief. She didn't believe in magic.

"I don't want to talk about it," I said, hoping to forestall comment.

"Cassie?" Madison clearly had not taken the hint. "You can't just walk in here like someone threw you on the grill and not tell us what happened."

"It's no big deal," I said, but as my gaze shifted to Angie, I could tell that neither girl was going to let me off the hook.

"Was it Nicolas?" Madison asked. "I heard he was trying to get a job with the fire department."

I sighed. I couldn't let people think that, especially if it would ruin his chances to get the job he wanted. He had enough trouble with the fire chief as it was. "No, it wasn't him. It was an accident. Mom's pregnant again."

"Congratulations," Angie said, "but what does that have to do with anything?"

Madison tilted her head to the side in confusion, but before she had a chance to ask, Kaitlin came by to take my order. She gave me and Madison a warm smile that faltered somewhat when she shifted her gaze to Angie. The two didn't get along and only pretended to try for my sake.

"Did you go home after your date last night?" Kaitlin asked Angie.

"What?" Angie's face promptly turned as red as her turtleneck.

"You wore that yesterday."

"It's not what you think," Angie said.

I didn't know what to think. Of all my friends, she was the one I was most certain was a virgin. Then again, she was just as certain I wasn't, so possibly, we were both wrong.

"How about a cheeseburger and coke?" I said, loudly, hoping to forestall any problems.

"Sure." Kaitlin went off to deal with another customer.

"I heard Belinda Hewitt's dead." Madison cleared her throat and cast her eyes anxiously about before adding, "They're saying it's a vampire attack."

I didn't know how word got around so quickly, but I decided, all things considered, that it might be better to confirm the rumors, especially if it helped my friends stay safe. So I nodded.

Angie rolled her eyes. "There's no such thing as vampires."

"Do you still have that cross I gave you back in tenth grade?" I asked.

"Somewhere," she said.

"Well," I said, trying to sound diplomatic, "it never hurts to wear it." I fingered the gold cross around my own neck. "The monster may be literal or figurative, but faith still protects us."

Those must have been the magic words, because Angie softened. Aside from owning a hotel, her father was a preacher at the Gateway Christian Church of Eagle Rock, so she tended to respond to calls for faith.

"I don't have one," Madison said, frowning.

"Get behind a threshold at night," I said. "That's really the best thing to do. Vampires can't come into a home unless they're invited."

Angie looked ready to bolt, but before she got the chance, a loud, angry voice caught our attention. It was coming from a nearby booth, one a little closer to the door, and I had to turn completely around to see what was going on.

I recognized the owner of the angry voice, though I couldn't quite recall his name–maybe Dan or Dave or something similar. He was a local, a year or two ahead of us in school, and had always been known for causing trouble. He abused teachers and students indiscriminately, and though I'm sure he had some deep-seeded issues which made him act that way, I wasn't inclined to charity when he aimed his abuse at my best friend.

"I told you, no salad dressing," he said, "and this water is dirty. There's something floating in it. No wonder you can't get a better job, if you can't even manage a simple order."

"I'm sorry," Kaitlin said, and I could tell she held onto civility by a thread. "Apparently, I misheard you. I'll be happy to get you a new salad and glass of water."

"Here, take this one back to the kitchen." Then, to everyone's astonishment, Dan threw the salad at Kaitlin, showering her in bits of cheese and lettuce, and getting ranch salad dressing in her hair.

The diner went silent, and everyone turned to watch the proceedings. I was trying to decide if I should do something, when Mrs. Meyer, Kaitlin's mom and owner of the diner, hurried out from behind the bar to confront the customer.

"I'm going to have to ask you to leave," Mrs. Meyer said.

"Why should I leave? I haven't had my lunch yet."

The diner was so quiet by then that the jingle of the bell, announcing the presence of a new customer, rang out like a gunshot. I looked up to see Evan standing there, studying the quiet diner as if trying to figure out what he had just walked into.

Neither Mrs. Meyer nor the abusive customer noticed him at all. "If you don't leave," Mrs. Meyer said, "I'll call the police."

Dan sneered. "Why don't you just get me some clean water?" With that, he threw the contents of the supposedly dirty glass at Mrs. Meyer, splashing liquid all down her front, and splattering a few drops on a nearby customer. "Call the police," Mrs. Meyer said to someone in the kitchen.

Evan moved away from the door, reaching Mrs. Meyer and the offensive customer in a few long, purposeful strides. As soon as the man saw him, the sneer fell from his face, and his eyes popped.

"Get out," Evan said. Just that. No threats, no raised voice, and not the slightest stirring of magic, which he rarely used in public, despite what many believed.

Dan scrambled out of the booth and out the door, moving so fast that his legs got twisted up beneath him, causing him to fall on his face just outside the diner.

A few people laughed, mostly tourists. The rest were a little too stunned by what they had just seen, or, more likely, thought they saw. I almost rolled my eyes, but figured it would do me no good.

"I need to talk to Evan," I said to my friends. "Sorry to cut our lunch short today."

I slid out of the booth, crossed the short distance between us, and touched Evan on the shoulder. "Let me give Kaitlin a hand, then I'll be right out."

"Fine."

Kaitlin hadn't moved, so I grabbed her by the arm and led her to the kitchen to help get her clean. We slid through the double doors, steered past a few cooks who were trying to figure out what had happened, and made our way to a hand sink near the back.

Kaitlin grabbed a clean towel, dampened it, and tried to scrub salad dressing off her face. "Someone turned up the crazy today."

I couldn't argue with that one, so I just took the towel from her and started dabbing dressing out of her red curls.

"I've got to quit this place," Kaitlin said. "It's not healthy."

"The cheeseburgers do have about a thousand grams of fat in them."

"I'm serious," Kaitlin said.

"I know you are."

"You look like you're having about as good a day as I am. Want to talk about it? We could hang out at my place after work."

"Can't," I said, "I've got a date."

"So do I. So what?"

I almost laughed, but since I suspected Kaitlin was having trouble with her boyfriend, I couldn't quite manage it. "I want to keep mine."

"So what happened to you?" Kaitlin asked, fingering my hair.

"My mom's pregnant again." I don't know why that's the first thing I told her.

"That's cool. I wish I had a big family."

I handed Kaitlin the towel again. "I've done what I can." She would need to wash it properly to get the rest out.

"Did you see what Evan did?" Kaitlin said, taking the towel and dabbing it at the front of her uniform.

The entire kitchen staff was busily trying to pretend not to listen.

"I don't know what you're talking about," I said.

"Sure you don't. He made that guy fall on his face."

I doubted it, but didn't think Kaitlin would believe me if I tried to explain. "All he did was walk in, and tell the guy to get out."

"Yes, but did you see the look on his face?" Kaitlin asked, and then, before I had a chance to respond, she plucked the crystal I had gotten her the day before out of her front pocket. "He came by this morning."

"Did he apologize?"

"Not exactly, but he said this thing wasn't very strong, so he took it and did something to it. Now it's almost hot."

"Really?" He had clearly put some real protections on the crystal, but giving away magic like that wasn't usually done.

"Did you know I had a crush on him in school?" Kaitlin went on.

"Um, no." I looked toward the door, dreaming of escape so I wouldn't have to hear more on the subject. "I'm glad you're not scared of him anymore, though."

"Who said I wasn't?" Kaitlin laughed.

I shook my head. "I'm going to head back, if you're okay."

"Sure, I'm fine. Thanks."

When I returned to the dining room, it looked as if nothing had happened, except, of course, that Evan sat in the booth recently vacated by Dan. I sat across from him, offering a forced smile he didn't return.

"What's wrong?" I asked.

"What happened to you?" Evan gestured at my hair and blotchy skin.

I groaned. Apparently, this was going to be an issue all day, but at least Evan might understand. "It was an accident. Mom's pregnant again."

"Oh." Something flickered across his face, so quickly anyone else would have missed it, but it reminded me of his reaction every time I told him my mother was pregnant again. He didn't like being an only child.

"What got her so worked up?" Evan asked.

"Oh." My face went red, and I found myself wishing I had a drink, so I could cover the awkward moment.

As if on cue, Kaitlin swung by with a couple of cokes, setting one down in front of each of us, though she only had eyes for Evan. She gave him her flirtiest smile, leaned in close, and said, "On the house."

I glared at her, but she didn't see. Evan, on the other hand, didn't seem to know what to do with her, which struck me as odd, since he had never had any trouble with girls in the past. Not that he had ever shown any interest in Kaitlin. I think she was too needy.

"Thanks," Evan said. "I can pay."

"I bet you can," Kaitlin said, still smiling. "Can I recommend the fried chicken sandwich?"

"Sure," he said.

"Coming right up."

Evan stared after her.

"It's your own fault, you know," I said. "She thinks you rescued her and made that guy fall on his face."

"I didn't," he said. I had assumed as much, but it was nice to have confirmation.

"They were about to call the police; you didn't have to get involved."

"The place is full. I didn't want to wait for a table."

I shook my head. "You haven't changed, have you?"

"In some ways, no, in some ways, quite a bit. But in case you were wondering, you haven't succeeded in distracting me. Why was your mom so upset? It's not because you're working for me, is it?"

I sighed, resigned to telling him the truth, or at least, part of it. "Juliana was spying on me last night when I dropped the love potion on my foot. She told my parents about it, with some embellishments, just for spite."

He nodded his understanding, but he didn't ask further questions.

"So listen," I said, "I assume you heard about Belinda?"

"That's why I'm here." Evan took a sip of the coke, closed his eyes, and added. "And for the food. I haven't had anything remotely sugary or greasy in three years. Master Wolf thinks that stuff interferes with the harmonious balance of natural energies."

"What does that mean?" I asked.

"No idea. Now, tell me about Belinda."

I took a deep breath. "She turned."

Surprise flickered across Evan's face, but before he had a chance to follow up on my statement, Kaitlin arrived with our sandwiches. Very intentionally, she brushed Evan's arm as she set his plate in front of him. "Let me know if you need anything else."

"How about some ketchup?" I said, loudly, from the other side of the booth.

Her smile faltered when she looked at me. "All right."

"She turned?" Evan prompted, when Kaitlin had disappeared.

"Yes." Quickly, I gave him a run-down of what I had seen that morning, and what I suspected. He didn't contradict anything I said, not even my confusion over the blood at the scene, which I had hoped he could shed some light on.

"Did she kill Nancy?" Evan asked.

"I don't know. I realize that when Belinda died, the threshold around her house disappeared, but the attack still probably happened in daylight. So I'm not sure what to think, and I don't want to start drawing conclusions until I have a few more facts."

"What's next, then?" Evan asked.

"Something needs to be done about the sheriff, we should probably talk to Jasmine Hewitt to ask her about the anti-venom vaccine, and it might be time to talk to some of Belinda's alleged boyfriends, to find out which one she spent the weekend with. I have a feeling Belinda was turned over the weekend, while she was at the cabin, because of the blood, and because the resort's log indicated she checked in Friday evening, before sunset."

"I've got an idea for the sheriff," Evan said. "I can take care of it this afternoon, after lunch."

I glanced at Madison, who was pretending not to watch Evan and me. A week or two ago, she had mentioned her suspicion that her hairdresser was one of Belinda's latest paramours, which gave me an idea. "And I think I'm going to find out if Madison's hairdresser takes walk-ins. If he doesn't have any good information for me, maybe he'll at least keep people from looking in horror at my hair."

II

It would be pretty daunting to compile a list of girls Evan dated in high school. So instead, I'll talk about some of the girls he did *not* date.

There was Laura Brown, who started dating Mark Price in the eighth grade and married him just after graduation. There was Heidi Jenkins, who didn't seem to understand the finer points of personal hygiene. Cindy Connor, the most beautiful and popular girl in school, was also among the meanest, so Evan avoided her.

Then, of course, there was me, and while I realize I was exaggerating his dating prowess, it didn't feel that way when, during our senior year of high school, he took Madison Carter to homecoming. Call me uncharitable if you like, but until I had befriended her late in our junior year, Madison's greatest social accomplishment had been invisibility.

I didn't have a date, though I went to the dance with a large group of my cheerleading friends, trying to pretend it didn't bother me. I suppose I was a little jealous, although the feeling didn't last long. I didn't know why Madison had agreed to go with him, but when I watched them together, I had to wonder if she had been too afraid to refuse. Odd, since Evan usually avoided those kinds of girls.

Sometime during the evening, Evan asked me to dance, and I asked him why he had invited her.

"It's nothing serious," he said. It was his standard line. "I just had a feeling I'd like her, if I could get to know her."

"That doesn't seem likely," I said.

He gave me a rueful smile. "No, it doesn't. You've spent some time with her lately, what do you think?"

"I think she's lonely, and she has a hard time trusting people, but I have no idea why."

"Well, if anyone can help bring her out of her shell, you can."

༄༅

Evan and I agreed to meet back at the diner when we finished our errands, so we could tackle an interview—or, more likely, a confrontation—with Jasmine Hewitt together.

To my surprise, Madison decided to walk with me.

"Don't you have to work today?" I asked.

Madison shook her head. "Tuesday is my day off. Do you mind if I keep you company for a while?"

"Not at all."

We walked in silence for a minute or two before Madison spoke again. "Is it just me, or is Evan taller?"

"It's not just you." I smiled at her in what I hoped was an encouraging way. "He won't bite, you know."

"That's not exactly what I'm afraid of."

"What, then?"

She drew in a deep breath. "I know you don't believe the rumors, but I swear he did cast love spells."

"Madison, seriously?" It was all I could think to say, and I didn't try to hide my exasperation.

She shrugged, and walked in silence for a long time. It took me a while to realize that she hadn't changed her mind, she simply didn't want the confrontation. I had been trying for years to draw her out of her shell, with some success, but we still had a lot of work to do.

"Why do you think he casts love spells?" I asked. "You only went on one date with him, didn't you? To a dance? Do you think he coerced you into going with him?"

"No, he didn't coerce me. It was actually... never mind. He didn't coerce me. And it wasn't a touch or a smile, like some of the silly girls said. It was the kiss."

"He kissed you?" For some reason, I found that hard to picture.

"Just the once. It was enough."

"All right." We were nearing our destination, but I waned to finish this before we arrived. "Let's say, for the sake of argument, that you're right. I still don't get why you're so afraid of him. Do you expect him to kiss you again?"

"No," she said, her eyes wide. "I'm not afraid for me. I'm afraid for you."

We reached Robert's shop, built into an old brick strip mall with a sign over the door reading, "Robert's Beauty Salon." I stopped, my hands on the door, and stared at Madison.

"We're just friends," I said. "Maybe not even that. I'm working a case for him, trying to figure out what happened to his cousin."

"Did you miss the way he looked at you and kept touching you?"

"I must have." I had noticed the touches, actually, though not the looks. The trouble was, it didn't make sense. Evan and I hadn't seen one another for three years, and then suddenly, out of nowhere, he develops an interest in me, when he never noticed me that way before? Not that I had ever tried to encourage him, but he had noticed practically everyone else.

"Just don't let him kiss you," Madison said.

On that note, I pushed open the door, which swung outward with a little tingle of bells. I wasn't prepared for the sight that greeted me inside. Robert, a tall, thin man in his early thirties, stood with his back to me, his scissors flying in seemingly random directions over a customer's head. But that wasn't the part that startled me. It was his bubble-gum pink hair.

Apparently, Madison wasn't prepared for it either, because she gasped.

Robert turned slightly, "I''ll be with you in a minute." Then he continued what he was doing.

I gave Madison an, "Are you sure about this?" look.

She shrugged and pointed to her own hair as if to say, "He did okay by me."

Half a dozen chairs at the front of the shop constituted a waiting area. Madison and I took the two nearest the door.

"Finished!" Robert announced with a flourish. He spun the chair around, and I saw, to my surprise, the mayor of Eagle Rock, James Blair.

James Blair is a sorcerer, though very few people are aware of it. He keeps a low profile, magically speaking, because his entire family is neck deep in politics. His sister is a judge, and his oldest son is a state senator. I don't know how powerful he is, but I do know what his gift is–human lie detector. I suppose that helps him in politics. Or, let's face it, that would help him just about anywhere.

"Cassandra," Mr. Blair said in a deep, carrying voice. "It's been a while."

It had been a while, though I was glad for it. The last time I'd seen him, he had been trying to set me up with one of his sons. He kind of gave me the creeps, but I'm pretty sure it wasn't the distinguished older gentleman good looks, or even the fact that he'd wanted to see me get together with one of his boys. No, I'm pretty sure it was the way he knew whether or not I was telling the truth at any given moment. It's not that I go around lying all the time, but everybody has something to hide.

"Cassie," I corrected, almost automatically.

He shook his head. "That's not true."

Like I said, he gave me the creeps.

"Nice haircut," I said.

"Thank you. Perhaps I ought to leave a nice tip."

While Mayor Blair paid Robert, Madison whispered to me, "See? The mayor comes here. He does a nice job."

"Yeah," I whispered back, "but what did he do to his hair?"

Madison shrugged.

The mayor gave me a smile and a wink as he walked out of the shop. Then Robert turned to us. "Can I help you?"

"I don't know," I said. "What did you do to your hair?"

"Cassie!" Madison looked away.

"What?" I know there are rules out there for what you should and shouldn't say to people, and I usually stick to them, but I like my hair, and thought it at least deserved an interview.

Robert shook his head and frowned deeply. It was the kind of frown that touched his eyes, which didn't look at all pink.

"It was the shampoo Belinda gave me. For a while, it was the best I'd ever used, and then suddenly this morning." He gestured helplessly at his hair.

That opened up a new range of questions, none of which I thought he could help me answer. One of those questions was whether or not to let him anywhere near my hair.

"What did you do to your hair?" Robert asked. He inflated a bit, and before I was even aware of it, he was leading me by the arm to one of his chairs. "Come on, sit down. I can fix it. It will be much shorter, of course, but I can work with this. You have such lovely, thick hair."

"Um-"

"Sit," he ordered.

I sat.

"I did Madison's hair last week," Robert said, gesturing to the waiting area where Madison sat, watching us. "Doesn't she look nice? I tried to talk her into highlights but she wouldn't listen."

"It's nice," I said. It didn't really need highlights, although if he didn't go over the top, I could see how a subtle infusion of color would be an improvement. That's not really what I wanted to talk about, though. "I've been hired to look into Belinda Hewitt's murder."

Robert started spraying my hair down with a squirt bottle. "And?"

"Were you seeing her?" I asked.

"I guess." Robert didn't sound enthusiastic. He may have been under the influence of a love potion at one time, but he definitely wasn't anymore. "I was actually going to break up with her after this." He stopped squirting and gestured at his hair. "But there wasn't much point, was there?"

"No," I agreed.

Robert picked up a comb and a pair of scissors. I closed my eyes.

"So, how long had you been seeing her?"

"About a month."

I heard the snip of the scissors very close to my ear, and imagined I could hear the long tendrils of hair clunk to the floor.

"When was the last time you saw her?" I asked.

Snip. Snip. "Friday morning. She said she was going out of town with some friends over the weekend. What does it matter, anyway? Didn't a vampire kill her?"

"Do you believe in vampires?" I asked.

"Belinda has a way of making a believer out of you." He brushed his finger over the gold cross at my neck. "Can't be me, though, can it? If I can touch your cross?"

"No, I suppose not."

We passed the next few minutes in silence. Then, with the same flourish he'd used to conclude the mayor's session, he spun me around to face the mirror.

I opened my eyes. It looked–different. I reached up to touch the wavy auburn tendrils that spilled around my ears. I'd lost a good ten inches of hair, but that wasn't Robert's fault. In fact, he had done a very nice job with what he had. It wasn't what I would have chosen, but it was a look I could live with until it grew out.

"You look great, Cassie," Madison said. Of course she would say that whether I did or not, but I chose to believe her. At least I didn't have the mayor's gift of detecting lies. Sometimes, it's better not to know for sure.

Just then, the bell chimed, and Evan strode through the door. I was surprised, since I thought we had agreed to meet at the diner. He looked at Robert and his bubble-gum pink hair without the slightest hint of alarm, though a small smile touched his lips.

"Come on, Cassie, we need to talk to Jasmine Hewitt."

"All right." I quickly paid for the haircut, then headed for the door.

"Bye, Madison," Evan said, "it was nice to see you again."

"Nice to see you, too," she mumbled.

"Bye, Madison," I said. "See you tomorrow?"

"Yes, see you."

I turned to go, but Madison still had one last thing to say. "Evan, you'd better not hurt her."

Turning back around, I saw that Madison was surprised by her own daring, but not more surprised than me. There are moments, in a relationship, that separate true friendship from the fair weather variety. This was one of those moments, even if it was driven by her misguided notions.

"I knew I liked you," Evan said. "Don't worry, I'll take care of her."

12

I GOT INTO MY FIRST CAR ACCIDENT THE DAY AFTER I EARNED MY DRIVER'S license. It wasn't a big deal, really, just a fender bender, but it had definitely been my fault. I was talking on my cell phone, and listening to the stereo at full blast, while backing out of a parking space at the Food Mart. By the time I realized the honking noise was directed at me, it was too late to stop.

I turned off the stereo, ended the phone call, and stepped out of the car. Most unfortunately, Jasmine Hewitt glared angrily at me from the other car.

She stepped out of her car, her eyes tinted nearly black, deep lines in her sour face. She was at least sixty years old and looked every bit of it, from her wiry gray hair to her gnarled fingers.

She pointed one of those fingers, tipped in red nail polish, at me. "Can't you see?" Her voice carried more than anger in it, and the next instant, the answer to the question became a resounding no.

"Hey!" I started rubbing furiously at my eyes with my hands, but it did no good. The world was completely black. I couldn't even detect the faintest trace of light, as you sometimes can even with your eyes closed tightly shut.

"At least you won't be a threat to anyone anymore," Mrs. Hewitt said with a laugh that sounded a lot like a cackle. All she needed was a broomstick and a pointy hat.

"Accidents happen," I said. "That's what insurance is for."

"Insurance doesn't bring people back from the dead, sweetie. What if you'd killed someone?"

"At less than ten miles an hour?" I sighed and checked myself. Reason was obviously not going to work with this woman, so I switched to threats. "Do you know who my parents are?"

"Should I?"

"Edward and Sheila Scot."

There wasn't an immediate response.

"Mrs. Hewitt?" I said.

"Oh hell," she said. I heard a car door slam and an engine rev up.

"Mrs. Hewitt?" I repeated.

"You deserve this," she said. "I think your parents will agree."

Then she drove away.

As it happened, my parents did not agree. I wish I could have seen the confrontation when my parents found out what had happened, but I was blind. Suffice to say, it was one of those not-so-subtle moments that has given my family a certain degree of notoriety in Eagle Rock.

When I was able to see again, the first thing I noticed was what everyone else in town was looking at—the large column of fire and smoke curling above Jasmine Hewitt's home. The flames never actually touched the house, but it was a near thing.

Later, the die-hard disbelievers swore it had simply been a forest fire, but they never could explain why not a single tree had been scorched.

ৎ৩

Once Evan and I were settled into his Prius, I decided I had to ask, "Do you know what happened to Robert's hair?"

A corner of his mouth twitched upward. "It was part of my community service project. I intercepted a shipment of shampoo to his shop last week, found it all spiked with love potion, and added an agent to counteract it."

"Wait a minute, all the shampoo was spiked? The ones he's selling in his shop? Will his customers' hair start turning pink?" I touched mine, anxiously, then remembered I hadn't gotten my hair washed.

"Most of it had a weak potion in it, something to make people more susceptible to romantic invitations. That was easy to counteract, but one had a note on it, saying something like 'for my special man,' and that one was far more powerful. I had to use more extreme measures."

"Oh." I would have to trust that he had done what he needed to do, but I still had one more question. "Did Belinda often sell love potions to the unsuspecting public like that? Slipping it into shampoo bottles, I mean?"

"Yes." Evan's jaw went rigid, and I could see the topic upset him. "She thought there wasn't enough love in the world."

We drove in silence for a few minutes, and then Evan broached another subject. "What got Madison's hackles up?"

My face turned a little pink. "Oh, she's just terrified of you; you know that."

"That's exactly why I'm curious."

I hesitated. Every time I'd brought up love spells with him, the conversation had gone badly.

"Don't worry," Evan said, offering me an encouraging smile, "whatever she said, I won't hex her."

"I know. She's just one of the people who's convinced you cast love spells."

"Ah," he said, looking more serious, "and she thinks you're my next victim?"

"Yes," I said. No point in sugar-coating it. "I explained we were just friends, and I'm seeing someone else, but she has this weird idea that you can cast love spells with a kiss."

"Does she?" If the accusation upset Evan, he didn't show it.

I found myself momentarily staring at his full lips. "So do you have some kind of magic kiss?"

"Oh, yes." Evan's serious expression melted away, and a mischievous grin took its place. "I can drive a woman to orgasm with a single kiss."

I snorted. I covered my mouth with my hand, somewhat mortified by the reaction, but his quip had been just the thing to break the dark mood that had been hanging over our heads ever since we found his poor, battered cousin. I needed to laugh, though I almost felt guilty for doing so with the image of her mutilated body still so fresh in my mind.

"What? You don't believe me?" Evan asked with wide-eyed innocence. "You should try it sometime."

I laughed again, this time pushing the guilt away. "There's an image. No wonder you never had trouble getting dates, and here I thought they were just in awe of you."

"Good thing you never had that problem."

"Yeah, good thing." Although, I noted with some chagrin, I did have another problem. The more time I spent with Evan, the more I did, in fact, want to kiss him. I had pushed thoughts of him out of my mind since high school, branding what I had felt as a silly crush, but I couldn't deny the spark of attraction still existed. Had Madison seen it? Was that why she warned me off? And did Evan, despite his lighthearted banter, feel the same spark? Did I want him to?

No, I decided, I didn't want him to feel that way. I had moved on, and Braden was a great guy. Not to mention one who couldn't, even accidentally, throw someone fifty feet and put him in a coma. I hated thinking that way, because Evan was far, far more than a long ago accident, but I understood better than anyone how accidents could happen. My mother had reminded me of that, quite painfully, earlier in the day. The scars were still fresh.

The house came into view then—a modest two-story dwelling that reminded me of Belinda's in all but the most important aspect: the plant life. There were a few shrubs along the path leading to the house, but that was about it.

A sign in the front yard read: NO TRESPASSERS. VIOLATERS WILL BE CURSED.

"That's friendly," I muttered. "I hope this ends better than our run-in this morning."

"What happened this morning?" Evan asked as he pulled into the short driveway.

I hadn't meant to tell him, although it had been a pretty careless slip, so maybe some part of me wanted him to know. I had felt pretty relieved when he suggested visiting Mrs. Hewitt together, since I didn't want to face her by myself again.

"I ran into her this morning," I said, "and asked her if she'd seen Belinda. She tried to curse me, but it's all right. I had some nettle on hand, so whatever it was, it's on her now."

Evan put the car in park and gave me a look I recognized all too well. It was the same look I had seen on his face the day he had hurt Paul Ellerson. Maybe I shouldn't have slipped. I shouldn't have had an ounce of compassion for the old witch, but she had just lost her daughter, and she had already fallen on her own curse.

"That is not all right," Evan said.

"She only ended up hurting herself, and besides, she must have been hurting pretty badly to do it, after what happened a few years ago."

"The fireball. I saw it." Evan clenched his hands into fists, then slowly let go. "Fine, but she'd better not give you so much as a dirty look while I'm here."

"Dirty is her natural facial expression," I said.

He laughed, and most of his hostility eased away. It was good to know he still had his sense of humor.

No sooner had we stepped on the path leading to the house, then the front door banged open, and Jasmine Hewitt stepped onto the porch, looking exactly as ugly and unfriendly as she had that morning. If she still suffered from the effects of the backfired curse, I couldn't see them.

"What are you doing here?" Mrs. Hewitt aimed a long, bony finger threateningly at me, and I saw that she still wore red fingernail polish. "The sheriff's already been here, and I won't talk to you."

Evan drew up alongside me, and very deliberately, slid his hand around my waist. Mrs. Hewitt's eyes widened somewhat, making me think she had not seen him until that moment.

"We're trying to figure out what happened to your daughter, Mrs. Hewitt," I said with as much respect as I could manage, which wasn't much. "I'd think you'd want to help us."

"You don't care what happened to my girl," Mrs. Hewitt said. "You want to know what happened to Nancy Hastings."

She kept shooting sideways looks at Evan, as though sizing him up. If she thought she could take him, she really had lost her mind.

"She is my cousin," Evan said, stepping slightly in front of me. "Now put those daggers back in your eyes before you hurt yourself. There's no reason we can't work together on this. We both want the same things."

"You have no idea what I want," Mrs. Hewitt said.

"Did the sheriff tell you it was a vampire attack?" I asked.

"He told me you said so." She couldn't have made it plainer that she didn't believe me. "I wouldn't trust the word of someone like you."

Evan started to say something, but I cut him off. I could handle a few insults; I'd handled worse, and from people I liked a lot more.

"Actually, Mrs. Hewitt, it was pretty obvious, since she had turned into a vampire."

"Liar." A shadow passed over Mrs. Hewitt's face and she scowled. "That's just not possible."

"I assure you," I said, "it is. Even someone like me can see when a person has turned into a vampire."

"You're a disgrace. If you didn't have your daddy to hide behind–"

"He wasn't with me this morning," I said.

Her eyes flashed. "You ran like a frightened child, and I notice you couldn't face me again without backup."

The kernel of truth in her statements made me hesitate. I could have armed myself with a few more protections and come alone, but even though she was far from the strongest practitioner in town, I normally dealt with her by using my family name. I had wanted to bring Evan only because she seemed beyond that kind of reasoning ability today.

Evan had apparently had enough, either because of her latest jab or my hesitation. "Are you upset because Cassie took you on and won, or because you know if you try anything again, you'll have to answer to me?"

She clenched her fists into tight balls, but she couldn't take on Evan, not by a long shot, even if she looked like she wanted to try. "My daughter did not turn."

A silence spread between us, thick and palpable. I think everyone was waiting for someone else to break it, and I, for one, was struck by Mrs. Hewitt's certainty. She had given her daughter the anti-venom potion, probably as a child. Of that, I had no doubt. Now, I needed to find out if the potion had failed, or if Belinda had found a way to counteract it, intentionally becoming a vampire.

"When did you last see your daughter?" I asked, breaking the silence.

"Last week. I met both my girls for lunch on Monday. And no, she never mentioned anyone she was seeing. I didn't ask after her love life. I disapproved, to be honest."

"Why did you disapprove?" I asked.

"Because she sometimes managed to make very powerful people very angry with her." Mrs. Hewitt wouldn't look at us, but we had seen the scrapbook, and knew the truth of her words.

"Thank you, Mrs. Hewitt," I said. "I think we've taken enough of your time."

"You can't trust him," Mrs. Hewitt called to my retreating back. "Men are all snakes and the ones with power are pythons, especially when it comes to girls like you."

"What's that supposed to mean?" I asked, but before I even had a chance to turn around, the door slammed shut, and Mrs. Hewitt disappeared inside.

"Come on." Evan's hand was at my back, a firm pressure ushering me away. "She's just a crazy, bitter old lady."

I let him guide me back to the car, but I felt uneasy. Her last words may simply have been the parting shot of a crazy old lady lashing out at the world, but coupled with Madison's observations, and his hand at my back, I couldn't help but wonder.

"I have a date tonight," I said as soon as we climbed back into the car.

"With Braden?" He started the engine and pulled out of the driveway.

"Yeah."

"Is it serious?" he asked.

"Yes."

"Okay." Just that simple word. He didn't sound upset or even resigned. Maybe I had gotten my signals mixed up; I never had been good at flirting, or noticing when men were flirting with me.

"I still have some shopping to do," I said, "since my mom burned my purse and all its contents. I need a new cell phone. It would be nice if you had one, too."

"Won't argue with that one, but it won't happen until I graduate."

"So, listen," I said, deciding to get down to business, "I believed Mrs. Hewitt when she implied she vaccinated her daughter."

"Me too."

"So what went wrong? Is there a failure rate? Or did she find some way to counteract the potion, so she could intentionally become a vampire?"

He hesitated just long enough for me to let my own unspoken fear rise to the surface. Belinda Hewitt, while a gifted herbalist, didn't have a lot in the way of magical talent. She wasn't dry, like me, but I did wonder if somehow the degree of magical talent was related to protection. Some potions didn't work at all on me, not many, but some.

"Sometimes, the potion fails if you only take one dose," Evan said. "That's why there's a booster three years later."

"Mrs. Hewitt might not have known that," I said. "The magical world doesn't exactly like to share."

"No, but in this case, it really is common knowledge. Master Wolf sent out pamphlets to all the magical households a couple of decades ago, giving detailed instructions for making and using the potion."

My jaw dropped. "He did?"

"Remember, I told you he's of the opinion we'd all be better off if we organized. There's this guy on the east coast, Alexander DuPris, that's been working towards magical unification for years, and Master Wolf follows everything he does. They've compiled a book of common knowledge–things they think all magic users should know."

I thought I'd heard my father mention the movement as well, with great contempt, but I didn't follow magical politics very closely.

"I didn't realize it was a matter of public record. Should I mention it to the sheriff?" I usually had some leeway in what I could tell the sheriff.

"No," Evan said, sharply, making me jump. "Sorry." His voice softened. "Look, a lot of people got pretty upset with Master Wolf when he passed around the information. We can't protect everyone, and right now we think the vampires don't know about it. The more people who know, the more likely they'll find out."

"What do you think?" I asked.

"I don't know. Master Wolf makes a good argument about the dangers of letting a sorcerer become a vampire."

I shuddered at the image. "One thing's for sure, we need to talk to a hunter. Things aren't adding up, and I can't put my finger on why. If Jason's tried to call me back, I won't know because I don't have a phone."

"Okay, we'll pick this back up tomorrow. I need to spend some time with my family this evening, anyway. Hopefully, your cousin will have called you by then. If not, we'll figure something else out."

"Sounds good. Meet me at my office at eight?"

"Master Wolf may need me to do a few things tomorrow morning, but I'll find you. If you're not at your office, I'll stop by the diner to use a phone."

"Okay."

"Just do me one favor. Don't let your date go on too late tonight. Sunset's around eight forty; you need to be behind a threshold by then."

13

I didn't know if I was in love with Braden or not. It had been a concept I'd played with for most of our time together, wondering what it even meant or whether it was simply something you decided to do. We had never used those words with one another, a fact for which I was grateful, because I didn't want to have to decide in a heated moment whether or not, "I love you," was something I wanted to say to him.

We had always been honest with one another, a concept some have had difficulty with, given the fact that we agreed to a non-exclusive relationship. But we had agreed to it; it's not like he cheated on me. When our lives had taken us down two different paths, we didn't make any false promises, but we still agreed to keep one another in mind. It was always fun, while it lasted, then he would go back to school, and I would return to whatever I was doing–first junior college, then my job as a deputy, and finally my attempt at entrepreneurship.

As for the fact that he saw other people and I didn't, well, it didn't bother me all that much. I think part of me enjoyed my quasi-single status. If I had ever wanted to, I could date someone, but if I didn't, I could always use Braden as an excuse to say no.

Lately, though, I had begun to wonder what I really wanted, both from Braden and from life. We had never even slept together, because I wouldn't take that step without a little more commitment. It didn't look like things would change anytime soon, either, not since he planned to attend law school in Chicago in the fall. In fact, he would be even further away than before, and while he had talked about returning to Eagle Rock when he obtained his law degree, that time still seemed so far off.

Meanwhile, I didn't know what I wanted from my own life. Facing the reality of what it was like to be a deputy had been hard. Maybe I would even have enjoyed being a cop in a different city, but my childhood dreams had me serving and protecting my family and friends, not a city full of strangers. Leaving Eagle Rock had never really crossed my mind.

Braden arrived promptly at five thirty, a tentative smile on his handsome face, carrying a bouquet of red roses. Red roses are a powerful symbol of love, passion, and fertility, but Braden didn't understand their potential, and I wasn't going to clue him in. They were beautiful and romantic.

He wasn't prone to giving me flowers, though, and I wondered if he had made the effort because Juliana had told him her lies.

He looked great, like an anchor of normalcy in the middle of a storm. He'd had his blond hair freshly cut, his face freshly shaved, and he smelled of my favorite aftershave. So why didn't I feel that spark of chemistry I'd grudgingly acknowledged feeling with Evan? It couldn't be simply because we had been together for three years, and were settling into a more mature relationship, because most of those three years had been spent at a distance. Besides, I had known Evan longer.

"You're beautiful," Braden said. "I love the new haircut."

I fingered my hair, still a little surprised to find it above my shoulders. "Thanks. You look nice, too."

He handed me the roses and gave me a quick peck on the cheek. I grabbed him around the neck as he pulled away, drawing him into a real kiss, setting the roses on my desk so they wouldn't get smashed. It felt nice, familiar, and even a little sexy, but I couldn't tell if any of that meant I loved him.

When we came up for air, Braden smiled and held out his arm. "Shall we? I made reservations at Hodge Mill."

I took his arm and let him lead me to street level, but when we left the building, I didn't see his car. Braden lifted his key ring with deliberate slowness and clicked a button. The answering click came from a new Mustang a few spaces away.

"You got a new car!" I squealed as I ran over to it. I love the smell of new cars. I opened the driver's side door and settled in behind the wheel, testing the feel of the controls.

"Ahem," Braden said.

I gave him an innocent look. "Yes?"

"I'll be your chauffeur this evening." Braden offered his hand to help me out of the car. I took it, allowing him to guide me to the passenger side.

A gentle summer breeze lifted my hair, and I looked toward the west, where the sun was playing tag with a low cloud bank. I fingered the cross at my neck, but was determined not to let recent events ruin this evening.

"Where did you get the money for this?" I asked as Braden pulled the car into the street.

"The down payment was a graduation present from my parents," he said. "I figured I needed something new for when I start law school in the fall."

That dampened the mood a bit. I didn't want to think about him leaving again in a couple of months, only about the time we would have until then.

"So," Braden said, "I hear you're dating Evan Blackwood?"

I fought the urge to groan. "Where did you hear that?"

"Your sister mentioned it. It's cool if you are, I was just curious. We established right up front that we weren't going to stop one another from seeing other people while we were apart."

"Juliana is mad at me, and she's spreading rumors. I'm not seeing Evan, we're just working together right now. He's really about the last person I would consider dating." *Not true,* my conscience whispered, *that's not what it looked like this morning when you were wondering what it would be like to kiss him.*

"Oh." Braden sounded more relieved than I expected, making me wonder if he had some idea about taking our relationship to a new level tonight, and if so, what that level might be. Kaitlin had hinted strongly that he might propose this summer, but really, was that likely? Maybe he would just tell me he loved me, in which case, I would have to decide on a response.

"So you're not seeing anyone?" Braden asked.

"No," I assured him, though I hastened to add. "I could have. It's not like you don't have other girlfriends." I let that last bit dangle as almost a question.

"I don't have other girlfriends anymore. Last week, I told Charlotte it was over."

"Oh." I looked out the window so he wouldn't see my smile.

We passed the rest of the ride talking about his weekend camping trip, a nice change from the more monstrous conversations I'd been having lately. For the space of the short drive to the restaurant, I let myself forget about the case, about my mom's pregnancy, and especially about vampires.

Hodge Mill was on form, as usual. They had us seated a minute after we arrived; water glasses showed up thirty seconds after that. Not that they were terribly busy on a Tuesday evening. Only about a quarter of the tables were filled, which was perfect for a private conversation.

An odd tension filled the air over dinner, and we had more trouble finding conversation than usual. Maybe it was because most of my life at that moment was mired in magic, and that was something Braden and I didn't usually discuss, but I think something else hung between us. We had reached a crossroads, but I didn't know if we would end up leaving it in the same direction.

"I hear you have a case," Braden said over dessert.

"Yes, trying to figure out what happened to Nancy Hastings and Belinda Hewitt."

"Everyone's saying a vampire attack was involved."

"Yeah."

"Should I be worried?" His eyes danced down to my cross.

"Yes."

"The priest at the Catholic Church was blessing bottles of water this afternoon, and there's been a run on crosses. I don't think you can buy one within fifty miles of here."

"Good." I let a smile spread across my face, thinking of the entire town gearing up for battle, although I hoped, fiercely, that none of them would have to fight. Maybe, with everyone armed and protected, the vampire would realize the town was too much trouble and leave. Although personally, I wanted to find him first.

"There are a few dissenters, of course."

"Of course." I thought about Angie, and shook my head. "But at least word is getting around."

"Listen." Braden's tone grew suddenly serious. "I know we've been avoiding the subject for years, but there is something we need to talk about."

"What?"

"Magic."

"Why?" I knew why, or at least suspected. If Braden was becoming serious about me, he probably wanted a few answers that I still couldn't give him, and probably never could.

"Because I got the impression that you wanted to live a normal life." Braden offered a forced smile. "I mean, you call yourself a normal detective on your business cards."

"That's true." I didn't know how to explain to him that living a normal life, and running a normal detective agency, weren't the same thing. With my family, I would probably never lead an entirely normal life, but because of them, I had to make sure people knew I didn't do spells, or whatever else they supposed magic users did.

"So then, why did you take a paranormal case?" Braden asked.

"It's what passes for normal around here." It wasn't as if I had been asked to perform actual magic, and besides, before I found Belinda, it was always possible that Nancy Hasting's death had nothing to do with the paranormal.

"Exactly." Braden sounded as if I had made a brilliant point, but I couldn't follow him. "Look, I'm not one of those people who hates the sorcerers around here. I probably wouldn't have started dating you if I did."

"That's good to know." I was liking the conversation less and less. I hoped he would make his point soon.

"But in this town, it's hard to get anywhere without magic. My parents own an antique shop, and they do well enough, but I've got bigger dreams. After law school, I was actually thinking about going into politics."

"Really?" I tried to picture myself as a politician's wife, but the image wouldn't stick. Last summer, he had been talking about going into corporate law and becoming rich, the year before that, trial law. For all I knew, he would change his mind again before graduating with his law degree. His eyes did gleam with excitement when he talked about his plans, but they'd done that before.

"Well, it's not set in stone or anything, but it's a thought, and I definitely couldn't do it in Eagle Rock."

"True."

"And you can't live your dream here, either," Braden said.

I blinked at him, confused, and wondered how he could know so little about my dreams. My daydreams often involved me waking up one day and discovering that I had some magic after all. Even my more sensible daydreams involved me proving myself to my family, which I couldn't do anywhere else.

"You've taken a case involving vampires," Braden said, taking my hand and giving it a squeeze. "*Vampires.* You can't do anything against a vampire, and you shouldn't have to."

I pulled my hand away. "There's magic everywhere, Braden, it's just more concentrated here. More difficult to ignore, though some people try really hard."

"I know," Braden said, "but there's also more opportunity in other places. I've been watching you slowly suffocate here, ever since we started dating. You don't like to let other people see, but when you left the sheriff's department, I finally understood."

"Did you?" My tone was icy, but he missed it.

"What are your plans if you stay here? Can you follow your dreams?" Braden asked.

I turned away, so he wouldn't see the impact his words had on me. Could I follow my dreams? Given the nature of my dreams, probably not.

"Look, I got a contact at a P.I. firm in Chicago, close to where I'll be going to school. He said they might be willing to train you, and take you on as an associate. I know it's not as glamorous as having your own firm, but they're established and get steady business, and after a few years, maybe you can strike out on your own."

Chicago was awfully far away. I wouldn't see my family very often, and after a few years, Adam and Christina would barely know me.

On the other hand, I probably could go far in a place like Chicago, especially if an established firm was willing to give me a chance. I could build a career for myself from the ground up, like any normal person. I tried to picture myself ten years from now, self-sufficient, the owner of my own firm, doing my best to help people in whatever small ways I could.

It sounded great, so why did it leave me feeling dead inside?

"Wait," I said, "are you asking me to come with you?"

"Yes, that's exactly what I'm asking."

He pulled his chair back and dropped to one knee. My heart beat a wild rhythm in my chest, but for some reason, all I could think was *oh no.* I hadn't even figured out what to say if he told me he loved me, and our recent conversation made me feel less certain than ever. At the very least, we hadn't worked out nearly enough details. What had we spent the last three years talking about, and had any of it been important? I didn't even know if he wanted children, or when. I did, eventually. As the oldest of seven, I'd always had children in my life, and couldn't imagine life without them. Braden was an only child, so how would he feel?

The worst part, though, was knowing he planned to leave town permanently. Of all the things we should have talked about, that was at the top of the list. Maybe he had only made the decision recently, given his new career direction, but he couldn't expect me to make the decision to leave everything I'd ever known in five minutes or less.

All of that flashed through my mind in an instant, making my cheeks burn and my ears fill with a strange buzzing sound. I almost missed his actual words.

"I love you," Braden said. "Will you marry me?"

I stared at a gold engagement ring with a small but tasteful diamond solitaire, and I knew I couldn't say yes, but I also knew I couldn't say no. He had given me too much to think about, and so, even knowing it made me sound like a damaged cliché, I gave him a resounding maybe.

14

CHRISTINA WAS BORN ON A STORMY AFTERNOON IN MAY, ABOUT A WEEK before I graduated from high school. We all had spring birthdays, ranging from February to May, which Mom's midwife assured us was perfectly normal. "Lots of women will become fertile at a certain time of year, and tend to have trouble conceiving at other times."

Despite the storm, the house was filled with excitement and energy at the prospect of a new baby–the seventh child. Mom had never made her desire to have exactly seven children a secret.

Mom always gave birth at home, with the assistance of Linda Eagle, a witch midwife (that's what she liked to be called). Somewhere around two in the afternoon, Linda shuffled down the stairs, gray hair coming unwound from the tight bun it had been in at two in the morning, and told everyone, "It's a girl. They're calling her Christina Pamela Evangeline Medea. Everyone's doing great."

We cheered, and I pulled the cake down from the top of the refrigerator. I had chosen the pink frosting, though Nicolas (or possibly Juliana) could have tinted it blue had my guess been wrong. I cut into the cake and we started passing it around, Adam managing to worm a second piece from me before Dad came down to join us.

"I want to see," Adam said, pulling on Dad's pants.

"Not now, Adam. In a couple of hours." Dad managed to get his pants free of Adam's grip, but then Adam latched on with a far more sinister weapon than his arms–his smile. "Oh, come on up, but one at a time. Cassandra, come with us so you can take Adam back downstairs."

So together with Adam, I got my first glimpse of the tiny, wrinkled, pink ball of baby. She was nursing when we walked in, but fell asleep a few minutes later. That's when I got to hold her. She was perfect and beautiful, in a poetic way. Poems usually ignored the amniotic fluid matting the small tufts of hair, or the loose skin that needed filling out. Both of these things would disappear in the next few days, though, and all that would remain would be the precious new life getting its first taste of the world.

After everyone had their peek, I managed the kids to give Mom and Dad some time alone with Christina. When I had the youngest ones bathed and in bed, I disappeared to my own room to study for my finals. That's when I heard them through the vents.

"I'm not sure," Mom was saying. "I can't tell if they're protected or not. I thought I would feel something. Maybe I should have one more, just to be sure."

I dropped my book, and put my ear directly to the vent.

"I'm not sure you would feel anything," Dad said. "It's the kids who we're protecting with the power of seven, not ourselves. Cassandra is one of those kids."

"Yes, but she can't add to the magic. I just...need to think. I don't have to decide tonight."

"Of course not," Dad said. "We've got years."

Somehow, Braden and I made it through the rest of dinner, and then Braden dropped me off at my car. He didn't kiss me good night, which I took as a bad sign, but hopefully, if it was meant to be, we would get through this.

By the time Braden dropped me off at my car, it was nearly dark. I probably had enough time to get home before full dark, but it would be a near thing.

My phone rang. Hoping it was Kaitlin, so I could tell her all about my evening, I answered without checking the caller ID.

"Cassandra Scot, where are you?" It was Dad. I looked up at the twilit sky and let my fingers fly to the cross at my neck.

"I told you I had a date." I tried to make light of it as I started the engine. "I'm on my way home now."

"Now may be too late. How can you be so careless? How did you plan to protect yourself if a vampire attacked you? Vampires are strong, and some of them are cunning." I heard the worry in Dad's voice, but far from making me feel loved, it made me angry. I knew how to handle myself. I had my cross, a bottle of holy water, and I was on my way home.

That's not what I said, though. In my attempt to be flippant, I think I crossed a line.

"Well," I put the car in drive and stepped on the gas, "I guess if I die, it won't matter if I count as one of the seven or not."

I don't know what made me say it. As soon as the words were out of my mouth, I stared at the phone in horror. I could hear Dad shouting something on the other end of the line, but I couldn't make it out. Deciding that anything else I might say would only make matters worse, I hung up and tossed the phone in the passenger seat. Then I banged my head against the steering wheel a few times.

The phone rang. This time, I checked the caller ID, and, seeing my parents' number, ignored it. After several rings, it went to voice mail. Then it started again.

Maybe I did know why I'd said it. The worry that the baby would replace me had been weighing heavily on my mind since I found out Mom was pregnant. I remembered the conversation I'd overheard, through the vents, the night Christina was born. It had been the first, but not the last. I had never told them what I'd heard. I had never even hinted at it. Maybe I thought if I ignored it, it would go away.

When the phone went to voice mail the second time, I punched in Kaitlin's number from memory. I didn't want to think about vampires or new babies, I needed to talk to someone abut Braden. Kaitlin would probably get angry with me for ruining her fairy tale image of Braden–she would probably even use the words "fairy tale"--but she was still the first person I wanted to confide in.

Her phone went to voice mail without ringing. Now that I thought of it, she had said something about a date with Curtis, so that wasn't entirely surprising. I still wanted to talk to someone, though, and Madison went to bed by nine o'clock. That left Angie.

Angie answered her phone on the second ring.

"Hi, it's Cassie. What are you up to right now?"

She hesitated. "I'm staying with my parents tonight–at the hotel."

That was on the way home, and since her family lived there, behind a threshold, it would be safe. "Would you mind some company?"

"Yes, I mean no. You can come over. Is something wrong?"

"Sort of, I'll tell you when I get there." I hung up, and turned the phone off. Then I tossed it in the passenger seat floorboard. Let my parents stew over what I'd said tonight. It served them right. Tomorrow they could reassure me that I was still a part of the family, no matter what, and I would forgive them.

Angie's parents lived in a set of apartments on the top floor of their resort/hotel. It was a three story building with a sort of rustic hunting lodge look. A large wooden sign on the front read "Table Rock Lodge." The lake was actually about a mile away, but on a clear night like that one, you could see the outline of the dark lake, dotted with the lights of hundreds of tiny boats.

Mrs. Mueller sat behind the front desk when I entered, reading a book. She had Angie's eyes and her slight frame, but her face was deeply lined, and she seemed to have a perpetual frown on it. In a way, it reminded me of Jasmine Hewitt, but with less overt malice. Mrs. Mueller's bark was far worse than her bite.

She glanced up when I walked in, the frown firmly affixed to her face. "Isn't it a little late? Angie has work tomorrow."

"I won't bother her long, Mrs. Mueller," I said. Mrs. Mueller and I had never gotten along well. She's one of those who judged me for my family before she got to know me. Even after she knew me, the shadow of my last name seemed to obscure every conversation.

"Go on, then," Mrs. Mueller said with an impatient wave of her thin, jeweled hand. "I think she's upstairs."

I took the elevator to the third floor, where the doors slid open to reveal a small lobby with a faded yellow paint job and little else worthy of note. The door to the apartment was directly in front of me when I stepped off the elevator. It was remarkable only in that it tried to blend into the ugly yellow around it, making it almost invisible. There was a doorbell just to its right, which filled the hall with muffled chimes when I pressed it.

A few seconds later, the door opened, and Angie stood inside, wearing a white bathrobe. Her dark hair hung in wet tendrils around her face, as if she'd just come out of the shower.

"Were you about to go to bed?" I asked, suddenly feeling guilty.

Angie shook her head. "I was going to go for a swim, actually. Officially, the pool is closed after dark, but I like it there. It's peaceful."

"Is it lit?" I asked.

"Only by the moon."

"There's no moon tonight," I pointed out. I had trouble imagining straight-laced Angie doing anything even as daring as taking an after-hours swim. She normally seemed to cling to the rules as though they were a lifeline.

"Then I guess it's not lit." Angie stepped aside. "Would you like to come in?"

Inside, Angie's parents had done little more purposeful decorating than they had done outside. The walls featured photographs of their four children, two of whom were now grown and raising children of their own. Angie came in second from the bottom in birth order. The youngest was still in school and living at home, but if he was in, I couldn't see any sign of him.

"So what's up? How was your date tonight?" Angie asked.

It was the opening I needed, but somehow, the words I needed to say got stuck in my throat.

Angie took a seat on an old brown sofa, bouncing a bit as she did. She pulled her robe around her a little more tightly. "You don't look good."

"Braden proposed."

Her eyes widened. "Isn't that a good thing?"

"I don't know. He started talking about going to Chicago with him, and then before I had a chance to take it all in, he was down on one knee. How can I make a big decision like that in one night?

"Do you love him?"

"I don't know. How do you know if you're in love?"

Angie shrugged. "I've never been in love, but I think it takes time."

"Honestly, so do I. I'm not into love at first sight or anything. I figure it's just sexual attraction and it helps, but love is more than that. But this isn't exactly first sight; we've been dating for three years."

"I'm sorry, Cassie. I wish I had some answers for you."

"I didn't need answers," I said, sniffling, "just someone to talk to."

"Hey, why don't we go for a swim?" Angie asked.

"Right now?"

"Yes, right now."

"I don't have a suit with me. I could go home and get one, but I don't think my parents will let me come back." No, once I got behind their threshold, I would not be going out again tonight. The hotel had a threshold of its own, since it was also the Mueller's home, but once I left, I would need to go straight home.

"I've got a spare suit," Angie said.

I eyed her, though I could not see the outline of her thin body beneath the robe. "I couldn't squeeze into one of your suits."

"No, it's not mine. Madison left it here the last time she was over."

"Oh." I considered that. "Well, that would probably be too big."

"So? There's no lights and the moon isn't out."

She had a point. What the heck? It might be the diversion I needed. Besides, if Angie was willing to go for a nighttime swim, then who was I to refuse? "All right. Just show me where I can change."

ᘓᘐ

Madison's black, one-piece swim suit looked strange on me. I spent a few minutes in the bathroom, pulling at the extra material, especially around my breasts and belly. If it hadn't been after dark, I never would have worn it, and even so, I decided to wear my regular clothes over it until I got to the pool.

"What took you so long?" Angie asked when I came out. She handed me a purple beach towel, but she didn't have one of her own, only the thick white robe.

"Are you wearing that down to the pool?" I asked.

"We don't all have the money for fancy swim suit covers. Come on, let's go."

We took the stairs down to the ground floor, where the doors opened onto the back patio. The only light sources were a faint glow from the hotel's interior, and the dim orb of an orange porch light. The pool itself was unlit, the water within black as ink.

I set my purse on a lawn chair at the shallow end of the Olympic-sized pool, and began to strip my shirt and pants. Angie made a bee-line for the low platform diving board at the other end, which I thought went up to twelve feet. The idea of jumping into twelve feet of blackness and having to feel my way up was unsettling.

Beyond the wrought iron fence surrounding the open-air pool were thick forests as far as the eye could see. I knew they ended at the lake a mile away, but I couldn't quite make out where the trees ended and the water began.

Angie flung aside her robe, tossing it carelessly over the back of a lawn chair. She looked oddly frail underneath, and somehow skinnier than I remembered. It was impossible, of course, but in the orange glow of the porch light, it looked as if she were wearing nothing at all.

Impossible. I shook my head and looked again. Even alone on a moonless night, Angie was the last person in the world who would be skinny dipping.

She climbed the short ladder to the low platform diving board, pausing before walking to the end to look around, as if in expectation. She revolved on the spot, a full 360 degrees, and even in the orange porch light, I could see for sure that she wore nothing more than she had on the day she was born.

I clutched at my cross and said a quick prayer.

A gated swimming pool like that one, set in a patio attached to a home, is protected by a threshold. Not a strong one, but one that should at least have been able to keep a vampire out. The trouble is, even the strongest threshold in the world is utterly useless if you invite a vampire inside.

Then Angie spoke in a loud, carrying voice. "Luke!"

Luke? Her boyfriend? I couldn't see him, but a cold dread washed over me anyway. There was only one reason Angie would have invited me over if she had plans to go skinny dipping with her boyfriend. I suddenly remembered her wearing a turtleneck two days in a row in the middle of June, and I knew what was about to happen.

"Angie, no!" The force of the words nearly made my throat hoarse. "Don't invite him in!"

She acted as if she hadn't heard me. "Luke! Come on in, the water's great." With that she danced out to the end of the board, jumped to activate the spring, and performed a perfect, graceful dive.

15

I DIDN'T KNOW LUKE VERY WELL AT ALL. HE HAD BEEN IN SCHOOL WITH US, a year or two ahead, but had only started dating Angie in the last month or so. Since then, I'd met him just once, and it suddenly occurred to me, it had been rather late in the day. The biggest difference between then and now, aside from the fact that we had been in a brightly lit public place, was his nearly incandescent eyes.

A vampire's eyes have the power to hypnotize, if you let them. At least, that's what I'd been told. You won't find many firsthand accounts of that power.

At that moment, Luke's eyes looked to me like the brightest and most beautiful stars in the night. They drank me in, and made impossible promises; on the other side of those eyes was life everlasting. Just fall into the eyes....swim into the eyes.

"That's it," came a low, soothing voice. "Just take off the cross and set it aside. You don't need it with me."

I still had one hand clutching the cross, but it was damp with perspiration. All thought was gone. There was nothing in my world but the stars in Luke's eyes.

Then he sang. I'm not sure if there were words to the song, but there was power. My heart danced with the notes, and my breathing slowed to help me keep pace. It was a familiar melody, though I'd never heard it before. He sang my heart and my soul, and after a minute or so, my throat opened in an answering tune.

Beneath my fingers, the cross started to feel warmer. It may have simply been from body heat, but as the song intensified, so did the heat beneath my fingers.

"That's it," came Luke's voice again. "Set it aside. We don't need it."

The cross burned white hot, searing my already burned fingers.

"No." I tore my eyes away from his. Thoughts clunked back into place. My will was my own again.

Not that will or thought seemed all that useful to me at that moment. I backed into the lawn chair where I'd tossed my clothes and purse, and began digging through the mess for the small bottle of holy water I'd packed that afternoon. My purse seemed bottomless, and as my search grew more frantic, I began tossing items haphazardly to the ground, until finally, my fingers grasped the bottle of salvation.

When I looked up, the vampire was gone. I spun, turning left and right in jerky movements, trying to find him. One hand clung to the cross around my neck, the other to the bottle of holy water. Then I saw him at the other end of the pool.

Angie was sitting on the edge of the pool, slowly swirling the water with one foot. Luke knelt behind her. Without the intensity of his eyes getting in the way, I could see him properly now. He had apparently come ready for the pool, because he wore nothing but a dark speedo.

Not all vampires are alike. They carry a bit of their former personality into their demon-possessed afterlife, but stories told of a great many vampires who enjoyed thralling their victims. Vampire venom turns men and women into slaves, ready to do their master's bidding for a taste of the drug they crave. In the end, they often beg for death, though it doesn't always come. The fact that a vampire can so completely thrall a victim means they don't have to kill every time they need to feed, thus controlling their population.

At that moment, Angie wasn't begging, she was giggling. Luke had her hair wound around his fingers and was drawing it slowly away, exposing her neck. He glanced my way for a fraction of a second, as if to make sure I was paying attention, then he plunged his teeth into her throat.

A vampire's bite is not a kiss, though Angie made positively indecent noises in response. She groaned and clutched at Luke's free hand–the one that wasn't keeping her hair at bay. She brought it down to her bare belly and held it there, gasping for breath.

My mouth went dry, but not so much from Angie's reaction. I understood, at least to a certain extent, how the venom worked. What really struck me at that moment was the slurping and swallowing noises. They filled the night like some twisted and magnified version of a baby demon sucking at its mother's breast.

The vampire lifted its head and looked at me, but I would not meet its gaze this time. *Fool me once*, I thought, *but not again.*

"You could run," he hissed, "but I'm awfully thirsty." As if to demonstrate, he bent down and licked at Angie's neck.

She shuddered. "Don't stop."

"It would be a shame to turn her so soon," Luke said, "she's been so useful."

I should have run. Logic dictated that I had no chance against this vampire. I couldn't save Angie, only myself. Trouble was, I knew I couldn't have lived with myself afterward. Luke must have guessed that about me, which was impressive since until that moment, I hadn't known it about myself.

I remembered the words Dad had said to me just a short while ago, before I'd gotten angry with him and done everything in my power to hurt him. "Vampires are strong, and some of them are cunning."

Thought escaped me again, but not because of his eyes. This time, it was simply a matter of resolve; a decision made that I could not take back. Hesitation was no longer an option. I removed the lid to the bottle of holy water and, rushing forward with speed I hadn't even known I possessed, I threw it at Luke.

I got his face, hair, and bare chest, all of which started smoking. He screamed and jumped away so fast that he was at the other end of the pool before I could blink.

"Let's go!" I shouted at Angie. I bent forward and tugged her to her feet.

"Why?" Angie sounded empty inside. I wondered how much of my friend still fought for sanity beneath that drug-induced shell.

"If we get inside, we'll be safe. You only invited him into the pool." I didn't know if that was true or not, but it was the only hope I had.

She clutched at my shoulders, using me for support as I tried to lead her away from the pool, and for the space of a few seconds, I thought I had her convinced, or at least, docile enough not to care. Then her fist closed around my necklace, and before I had a chance to react, before I could even flinch, she yanked it off and flung it into the pool. It didn't even make a sound as it hit the inky waters and sank beyond my reach.

Angie let go of me and stood on her own power, looking quite whole and sure of herself. She was so in the power of the vampire, she didn't know where his will ended and hers began. "It's gone."

The icy horror did not have a chance to settle in my heart before Luke was on me. He came up behind me and encircled me in strong, impenetrable arms, almost like a lover. Almost. No blood flowed through his cold, dead veins. It felt to me as if a little bit of January had blown into June. I shuddered, hard, though I don't know how much the cold had to do with it.

"Hush," he said, his mouth so close to my ear that I felt his chill breath on my face.

I closed my eyes. There were no weapons left to me. The cross was gone. The holy water was gone. In the end, it didn't matter how powerful my family was. They weren't there to protect me. There was nothing between me and a fate worse than death except, perhaps, the anti-venom potion I had taken so long ago I could no longer remember. Would it fail me as it had failed Belinda? If not, if his venom could not touch me, then I would die. It was the best outcome I could hope for, the one for which I prayed, silently.

I tried not to think about the possibility that I would become his thrall, but the fears rushed through my head, unbidden and unstoppable. Would he finish it right there, I wondered, or would he play with me as he was doing with Angie? When it was all over, would he turn me, and send me to attack my family? Would the demon inside me kill any of them before they killed me, as they surely would?

Christina's sweet face flashed in my mind, Adam's charismatic smile, and Elena's haunted grace. At that moment, I would have given anything to have seen a single one of them, even Isaac, with his taunts, sneers, and attempts to curse me. If Juliana had been there, I would have flung my arms around her and forgiven her for spreading lies about me. In the end, what did it matter?

"This won't hurt," Luke said. "You'll even enjoy it. Here, let me show you."

He raised my left hand up, over my head, to his lips. I couldn't see, but I imagined a mouth full of jagged razor blades. When he tore into my thumb, the vision turned to truth, and my thumb cried out in pain. It took all my strength not to cry out for real. "That's better, isn't it?" he said. He released my thumb and allowed it to fall to my side.

No, it wasn't. My thumb still stung where he had tasted it, but I didn't trust myself to speak, or to show the tiniest hint of emotion. At that instant, two important truths clunked into place.

First, the anti-venom potion seemed to be working. Whatever had happened to Belinda in the end, it did not seem to be happening to me now. The pain in my thumb, the blood still oozing from the wound where my index finger tried to stem the flow, and the sharpness of my mind all indicated that for now, at any rate, I wasn't in danger of turning.

Second, Luke didn't know about the anti-venom potion. If he did, he would have noticed my sharp intake of breath or the flow of blood. He would not have expected me to respond to him as Angie had. He would have guessed that Cassandra Scot would be immune to him.

As weapons went, it felt feeble, but it was all I had. For the first time in my life, I appreciated the veil of secrecy that shrouded my family's most powerful magic. If we had gone through town, shouting about the potion, Luke would have known. He would have given up his bizarre seduction routine and killed me in an instant. Instead, if I could keep the act up convincingly enough, he might let me go, believing he had me as his willing slave.

All I had to do was keep my mouth shut, to pretend to be in heaven rather than in hell, and to act as though I wanted a bloodsucking vampire to drain me dry.

He released me, but I stayed put, determined to keep up the ruse that I was under his power. Angie came to stand by my side, and Luke strode in front of us, leering. I avoided looking into his eyes, though he did not make it easy.

"Angie told me you had a date tonight," Luke said. "She didn't think she could get you here until tomorrow."

Despite my fear, my first thought was to ask why he wanted me here, but I managed to bite my tongue. It didn't matter. He had wanted me, and without either of them having to try, I'd walked into their trap.

Angie took a step forward, and I resisted the urge to pull her back. She flung herself at the vampire and tossed her hair aside, inviting him to bite. From this distance, I could see bruises and scars where she had been bitten half a dozen other times. No wonder she had worn the turtleneck two days in a row.

"Not now," he said, "I want to play with your friend first."

I knew vampires were strong, but even so I wasn't prepared for the ease with which he lifted me off my feet and tossed me into the pool. I might have been a tiny pebble rather than a fully grown woman, flailing gracelessly as I hit the water with a loud splash.

The water was warm, deep, and dark. Beneath the surface, I could not tell which way was up, nor which was down. I kicked off in a random direction, my lungs constricting from the unexpected dunking. I hadn't had a chance to take in a lung full of air before losing my connection with the oxygen I'd always taken for granted.

At least I hadn't fallen far. I expected to find fresh air in a matter of seconds, but it didn't come. I kept kicking and kicking, always expecting to find the fresh air I sought, but it wouldn't come. Frantic, I switched directions, and this time my hand brushed against something hard–the edge of the pool. Grateful for the landmark, I used it to feel my way to the top, where I drank in a refreshing breath of air.

The vampire was there when I gasped for breath, his yellow eyes boring into my soul. They didn't hypnotize me as before. I can only assume that he didn't feel the need, since he thought I was under the spell of the venom. I looked away as soon as I could, but there was nothing friendlier to see in the rest of his face. Certainly not his pointed fangs, stained with something dark and deadly.

With a casual sweep of his hand, the vampire pushed aside the loose strap of my large swimsuit. "If we want to have more fun after tonight, it will have to be the shoulder. Your family would notice the neck." They might have noticed the thumb, too, but I didn't point this out to him.

Then he bit. I closed my eyes, dug my nails into my palms, and clenched my jaw tight. The pain was that of a hundred tiny knives ripping open flesh, tearing muscles, and scraping them raw.

A scream tried to force its way up my throat, but I fought it with every ounce of strength in my body. I focused on the fight with the scream, because I was losing the fight with the vampire, and I did not want to dwell on the pain, which consumed the whole of my existence.

Tears flowed from my eyes, but bent as he was over my shoulder, Luke did not notice. He might not have noticed anyway, in the dark and the damp.

Then the slurping began. What had sounded like demonic nursing when I'd heard him do it to Angie, now sounded like a chorus of fear, digging through pain to reach my soul. My heart shuddered. I could feel the blood being drawn up and out through the veins in my shoulder. My head felt light, and it became hard to breathe.

Time passed. It might have been a few seconds or an hour, but it passed. Each second was a fresh fight with the pain, with the fear, and with the desperate scream in my throat. How long could I hold out? Surely, it wouldn't be so bad to scream. Then he might end it more quickly. Death would be a welcome relief.

I wasn't immediately aware of the moment he released me. One second, I was wrestling with my need to scream, debating the merits of death, and the next, I looked up at the starry sky. I was floating on my back in the water, whimpering. It wasn't a scream; it was more a compromise.

"Tomorrow," he whispered in my ear. "Return to this place tomorrow night."

Then he was gone, though not far. I managed to turn my head just enough to see him standing by Angie, the latter on her knees, begging him to taste her.

"Tomorrow," Luke whispered. "Tomorrow you and your friend will come back here."

I touched my right shoulder with my left hand and felt the torn, damaged flesh there. Among vampire venom's other magical properties, it acts as a coagulant and healing agent. This is useful when you want to spend days playing with a victim before they die. Without it, they may bleed out the first night.

So I wasn't thralled, but it looked like I might die anyway. He hadn't drawn enough blood to kill me, but it continued to drip into the pool from my open wound.

The stars looked out of focus and hazy, as if obscured by the glow of a city's lights. My body felt heavy; the muscles relaxed, and I began to droop into the pool.

In the next second, Angie was there, supporting my body and helping me to the stairs leading out.

"I know how you feel," Angie said in a low voice. "I'm sad when he leaves too, but there's no reason to drown yourself. He'll be back tomorrow."

"Yeah." I didn't tell her that I wouldn't be. Whether my absence would be due to death or the desire for life, I did not know.

With shaking limbs, I crawled out of the pool. I had left my purse on a lawn chair a few feet away, but it seemed so far. If I could reach it, I could get my cell phone and...

An image flashed in my mind: a cell phone lying on the floorboard of the passenger side of my car.

"I need help," I managed to say to Angie. "I'm losing blood."

She leaned over me, damp hair hanging around her face. "What happened to your shoulder?"

I gaped at her. "The vampire."

She laughed. "You always did have an overactive imagination."

In my pain-shocked mind, I didn't know if it was Angie herself or the venom that allowed her to so stubbornly refuse to see what was happening. Looking back, I think it may have been both.

Her face swam out of my vision, but I was sure it would come back in a matter of moments. I heard her around the other end of the pool for a few seconds, then I heard her footsteps coming closer and closer. Any minute now, she would stop by my side, maybe with a towel or something to help stop the bleeding. But the footsteps didn't stop. They went past me, through the patio door.

The banging of the door behind her sounded like the lid of my coffin closing.

I closed my eyes and steeled myself to do something–anything. With agonizing slowness, I managed to get myself up on hands and knees, and inch toward the lawn chair. The phone wasn't there, but my car keys were. If I could get the keys and then get to the car...

But the ten feet to the lawn chair took an age to cross, and when I looked back, I saw a trail of blood. The hand digging through my purse closed on the car keys and pressed a button to unlock the doors. I heard the tiny chirp. Then I saw black.

16

I woke slowly, sensations returning to my body one at a time. The first thing I felt was hard, cracked pavement pressing against my belly and legs. It smelled strongly of chlorine and something else, something a little bitter. I moved my hand, felt a thin metal ring, then heard the jingling of a set of keys.

"Sh-she's ok." The voice was shaky and out of breath, as if its owner had just run a long race. I didn't immediately recognize it.

"Cassandra?" That was Dad. He knelt down in front of me, and I managed to open one bleary eye to focus on his fear-lined face.

I closed my eyes again. It wasn't real. Dad wasn't real. The vampire wasn't real. The world wasn't real. If I could just fall back into sleep, I would wake up in my own bed, enfolded in the loving embrace of my fortress of solitude.

"Cassandra?" That was Mom. I felt her hand on mine, and the keys slipped into her waiting fingers.

"M'okay," I managed.

"Can you sit up?" Dad asked.

I didn't want to, but I tried it, scraping my knees against the rough cement. Lifting myself into the lawn chair didn't seem possible, but I did manage to square myself on the ground and take a look around.

Juliana was on her knees a foot or so away, gasping for breath. Either she had gone on a healing spree before she had gotten to me, or she hadn't gotten there a moment too soon. She pulled a lock of sweat-drenched hair behind one ear and slumped down on the ground next to me. Then she flung one arm around my neck and started whimpering.

"D-don't scare me like th-that."

I patted her hair absently for a while, letting sensation return to my body. It ached all over, but the acute pain was gone, and strength was slowly returning.

"How did you know?" I asked.

She didn't answer. None of them did, but I guessed. Juliana had been crystal gazing again. I sighed in a resigned sort of way, but I couldn't get angry with someone for invading my privacy when she had just saved my life, however much I may have wanted to.

"It was Angie," I managed. "I came over to talk, thinking I'd be safe behind her threshold, but she knew the vampire. She invited him in."

No one answered, which was just as well. There wasn't anything to say that wouldn't make me feel worse than I already felt. I stared at the pool, which, I suddenly realized, was glistening with light reflected from a new source. It didn't take me long to find it. Dad balanced an orb of light above his head, casting bright white illumination across the entire patio.

The scene looked worse than I would have thought. A cloud of blood filled much of the shallow end of the pool. More blood traced my path from the steps to the lawn chair, where I sat huddled with Juliana.

I could only imagine what I looked like, though I felt all right, and was feeling better the more time passed. Juliana's breathing was easing too, though she had her share of my blood in her hair and on her clothing. She had decided to wear white shorts that day, an unfortunate choice.

Mom followed my gaze. "We can't leave this."

Of the things that a sorcerer can use to gain control over another human, blood is the strongest. Certain spells can be woven around hair, skin, fingernails, and saliva, but blood trumps them all, and I had just left behind enough for every sorcerer in Eagle Rock to take a sample.

"Get the chalk and salt," Dad said. "I'll heat the water."

Mom ran off, I assume to her Sprinter, while Dad sat by the edge of the pool and put his hand in the water. Within seconds, the already warm pool began to steam and bubble.

"Come on," I said to Juliana. "We need to move back." With difficulty, I got to my feet. My knees weren't sure whether they wanted to support my weight at first, but I talked them into it. Then I offered Juliana a hand. She took it, wobbling slightly, and together we backed away from the pool as far as the fence. There, we collapsed together and waited for our parents to begin their spell.

Mom returned with an old black diaper bag that she calls her potion bag. She set it by the pool, then fumbled around for the salt, which she immediately tossed into the boiling water. Then she took out the chalk and drew a large pentagram over the place where I had lain motionless a few minutes earlier. She drew a circle around the pentagram and blessed it with a few whispered words. I had seen her do all of this a hundred times before, though I admit I didn't understand the finer points of how it all worked.

"Ready," Mom said, standing in the middle of the circle.

Dad joined her inside the circle and took her hand, linking their magic together. I saw when it happened, because a shudder ran through both of their bodies.

I shuddered as well. It was hard to watch them clean up my mess, as it was one of those not-so-rare moments when I felt utterly powerless. Juliana leaned against me, still weak from her exertion, and I patted her hair comfortingly. She was six years younger than me, practically a child, and yet I had needed her to come to my rescue. Not only that, but I had put her at risk, drained her battery. She would recover from tonight, but what if there were other nights?

"Let's go," Dad said.

I blinked. The blood was gone. All of it–the cloud in the pool and the trail on the ground. It looked as though I had never been there. Even the chalk circle had been wiped clean, and I hadn't even seen it happen.

I stared at the spot where the attack had taken place, remembering every moment of it as if it were happening to me all over again. There was Luke, standing over me with his glowing eyes. There he was again, standing over Angie, slurping her life's fluid. There he was in the pool, razor sharp teeth ripping into my flesh, eliciting a scream that never escaped my lips.

I rubbed my eyes, willing the images away. If only I could wipe the memories quite as easily as my parents had wiped the blood.

17

MOM DROVE MY CAR HOME. WE PASSED THE TWENTY-MINUTE DRIVE IN complete silence, my head firmly pressed against the passenger side window. Partly, I was avoiding her gaze and any unwelcome conversation that might accompany it, but mostly I was trying to escape the world. I squinted up at the stars, wondering if one of them granted wishes like in the fairy tales I'd read as a child. *I wish I may, I wish I might,* I thought. But I stopped there. I wasn't even sure what I wanted.

Everyone was gathered in the living room when we walked in, I still in the over-large swimsuit, carrying my clothes and purse at my side. Gathering as much dignity as I could manage, I pushed past them, letting their shouted questions and comments roll off of me. The only thing I wanted was a shower, my most comfortable pajamas, and bed.

My plans did not work out. No sooner had I slipped into the pajamas, then there was a knock on my bedroom door. I knew it would be my parents before I answered. I even knew it would be both of them, together, and that they had no intention of letting me sleep until we had worked out a few things that had been weighing us down over the past couple of days.

"Come in." I flung myself down on my bed and pretended to be in the middle of reading a book. My parents couldn't have been less fooled by the nonchalance if the book were upside down.

"We need to talk," Dad said.

I couldn't think of a thing I wanted to say. I had acted recklessly, all because of my own private feelings of doubt about Mom's pregnancy. Well, they weren't so private anymore.

"Why did you go to Angie's?" Dad asked. "You said you were coming home."

He had to know. Was he going to make me say it? I wouldn't look at his face. Instead, I studied the pocket of his black robe, embroidered with his initials, E.S.

"Has Jason called?" It was a lame and desperate attempt to change the subject.

"No," Mom said. "I've left three messages myself. Don't worry about him, I'm sure he's just busy."

"If we have to, we'll kill the vampire who attacked you ourselves," Dad added.

I closed my eyes and clenched my hands into fists. "If we don't get him by tomorrow, he might just finish Angie off."

Mom and Dad looked at one another significantly, and Mom twisted the belt of her pink floral robe around one finger. "We'll try to help her."

"Cassandra, you're trying to distract us," Dad said. "I want to know why you said what you said to me on the phone."

I couldn't find a way to dart around that one, so I tried for a partial truth. "Mom always said she wanted seven kids. She was quite clear about it, and about why. I figured if you had another one, it was because you didn't think I counted."

"Aren't you a little old to be worried that a new baby is going to replace you?" Mom asked. "I thought we covered this when you were two, and we told you about Nicolas."

"Fine, I'm crazy. Let me go to sleep." I pressed my face into a pillow.

"We really ought to talk about this," Mom said. "You know we love you, right?" There was tension in her voice, as if she were desperate for me to understand.

"Yeah, I know." Lack of love had never been the problem in our house. It overflowed with love. It was respect and acceptance that I had been missing, something she would be hard pressed to give me in an evening pep talk.

"We'd do anything for you," Dad said. "All you have to do is ask." There was a note of desperation in his voice that did not quite infuse me with confidence. Besides, after the way they had treated me the other day, overreacting because of an alleged relationship with Evan, I didn't know if I could trust them.

"Anything, huh? Would you stand aside and let me make my own choices?"

"Yes," Dad said.

The answer had come too easily, so I upped the stakes. "Even if I chose to go out with Evan Blackwood?"

Neither of them spoke for a long time. Mom seemed supremely interested in a spot on the wall, while Dad feigned interest in the book I had pretended to read.

"I thought you were dating Braden," Mom said.

"I am." Although after our disastrous date that evening, I didn't know how much of a future we had. I thought of his proposal again, wondering how badly I had hurt him, not saying yes right away, but how could I have said anything else? All of a sudden, he wanted me to change my life for him, and then, without giving me a chance to catch my breath, he asks me the most important question of my life.

Besides, a guilty part of me asked, how could I say yes to him, when I had fantasized about kissing Evan earlier that same day?

"If you're dating Braden," Mom said, reminding me that we hadn't finished our uncomfortable conversation, "then I don't understand the question."

"It's simple enough," I said. "I could change my mind, and I want to know if you trust me to make my own choices."

"Yes, we would," Mom said. Dad glared at her, and she shot him a dirty look.

"We do always have your best interests at heart," Dad said, ignoring Mom's look. So, in other words, *no.*

"Is there a point to this conversation?" I asked. "Or is it just slow torture?"

"We just want you to know we'll always be there for you, no matter what." Mom stood. "Good night."

She was halfway to the door when I said, "Braden asked me to marry him."

"He did?" Mom paused. "What did you say?"

"Maybe. He wants to move to Chicago, and I didn't know how I felt about it. I'd always thought he wanted to move back here after school."

"Oh." Mom returned to the bed, and perched on the edge. I couldn't tell if she sounded pleased or not.

"You won't be around to protect me in Chicago," I said. "You'll have to trust me."

"We do," Mom said, "but there are some things you might want to think about. Reasons you might not want to live so far away."

"Such as?"

"What if you got pregnant?" Mom asked.

"I think that's a long way off." Actually, since Braden and I had never discussed children at all, I had no idea how far away such a thing might be. "Why would it be a big deal, anyway?"

"What if the baby ends up being a fire starter, or empath, or healer?"

The idea had honestly never occurred to me. The only thing I could think to say was, "That's not likely, is it?"

Mom's silence was answer enough.

"I can't think about this right now." Out of frustration, I flung the book to the floor. It fell open, revealing a spell to conceal oneself from magical scrying.

Dad glanced at it. "Were you trying to stop Juliana from looking in on you?"

I nodded, mutely.

"Even after what happened tonight?" he went on.

I glared at him. Yes, for one evening it had been convenient to have someone looking in on me. That did not mean I wanted Juliana to watch me every night of my life.

"Fine, we'll talk later." He stood, and after a moment's hesitation, so did Mom.

"I love you," Mom said.

They kept saying that, but as they left the room and closed the bedroom door behind them, I realized that they had never come right out and told me that I was and would always be a part of this family.

ꙮ

Mom and Dad had a fight as soon as they retreated to their own bedroom. It was one of those times when I desperately wished I could not hear them through the vents. Sometimes, it was better not to know what others said about you.

"You have to let go," Mom said. "She's a grown up."

"She's my little girl," Dad said, "and she doesn't know what's best for her."

"Do you?"

"I know she can't take care of herself. You, of all people, should know what's out there waiting for her. And, God, *Evan Blackwood*? I thought that nightmare was over. I guess ignoring it wasn't the best strategy after all."

"She is thinking of marrying someone else," Mom said.

"She didn't say yes, and besides, if Evan decides he wants her, how would she even resist?"

"We'll always protect her."

"I know," Dad said. "I'm just not sure, and I'm not ready for this."

Mom started sobbing then, and I couldn't make out what she said through the tears. I didn't want to hear it anyway, I decided. I grabbed my iPod, put headphones over my ears, and turned up the volume. For a long time, I lay there like that, willing sleep to come, despite the thrumming in my ears.

Yet sleep remained elusive. For some reason, I kept thinking about yellow eyes and razor sharp teeth. No sooner would I drift into my usual state of dreamless oblivion, then something would scare me back to reality. Finally, around one in the morning, I gave up, and made my way to the kitchen to find some way to take my mind off things.

It had been a while since I had brewed a wakefulness potion, but as soon as I entered the kitchen, it seemed like the thing to do. The potion primarily consists of ginseng, grapefruit juice, sea salt, and a few essential oils. It requires no special magical ability, only a recipe and a bit of heart, as my mom would say. I always enjoyed brewing those simple potions I could make without help; it made me feel some connection to the magic long denied me. Sometimes, I would even brew potions requiring magic at key points, but I always felt on shaky ground when I had to ask for help, so I didn't do it often.

"Having trouble sleeping?"

I jumped and splattered some of the potion on the stove. I wiped it with a towel, and turned to see Nicolas, dressed in a black robe a lot like Dad's. He looked like he was having trouble sleeping too, and in fact, the circles under his eyes made me wonder how long it had been since he had gotten a decent night's sleep.

"What are you doing up?" I asked.

"Oh, you know, trying to figure out what to do with my life. That sort of thing. Did you make enough for two?"

"Sure." I ladled out two cups of the potion, and turned off the stove.

Nicolas took a sip. "Perfect. Just like Mom makes it."

I brushed off the compliment. "Did you find out about the fire-fighter thing yet?"

"I've got to take a bunch of tests. Strength, stamina, and a drug screening. Plus there's a three-month training course."

"Is that a problem?"

"No. They said I could do it, but I just have this feeling that the chief is going to set me up to fail."

"You'll do great," I said, not because I was certain, but because it was my job as his big sister to reassure him–also to tease him endlessly, but only at appropriate times.

"So what's got you up at one in the morning?"

"Post traumatic stress?" I suggested. "I don't know, for some reason I just keep thinking about this giant vampire. Can't imagine why."

He looked into his mug. "I wanted to go, but someone had to stay with the kids, and they thought Juliana's gift might be more-"

"It's fine," I said. "Everyone doesn't have to protect me all the time."

"No reason to snap at me."

He was right, but he had managed to say just the wrong thing when I was already beginning to feel less like a daughter/sister, and more like the family's mascot.

Suddenly, I knew what I needed to do. The revelation came on me in a rush, and it half shocked me, half thrilled me.

I had to be the one to kill the vampire. I mean, I knew just where he would be the next night. He had told me to meet him back at the pool. I could go there, hide in the trees with my bow and arrow...he would never have to see me.

Of course, if anything went wrong, I would be dead before I could reload. I had exactly one shot, and I hadn't practiced regularly in weeks. My dedication to the sport of archery came and went in spurts.

But I needed to do it. I needed to fight my own monster. How else could I look my family in the eyes again? How else could I prove myself?

I sat up straighter, staring past Nicolas at the art on the refrigerator door. There was a stick figure drawing of the entire family–nine figures, 5 with long curly hair and 4 with short hair. One of the curly haired figures had a smaller stick figure drawn across its stick tummy.

"Cassie, what are you thinking?" Nicolas asked. "Whatever it is, I don't think you should do it."

"Not now." I looked down at the wakefulness potion, which I hadn't sipped at all. I didn't need it any longer, so I tossed the contents in the sink. "I'm going to bed."

"Good night?" Nicolas made it a question.

"Good night."

Upstairs, in my fortress of solitude, I gathered the pieces of my plan around me. There were a number of flaws in it, including the fact that my parents and sister were actively spying on me, but I was sure I could find a way to work around that. I just needed a good night's sleep and a chance to think. Now that I had a plan, I thought I might even manage it.

18

I'm not completely stupid. Yes, I had a moment when I briefly envisioned killing the vampire single-handedly, but by morning, I knew it couldn't quite work like that, not if I wanted to live–and I did. I just couldn't ask for help from anyone in my family, because they probably wouldn't allow me my shot at the vampire, and because I wanted to prove my independence.

Luckily, there was someone I could go to for help, someone who also had a vested interest in killing this vampire. I just had to find some way to talk Evan into letting me join the hunt.

I didn't have much time, which meant I couldn't wait for Evan to show up in my office sometime in the uncertain future. I would have to go to him.

I dressed quickly, opting for more sensible jeans and tennis shoes over my usual businesslike attire. Heels and tight shirts only helped heroines fighting vampires on camera; the rest of us needed to make more sensible choices.

The real trick was acting as if everything was perfectly normal, so that no one would think to take out a crystal ball as I left the house. Whether or not my parents were remotely fooled, I'll never know, but they did back off, perhaps feeling we needed a cool down after the previous night's discussion. As long as they left me alone, that suited me perfectly.

I only stopped in the kitchen for a piece of toast and glass of orange juice before stowing a book and a few supplies in an old backpack and heading out the door.

Despite my certainty that talking to Evan was the right thing to do, I knew this wasn't going to be an easy conversation. For one thing, I also needed him to work a concealment spell for me, so my family wouldn't know what I was up to. In fifteen years, I had never once asked Evan to do magic for me, and I wasn't entirely sure he would, even for a friend–or whatever I was to him. My parents had sometimes traded favors with the other magical families for spells and potions, but if it came to that, I wasn't sure what I had to offer that Evan didn't already have.

I had also never been to Henry Wolf's house, though my parents had invited him to our home many times over the years. My GPS didn't know how to get to his place, and of course, he didn't have a phone. The only thing I knew for sure was that he lived west, and that his house was directly on the lake.

Table Rock is a man-made lake that stretches through southern Missouri and northwestern Arkansas. The lake is narrow, winding through the hilly landscape like a many-headed snake. At most points along the 745 miles of coast, the opposite shore is clearly visible.

The lake is also the reason that there are so many magical families in such a small area. It is not at all normal to find such a large concentration of practitioners, because sheer numbers get you noticed, something most prefer to avoid. Yet here, and in a few similar places around the world, sorcerers willingly trade a bit of notoriety for the power of a node, a concentration of energies that sorcerers can tap into and use in their magical workings.

That's from a textbook. I have never experienced the tiniest twinge of magical ability, so I really don't understand what it means. All I know is that somewhere beneath the westernmost tendril of Table Rock Lake lies a node, and practitioners thrive on it.

Henry Wolf lived as close to that node as he could without growing gills and living underwater. Since Evan was still his apprentice, he lived with him, so that's where I needed to go.

I sped along the lakeside roads, which turned into the forest and back out toward the lake in harmony with the curves of the land. I had a vague sense that it wasn't terribly far away, so I kept my eyes peeled, especially when the road turned to give me a view of the lake. The only thing I knew for sure was that he lived right by the water.

I had just turned into a deep patch of forest, trees sloping up to my left, and down into a deep gulf to my right, when the ground slipped from beneath me.

That's the only way I can describe it. My heart lurched with the road as I slammed my foot on the brake, but then the pavement bucked upward, smacking my car dangerously to the right.

White knuckled, I twisted the steering wheel hard to the left, but the wheels didn't seem to respond. The ground began bucking and shifting with dangerous malice, alternately tossing the car into the air and then batting it back down. My feet flew from gas to brake, my hands gripped the steering wheel for dear life, but nothing I did seemed to make the slightest difference.

When the car's back wheels went over the edge, I screamed. It's a useless, girly thing to do when you're in the middle of the woods, your voice being drowned out by the roar of an earthquake, and no one could have heard you even without the ground shifting, but it felt good. After holding it in the night before for so long, giving in to the scream at that moment felt like the perfect release of tension.

Except it didn't really release anything. It made my heart pound faster and I began to see spots.

Then my front wheels followed my back wheels into the ditch.

The car rolled down the sloping sides of the ditch for a few feet, before landing, hard, against a giant oak tree. The car crunched, the windshield cracked, and I felt a sharp pain in my right foot.

At some point during my slide, the ground must have stopped shaking, because all was still as I sat there in the wreckage of my powder blue Jaguar, trying to work out what to do next.

Above me, the sun ducked its head behind some clouds. Nearby, a bird started to sing, and a few seconds later, others joined its song.

Experimentally, I lifted my right foot, which had gotten wedged under the gas pedal. It protested loudly, but I didn't think it was broken–just sprained. Sometimes, you have to thank God for small blessings.

My car had come to rest at a sharply upturned angle, and there was no way I was going to be able to drive it out, so with monumental effort, I wrestled the door open. Gravity worked against me, but I managed to prevail. Grabbing my backpack from the passenger seat, and bracing myself for the pain I knew would accompany the motion, I rolled out.

The ground beneath me was a mass of giant roots that made it hard to get any kind of footing, not that my right foot was of much use anyway. Every time I moved it, there was renewed pain, but I couldn't stay in the ditch, so, slinging the pack onto my back, I prepared to climb.

All things considered, it didn't take long, but it felt much longer. The road was only a few feet above me, but every step hurt. I used large roots and small trees for leverage as I made my way up to the smooth, unblemished surface of the road.

Smooth and unblemished? I checked again. There was no sign that an earthquake had just bucked me off this section of road a few minutes ago.

I heard a car approaching, and scrambled out of the way, ready to flag it down for help. I had my cell phone in my pack, but I wasn't ready to call my parents yet. This was a significant hiccup, but I would not yet concede defeat.

The car was a green Ford Focus. I recognized it only because I had run into it once, five years earlier, just before its owner had cursed me blind. Jasmine Hewitt passed at top speed, paying me no notice as she raced to whatever errand awaited her.

Odd, I thought, *she lives a pretty good distance from here.*

Now what? I couldn't walk far on my damaged leg, but there was no telling how long it would be before another car drove by. Once again, I thought about the cell phone in my backpack, but did not immediately reach for it.

It couldn't have been more than a few minutes before I heard another car approach. This one was traveling much slower, and as it rounded the nearest curve, I recognized Evan's metallic blue Prius.

I waved, but he had already seen me. He pulled the car to a stop directly beside me, and the passenger door swung open, of its own accord, inviting me in. Without hesitation, I accepted the invitation.

"What are you doing out here?" Evan asked. "I told you, I'd meet you in town. It's dangerous out here."

I tried to decide if he was angry or worried, but couldn't work it out. "I noticed. My car's in a ditch over there. What was that?"

"A ward," Evan said, confirming my suspicion.

"I was on a public road. Mr. Wolf's wards are too sensitive."

"You didn't trip it, Jasmine Hewitt did. You just got caught in the backlash."

"Is that old woman crazy?" I asked, remembering her hurrying away as if the hounds of hell were after her. If she had done something to provoke Evan or Mr. Wolf, maybe they were.

"Are you hurt?" Evan asked, taking inventory of my body from head to toe. He ran his hands along my arms and legs, checking for breaks or sprains, but the contact unsettled me.

"I'll be okay,"

He didn't seem to believe me. His hand was in my hair, searching–for what, I had no idea. Then his eyes traveled down the length of my body to my right foot. "You are hurt."

I almost asked if he had x-ray vision or something, but thought better of it. If I wanted his help, the last thing I needed to do was start prying.

"It's just a sprain," I said. Juliana would be able to fix it in about two seconds, if I went to her.

"Which means the answer is yes, you are hurt. Have you called for a tow truck yet?"

Now that he said it, that seemed like the obvious thing to have done. "I, um, didn't think of it," I admitted.

"Are you sure you didn't hit your head?" Evan reached his hand toward me again, but I intercepted it. He had a rather intense look in his eye that reminded me of what Madison had said the day before.

Despite my uncertainty about Braden, and my attraction to Evan, I wasn't ready for Evan to take Braden's place in my life. Assuming he wanted to, of course. I might have been reading the signals all wrong, and part of me hoped so, because I had a feeling Evan would be relentless when he set his mind to something.

He did seem to be taking every chance he got to touch me, but no, there wasn't anything implied there. It was just... he was just checking to make sure I was all right.

"It was just shock." I pushed his hand away, and rifled through my backpack for the phone. Evan waited patiently as I dialed information, got the number for a tow truck, and told them where to find the car.

While I was on the phone, Evan put the car in park and stepped out, walking over to the ditch to survey the damage to my car. After a few minutes, he shook his head and slid back into the driver's seat. By then, I had finished my call.

"I'll get you a rental for now," Evan said.

"Thank you."

He put the car into drive and started forward. "I'm going to take you back to Master Wolf's house so I can fix that foot."

I nodded and again said, "Thanks."

"Now, what was so important it couldn't wait a few hours?"

Here it was, the moment of truth. I glanced around at the quiet road, shaded by tall trees. "I have a favor to ask you. Actually, two favors."

"Okay." He sounded dubious. "You need to be careful with that. You don't want to be in my debt."

"I know that," I snapped. Then, more calmly. "I thought we could make a trade. Maybe I could finish this investigation for you for free or something." I didn't know if that would work or not, since Evan had as much difficulty making money as my parents–which was none at all–but it was all I had.

"What do you want me to do?"

I dug into my backpack and pulled out the spell book entitled, "Magical Concealment." Evan raised an eyebrow when he saw the book, but didn't say anything.

"First, I need a spell."

"Put that away," Evan said, very quietly.

My face fell. The quick dismissal, without even asking me what I wanted the spell for, came as a bit of a shock. With trembling fingers, I shoved the book away and zipped the pack. "I'm sorry."

Evan shook his head. "You don't understand. There's no way in the world your parents are going to let me read that book. I'm surprised they let you take it out of the house."

My face flushed, and I shifted uneasily. "Well, technically, I'm not supposed to." In fact, I never had before, but I had never really wanted to before. It's just that I knew exactly what I needed, and I couldn't be sure Evan had access to a similar spell. I wasn't even sure it would be right to ask him, since it was my favor. Whatever spells he used were his secrets.

"Come on," Evan said. "It'll be easier to talk at Master Wolf's. And I think he's out resetting his wards."

We drove in silence for a couple of miles, giving me time to consider my approach. He hadn't dismissed me outright, but he was definitely wary. Well, that was only to be expected. I could work with that. I only hoped he didn't flip out when he heard the other favor I needed.

When Evan steered off the road, I thought he was making a wrong turn. I would never have seen the tiny dirt path if I hadn't known exactly what I was looking for.

"This is where he lives?" I couldn't believe it. I had never known anyone with Mr. Wolf's kind of power to live in such a backward manner.

Evan nodded. "He believes modern technology interferes with magic."

I vaguely remembered my father saying something about that, but the idea seemed crazy to me.

Evan's car bumped down the old dirt road, tossing up a cloud of dust that made it difficult to see. After about half a mile, Evan stopped the car and put it in park.

"Here we are," he said, stepping out of the car.

I opened the passenger door and swung both legs out, wincing a bit as I once again agitated the right foot. I started to grab the door for support as I stood, but before I had a chance, Evan put an arm around me and easily helped me to my feet. It didn't hurt. In fact, it didn't feel as if there was any pressure on my feet at all.

Glancing down, I saw that my feet were several inches off the ground.

"Thanks," I said, weakly. It had not escaped my attention that Evan had not needed to put his arm around me at all.

Mr. Wolf's "house" was an old wooden cabin framed by a narrow stretch of grayish-blue lake. At first, I thought it looked like the lake-side cabins rented out to tourists, but then I noticed the complete disconnection from the modern world. There wasn't so much as a porch light. No electrical or phone lines fed into the home. Off to the side, a few yards from the house, I saw a building that distinctly looked like an outhouse.

The porch was friendly enough, though. It was long and wide and had a lovely wooden bench swing. Evan did not release me until he had guided me into that swing.

"I'll be right back," he said.

For a few minutes, I just enjoyed the cool morning breeze, ignoring the trepidation in my heart about what the rest of the day might hold. One thing at a time, I reminded myself.

Then Evan emerged from the house, holding a few white candles, some rose petals, and a jar of ointment. In a flash, all the materials flew into place in a circle around the swing. In the same instant, I looked down to see that my right foot was bare, while the tennis shoe, stuffed with a sock, lay a few feet away.

"Wow," I said, despite myself.

Evan didn't answer. He just began rubbing the ointment into my foot. He took his time, massaging it into the skin in slow, deliberate movements.

"I didn't mean to sound harsh earlier," Evan said, his voice softer than usual, "but you can't undo any of the enchantments your parents put on their books, and believe me, there are enchantments."

I knew there were. My parents had mentioned it before, though they didn't get specific and always assured me that I could read whatever I liked.

"I can read it," I said.

"Yes, but they told you not to take the book out of the house. I imagine the enchantments are keyed to location."

"Oh."

"And even if that's not the case, it's not right for me to read that book."

"Oh." I knew he was right, and I felt ashamed. I only hoped my parents never found out.

Evan finished rubbing in the ointment, then capped the jar. "Tell me what you need. I may still be able to help." He took a seat next to me on the bench swing, and gave me what I'm sure he thought was a welcoming smile, though it only made me more uncertain about my whole mission.

Taking a deep breath, I plunged into my rehearsed story. "My sister, Juliana, is spying on me. She was crystal gazing, and saw me the other night, when I dropped the love potion on my foot."

"So you came to ask for help with a concealment spell because your little sister is spying on you?" Evan did not sound convinced.

"Sort of." Now I needed to find a way to tell him about the other thing, and I found I was too anxious to sit. I cast my eyes down, unable to bear the scrutiny. "Um, can I stand?"

Evan shrugged. "Try it."

Tentatively, I put some weight on my right foot. It twinged a bit, but did not hurt, so I stood fully upright. Whatever was in that ointment, it worked as well as anything my parents knew how to make.

"You may need another treatment later this afternoon," Evan said.

I nodded. The burn ointment would have worked the same way, if Juliana hadn't interceded and given me a full-body healing a few hours ago.

"You're stalling," Evan said.

I took a deep breath to prepare myself. "The thing is, I know where to find a vampire–I don't know if it's *the* vampire, the one who turned Belinda, but it definitely needs to be dealt with, or it's going to kill a friend of mine."

His face registered surprise, and perhaps a hint of triumph, though nothing could truly right this wrong.

"Why didn't you just say so?" Evan asked. "And what does this have to do with a concealment spell?"

"The thing is, I want to be the one to kill it."

I thought Evan would react badly. I thought he would talk me out of it, or even magically bind me to prevent me from going. I did not expect his bellow of rage.

"What?"

I scooted away, until my back pressed against a wooden post. "I-it-well, you see-"

Evan was up too, so quickly that I didn't see him stand. He grabbed me by one arm, and spun me around so that my back was pressed against his chest. With one arm around me, holding me close, he gestured with the other. "Do you see that old oak tree over there?"

He pointed to a proud old oak tree that overshadowed the plant life around it. No other trees grew nearby.

"Y-yes."

With deliberate slowness, he closed his hand into a fist. As he did, the enormous old tree broke apart, creaking and splintering, into a million tiny pieces. I froze, unable to take my eyes off the sight, not even sure if I was really seeing it. The ground shook as the tiny toothpicks spilled to the ground in a massive heap, cascading towards us with frightening force.

I screamed. Evan's grip on me tightened, but I didn't dare move. The tiny splinters of wood stopped well away from the house, but then I had known the damage inflicted by this action would not be physical. For the first time in my life, I had a real glimpse of Evan's power. I wonder how many people ever had. No one in my family could have done anything like that, not even if two or three of them linked together. The realization left me weak-kneed and trembling.

"Why did you do that?" I whispered.

"Because," he said, "I can. And even I would have trouble against a vampire."

If he hadn't been holding me, I probably would have sunk to my knees. As it was, I leaned against him, irrationally seeking support from my own tormentor.

"It's not like I wanted to go alone," I said. "I'm not suicidal, I just want to be the one to kill it. I'm good with a bow and arrow."

"No," Evan said. "I'll take care of it. I'll bring in my uncles and my father."

"You don't understand," I said. "The vampire is Angie's boyfriend. She invited him in last night, while we were at the pool."

Evan's grip on my arm tightened. "He attacked you?"

"Yes."

"And you escaped?"

"He didn't know about the anti-venom potion. He thinks he has me in thrall."

Evan loosened his grip on my arm, turning me around so I could face him. His eyes were stormy, and I saw something in them that sent chills down my spine, even though I knew his anger was directed at a vampire, or at an attack he had been unable to prevent.

"What did he think when you started screaming?" Evan asked.

"I didn't scream."

"You just stood there, pretending?"

"Yeah."

"That sounds like an academy award performance."

"It did hurt like hell. Then he left, and I nearly bled out, but-" I stopped myself just in time. I had never told Evan about Juliana's gift, and I wasn't about to let the secret slip out now. "My parents came."

If Evan caught the slip, he didn't say anything. He did give me a skeptical look at the idea that normal healing potions would have helped me get from the brink of death to perfect health in twelve hours, but he didn't ask.

"He's going back for Angie tonight," I said. "Both of us, actually. He told me to be there. If I don't go and stop him, Angie won't have a chance."

"Cassie, look at me," Evan commanded.

Licking my lips nervously, I looked at him. His eyes weren't quite as stormy, but they were intense.

"You don't have to prove yourself to me."

"I know."

"You don't need to prove yourself to your family."

"You don't think I can do it," I said, flatly. "I have a plan. There are lots of trees to hide in around the pool, and he won't even see me. I'll get an arrow in his heart before he has the chance."

"What if you miss?"

"That's why I need backup. I came to you because my parents would never let me go at all."

"Your parents are right." Evan stepped away from me and folded his arms across his chest.

I closed my eyes and took a deep breath. "Look, I know I'm going to sound paranoid, but I do feel like I need to prove myself. There are things I've overheard my parents say... it's hard to explain, but I have a very bad feeling about my mom being pregnant again. We won't be seven anymore."

To my relief, Evan didn't argue, although what he did say was almost worse. "I hope you're wrong, but I always thought you had some intuition. If you've got a bad feeling, I trust it."

I held up my hands to ward off the assertion. He had said it before, and he might even have been right, but as far as gifts go, intuition is slippery. It's only clearly identifiable in extreme cases, and I didn't qualify, so I didn't want to think about it... or get my hopes up.

"We'll skip the debate," Evan said, "but I'm not sure how putting yourself in danger on the off chance you might kill a vampire is going to help."

I winced at his phrasing, but held my ground. "I don't want to be pushed out. I want to prove I'm a part of the protective magic, and if Mom wants to restore it, she'll have to try for nine of us."

Evan didn't answer for a long time. He stared off into the distance, at a spot somewhere over my shoulder that I couldn't see. I had to resist the urge to turn around and follow his gaze.

Evan let out a long breath. "I understand that you want revenge, and that you have something to prove to your family, but I think you're selling yourself short. You're intelligent and compassionate, and your family has to see that."

Blindsided by his flattering assessment, it took me a while to respond. "I think they do, I just don't think they see it as important as other qualities."

"Do you?" he asked.

I didn't know, and I didn't want to analyze my feelings right then, so, taking a deep breath, I offered him one last word. "Please."

"*If* I let you do this, you have to promise me one thing." My heart started to beat faster. Was he really considering letting me help? "What?"

"You do what I say at all times. I've got a couple of escape ideas in mind, if all else fails, but I need to know you'll cut and run if I give the word."

I nodded, and held my breath.

"Then let me see how you handle a bow and arrow. I won't make my final decision until then."

19

I spent the day with my bow, while Evan spent the day brewing potions. It didn't take long for my arm to become sore, but apparently, one of the first potions Evan decided to brew was to increase endurance. He brought it out to me as I sat on a bale of hay and rubbed at my aching shoulder.

"I'm also working on strength and speed," Evan told me after I had finished the foul-tasting endurance concoction.

My stomach rebelled at the idea of taking two more potions, but I nodded.

"I just have to tweak them a bit so they won't cancel one another out," he said.

"Doesn't that kind of defeat the purpose of me being the one to kill it?" I asked.

He set his face in a grim line, and I knew I had said the wrong thing. I needed to watch it, because he still hadn't given me his final approval.

"You're not doing this alone, you're doing it with me. I'm not sure what you thought my role in all of this would be, but I'm sending us both in there with everything I've got. I only wish we had time for me to brew stronger versions of these potions."

I didn't say anything, but I held my breath while Evan studied the target I had been aiming at. Ten arrows formed a tight pattern, obscuring the bulls-eye painted over a straw man's heart.

"You're good," Evan said, "but don't get too cocky. There are a lot of things that can go wrong."

I wiped sweat from my brow and nodded. "I know, I'll only have one shot."

"Not exactly," Evan said, his brow furrowed. "If you miss the first time, he'll be on you in a flash. I can hold him, but only for a few seconds. Vampires can't be held by telekinesis the way others can. He'll break free."

"You could always shove a stake through his chest," I suggested.

To my surprise, he shook his head. "I can be fast or I can be accurate, but I can't do both at the same time. I'd be more likely to hit him in the eye."

"What if you aimed for the eye?"

He ignored me, which was the right thing to do. "You can get off another shot or two while I hold him."

"And if that doesn't work?" I asked.

"I've got one more trick," he said. "A crystal that traps sunlight. It doesn't last long, which is why I want to hold it in reserve, but we might have five minutes to get out. The speed potion will help with that, and my car won't be far away."

"Will he be able to follow?" I asked.

"Only if he knows which way we went, but even then, it'll be hard. I checked some of Master Wolf's references a little while ago, and vampires are insanely fast over short stretches, but they can't sustain the speed. They can't follow a car for long."

"So are we doing this?" I asked.

"Probably, but I reserve the right to change my mind until sunset."

ꕥ

He didn't change his mind. I was in position well before the sun set, my back leaning against a tree, all my senses straining for the smallest sign of a demonic presence in the woods with me. Evan lurked nearby, a few trees away, but we didn't speak, and as the sun began its descent, I had trouble seeing him.

When the sun disappeared entirely, I strained against the dim glow from the porch light and hotel windows to find my target. He had come in through the gate the night before, but all I saw there were more trees and more dark.

I nearly jumped out of my skin when I saw two tiny pinpricks of light that reminded me of the vampire's hypnotic stare, but they turned out to be from a car driving down the road. They grew steadily larger, shining light on the nearby trees, until they stopped in the hotel parking lot. I hoped whoever it was got inside quickly.

A few minutes later, Angie came out, wearing the same white robe she had on the night before. I had a sick sense I knew what she had on underneath, but I did not wait for her to disrobe. Instead, I scanned the woods around me more frantically. If she was here, then so was the vampire.

"Luke!" she called.

My heart hammered. Was he already here, in the woods? Had he seen me? I had purposely chosen a spot away from the gate, which was the direction he had entered from the night before.

A wind rustled the leaves above my head. I had my arrow cocked and ready.

"Luke!" Angie called again. "Come in, the water's great."

Then I saw him once again, at the south end of the property near the gate. He jumped over the fence in one smooth, fluid movement, landing directly beside Angie, but he did not touch her. He was looking around, and I knew exactly what he was looking for.

"Where is Cassandra?" the vampire asked.

"We don't need her," Angie replied.

He growled, a low, bestial sound. It reminded me, though I did not need a reminder, that Luke was not human. He might look human, but whatever humanity had been in him disappeared the night he turned.

I stepped around the tree to get a good angle, lifted the bow, took careful aim, and...twang! The arrow slid through the air, silently stalking its target.

After a few seconds pause there was a loud thunk, but not from the arrow hitting home. I'm not sure if my aim was off or not, but I had not properly accounted for the wrought iron fence in the way. The arrow hit one of the posts.

Of course, Luke heard it, and was by the fence before I could blink. Knowing I had only seconds, I reached into my quiver and took out another arrow as he bent down to pick up the first. I worked to still my breathing as I cocked the arrow, but my heart caught in my chest when Luke lifted his head to stare directly at me.

He lunged forward, a movement that should have ended in my throat being ripped out, but instead he began an intense struggle with the air around him. Evan to the rescue. This was my last chance.

My hands trembling, I got the other arrow in place, lifted the bow, aimed, and fired.

Luke lurched to the side just as the arrow left the bow. It hit him, but in the arm rather than the heart.

I didn't hesitate a second before getting out a third arrow. I knew I didn't have another chance. Evan and I had gone over this again and again, and it was unlikely that he would be able to hold the vampire for more than a few seconds.

But I wasn't done yet. I wasn't trembling any longer. I snatched the third arrow out of the quiver, took a step closer to the vampire, and sent it hurtling toward him.

Luke broke free of the invisible force holding him, and started toward me just as the arrow left the bow. He and the arrow met in mid-lunge.

This time it struck true. There was a moment when he seemed surprised. He looked at the arrow in his chest in utter disbelief, the strength and speed of his movement carrying him forward until he dropped at my feet.

He didn't die right away. As I looked down into his now pale yellow eyes, he reached out a hand to grab my almost fully healed foot.

Thanks in part to his weakened form, and in part to the strengthening potion I had taken earlier, I did manage to pry my foot free, but in the process I lost my balance and began to fall on top of the vampire.

I didn't quite finish the fall. Something caught me halfway down, and I found myself flying backwards through the air. I landed hard on the forest floor, then skidded a couple of feed until I felt Evan's arms around me. He was panting with exertion.

I let the bow drop to my side, and just sat like that for a full minute, letting the adrenaline rush subside, letting myself feel safe again for the first time since the vampire had attacked.

Behind me, Evan's chest rose and fell in an increasingly steady rhythm. When his breathing returned to normal, I allowed myself to turn slightly to face him. "That was close."

He did not answer. For a fraction of a heartbeat, he looked like he wanted to kiss me. I could feel his breath on my cheek, and even in the dark I could see his eyes boring into me.

In the intensity of the moment, I forgot all about Braden and my parents' disapproval. Evan was firm and warm and he had just saved my life. Whether it was the relief or the adrenaline or something else, I may never know, but I turned my face ever so slightly to meet him.

The kiss never came. With our faces a mere inch or two apart Evan broke away, muttering something under his breath.

Sense returned, and I leaped to my feet, brushing the contact off myself. "W-we need to get his head," I reminded Evan.

Evan had brought the ax. He picked it up, slung it over his shoulder, and together we walked to the vampire corpse. The light had finally left his eyes, but you can't be too careful with a vampire. If the stake (or arrow, in this case) is removed, there is a chance they can heal. Removing the head makes their death more certain. Technically, you could go for decapitation in the first place, but that's harder to pull off than the stake.

"Let me," I said.

Wordlessly, Evan handed me the ax and stood back as I began to swing. I didn't have a good grip on the ax the first time; my hands were too close together, and I ended up putting a gash in the corpse's forehead. Drawing the ax back up, I widened my stance and my grip, then swung again. And again. And again. I'm not sure when I did manage to sever the head, because I lost myself to the swish and thud....swish and thud.

"Cassie, stop," Evan said after a while.

I came back to myself. Leaving the ax where it had landed last, I glanced back at Evan, but he wasn't looking at me. He was looking over my shoulder. I turned and spotted Angie on the other side of the wrought iron fence, still unabashed by her nakedness, staring at me in stunned disbelief.

I started toward her.

"Stay away from me," Angie said.

"Angie, wait." I started toward the fence, but she backed away.

"I'm getting the police." She turned and fled inside, not bothering to pick up her robe.

"She's still being influenced by the venom," Evan said. "It'll take a couple days to wear off."

"Yeah. I wonder if I should wait for the sheriff, though."

Evan shrugged. "It's up to you, but leave me out of it."

I nodded. I knew it wasn't that he thought he had done anything wrong, it's just the arrogance of his kind, thinking that normal laws don't apply. Or any laws, as far as I can tell. It's not like there's some magical oversight committee out there.

"Take me home," I said. I could explain all this to the sheriff in the morning.

20

NOT UNEXPECTEDLY, MY PARENTS, NICOLAS, AND JULIANA WERE ALL waiting in the living room when I got home. There was a tense moment when I stood in the entryway, keys dangling from one hand, backpack gripped loosely in the other, staring at my foot as it dug into the dark brown carpeting. I wasn't sure if they knew what I had done or just guessed, but from the looks on their faces, I wasn't going to escape the room without a tongue-lashing.

Then it began. All of them at once, yelling so loudly I couldn't make out a word of it. I kept my eyes on Mom throughout, wondering if she would be able to hold in her untrained power. She must have had a breakthrough, because as red as her face grew, she reined it in.

"Hey!" I shouted, loudly enough to be heard over the din. They ignored me. Well, I wasn't going to let them treat me like that, so I strode past them toward the hallway.

I never quite made it there, because out of the corner of my eye, I spotted a stranger leaning against the entrance to the kitchen. No, not a stranger. He looked familiar, but I had not seen my cousin, Jason, in eight years, since he had been fifteen. He looked much older now, tall and very, very large. He might have been intimidating if it had not been for the amused sort of smile on his face. He caught my eye, and winked.

"Enough," Dad said, finally. Everyone quieted down. Then he rounded on me. "Can you explain why you decided to keep us from finding out where you were? Or better yet, how you pulled it off?"

"No," I said.

"We know you went after the vampire," Dad said. "Didn't you think we'd guess?"

I shrugged. "I killed him."

Behind me, someone started clapping, and I saw I had an unexpected ally in my cousin. "It was nice, too. For a minute, I thought you'd had it, but then you pulled it together on the third shot—against a moving target and everything. Sweet."

"Um, you were there?" I asked.

"I got about a hundred phone calls yesterday," Jason said. "Didn't you think I'd show up?"

"When did you get here?" I asked.

"This morning," he replied. "Someone hasn't been checking her messages today."

That was true, I hadn't been. I had called Kaitlin to cancel lunch, but had otherwise kept the phone off all day.

"We guessed where you were going tonight," Dad said, "so we sent Jason to save you from yourself."

"I didn't need it, though, did I?"

"Of course you did," Dad said. "You went up against a vampire all by yourself-"

"Oh, no, Uncle Edward," Jason said. "Didn't I mention? She had help."

Everyone turned to look at him. I bit my lip, praying he wouldn't go on, but my prayers were not to be answered.

"Yeah," Jason said, "tall, long dark hair tied in a ponytail, about Cassie's age."

"Evan," Nicolas said.

"Strong, too," Jason said, apparently oblivious to the chill in the room. "I've met telekinetics before, but none that could hold a vamp, even for a heartbeat. This guy actually managed to give Cassie time to reload–twice."

"Evan is impressive," Dad said, "but he had no business putting you in danger like that."

Jason laughed, still clearly oblivious to the tension in the room. "Oh, he was probably just trying to show off. I left when they started making out."

Why isn't there ever a hole in the floor when you need one? I hid my scarlet face in my hands and shook my head. The trouble was that this time, it wasn't exactly a lie. He hadn't seen what he thought he had, but there had been that moment when we nearly kissed.

Juliana whistled. "And I thought you were happy with Braden."

"Oops," Jason said, though his smile didn't falter, "didn't realize that would be a touchy subject."

"It's not what it looked like," I said.

"It doesn't matter," Mom said. She put an arm on Dad's hand. "Edward, it doesn't matter. She's fine. She did get some help. She didn't just go off on her own."

Dad didn't look angry anymore. He looked worn out. For the first time, I noticed his eyes were red, as if he hadn't slept well lately. "Why Evan? Why couldn't you have come to us? Now you owe him a debt."

"No, I don't. A vampire killed his cousin, so he had as much stake in the kill as I did." I winced, when I recognized the pun, but no one else seemed to have noticed.

"And the concealment spell?" Dad asked.

"I've been helping him track down his cousin's killer. Now, I'm doing it free of charge." Luckily, Evan had been open to the arrangement, and sensitive to the fact that I did not want to incur a magical debt.

"Well," Jason said loudly from the kitchen, "I thought she did a great job. She trained, she knew her target, she went with a plan, and she brought backup."

At least someone had been impressed.

"You did well," Mom said after a moment's hesitation.

I stared at her, a little warily. She met my gaze levelly, and offered a smile. "You've grown up. You can take care of yourself."

"Thank you. I better go to bed."

"Good night," she said.

ᘓᘏ

I didn't make it as far as the second floor landing before Jason intercepted me. "Sorry about that," he said. "I stuck my foot in, didn't I?"

"It's okay. Thanks for having my back, anyway. And for not getting involved when you didn't have to."

"Hey, I know what it's like to want to prove yourself. I tried that when I found my dad a couple of years ago."

"I didn't know you were looking for him." For that matter, I didn't know much at all about the circumstances around his parents' divorce. Mom and Aunt Sherry had always been tight-lipped about it, so I had assumed it was one of those painful situations best left alone. Aunt Sherry didn't come around much, anyway. Like Belinda, she was a gifted herbalist, so she spent most of her time with her gardens and greenhouses in Arkansas. She might have lived closer, but Belinda's claim as the community herbalist was absolute, and Aunt Sherry is non-confrontational to an extreme.

"Yeah, well, take my word for it," Jason said. "Don't bother trying to prove yourself to anyone."

He was probably right, but I wasn't quite ready to hear it.

"Anyway, I wanted to tell you to be careful. There's almost never one vamp in town. I'm going to hang around for a few days, try to track the line to its source."

"How do you do that?" I asked.

Jason smiled. "Good old fashioned detective work. Know anyone who could help me? I can't afford to pay except in adventure."

I'd had plenty of adventure in the last forty-eight hours, but I couldn't bear the idea of not finishing what I started. Besides, Jason was cool. He was easy to want to be around.

"I don't need any money," I said. "Mom and Dad turn lead into gold for a living."

"Yeah, they send me money sometimes. I'm not sure they understand how much things cost, though."

Truthfully, neither did I. "Do you need more?"

"Nah." Jason shuffled his feet a bit. "Look, why don't we find a place to talk? I have a lot of questions for you, and I'd rather ask them someplace I can have some of your mom's homemade candies and wine."

"No one will be in the library at this hour."

"Great, I'll catch you there in a few minutes." He started to head down the stairs, suddenly stopped, and turned back to me. "Wait, are you old enough for wine?"

I blinked. Technically, I had only been legal to drink alcohol for a couple of weeks, but my parents served us their homemade wines as early as twelve. I guess it's just one more way that the magical families in the area consider themselves above the law. "Um, yeah, I'd love a glass of wine."

"Back in a flash," Jason said.

I wandered into the library, while he headed down the stairs. There were only smoldering coals in the fireplace, so I added a few logs and kicked it up a bit. The flames were dancing by the time Jason returned with the wine and chocolates.

"I don't know where your mom learned to cook," Jason said, "but she could teach mine a thing or two. I grew up on fast food and microwaves." He poured a glass of wine and handed it to me.

I swirled it a bit, and took a sip, but it didn't taste right. It was sweeter than usual, and had a hint of something I couldn't identify—peppermint? "Did you put something in this?"

"Just something to help you relax. Most people don't like to relive vampire attacks. This makes it easier."

"You slipped me a sedative?" I put the glass down on an end table. I couldn't believe it, not from Jason. He'd seemed to think I was okay, or had that all been an act? "That's not cool."

"Not a sedative, exactly," Jason said, not looking at me. "It'll help you remember without making you relive it. It actually helps prevent post traumatic stress."

I shook my head and scowled at him. Just what I needed, another relative thinking I needed protection from myself. "Thanks, but I don't need it."

"You need it," Jason insisted. "I've been in this business longer than you. It's got nothing to do with you, and it doesn't mean you're weak. You're human, and anyone who went through that would be in danger of having post traumatic stress." Jason held up his glass. "Which is why I take the potion every time I fight a vamp."

"Oh." I stared at his glass, trying to imagine the strong, confident Jason needing a potion to help keep him sane.

"I'll trade with you if you don't believe me, but I really think you ought to take the potion."

I believed him. I picked up my own glass and took another sip.

"That's better." Jason drank deeply from his own glass. "You know, you really shouldn't jump to conclusions."

He was right, of course. Jumping to conclusions is especially dangerous in detective work.

"I've just been on edge lately," I said. "I don't know why. I can't sleep."

"Bad dreams?" Jason asked.

"Not exactly. I don't really remember my dreams."

"Not at all?"

"Sometimes I get a flash or an image, but that's about it."

Jason took a seat in one of the high-backed armchairs closest to the fire, and I sat across from him, continuing to sip the wine. He didn't say anything, and I knew he was waiting for me to be ready to tell him what I had seen over the past couple of days. There was no rush. We drank the wine and each had one of the chocolates–I took the turtle cluster.

Then I started telling him what I had seen in as much detail as I could remember, which was quite a bit. When I finished, we fell back into silence for a few minutes.

"Things aren't adding up," I said into the silence. "I'm not sure if the vampire I killed tonight is the one who turned Belinda, but either way it doesn't explain Nancy's death in broad daylight. Plus, why did Belinda turn?"

"The vaccine has a very small failure rate," Jason said, "even when given twice."

"Is that what you think happened?" I asked.

He shook his head.

"Is there an antidote?" I asked.

He gave me a tight-lipped shrug, which I took to mean yes, but officially, I didn't tell you. I understood. The vampire hunters had their secrets as well.

"So Belinda may have wanted to become a vampire? Done it intentionally? That just seems so wrong. And I just can't help but remember all the half-healed bite marks all over her body. I mean, from head to toe."

"Torture," Jason said, almost too casually. It made me think he knew the word from personal experience.

"Oh," I said, with dawning understanding. "She might have been forced to take the potion? But then, who brewed it? Can vampires use magic?"

"Yes." Jason made the word sound final and ominous.

"That doesn't sound like a good combination." I tried to sound casual, but I didn't feel it.

He didn't answer right away. When he finally did, it was in a hushed tone. "Look, there are some things I can't tell you. You know how it goes."

"Oh yes," I assured him. "Secrets and lies."

"Exactly. My order depends on secrecy. Our mortality rate is high enough as it is."

"You don't have to tell me anything," I said, "but I am on this case."

"There are a few things I can say. First of all, you have to understand that vampires are highly territorial. Their personalities differ, so you'll get some who want to be masters of a horde of vampires, and others who guard their own territories alone. The latter usually settle in rural areas, and don't like any other vampires to trespass. They survive by subtlety, which is harder when more vampires are around. They'll take a sip from many different people, rarely killing, because that creates a new vampire, although accidents happen. In those cases, the would-be sire will often cut the head off the body to stop the new vampire from rising. They actually kill one another more often than we do."

He paused, and I sensed there was something he wasn't telling me, but something he wanted me to figure out for myself. That way I would know, and he wouldn't have broken his word to the order. I found myself understanding him, and even appreciating the situation.

He let me have all the time I needed. I took another chocolate while I tried to put the picture together in my mind.

Somewhere out there, a vampire, either alone or with a small number of followers, had carved out Eagle Rock as its territory. This vampire would have survived in the area for a long time, undetected, which meant he was clever and, well, powerful. He couldn't have successfully held a territory with so many practitioners otherwise.

Some vampires can do magic, Jason had said. Luke couldn't, which made me think he wasn't the master around here. Someone else had to be the master, someone smarter and stronger.

Finally, I spoke. "So theoretically, if a vampire is also a sorcerer, what additional powers might he have?"

"Theoretically, he might have any powers a sorcerer would have."

"So," I said, straining to think, "he could cast an illusion, work spells, brew potions?"

"Those are the sorts of things a sorcerer can do."

"Could he turn into a bat and fly away?" I asked.

"Possibly," Jason said.

"Could he mix up some super-strong SPF 2000 sunblock and go out in the daylight?"

Jason didn't answer, which I took to mean yes.

"Really?" I hadn't been entirely serious, but now I found myself rethinking everything I thought I knew about vampires. "But wait, if they're immune to sunlight, then anyone could be a vampire. Are they also immune to crosses and holy water?"

"Faith is a special kind of magic," Jason said.

"Small comfort." Then another thought occurred to me. "Is vampire hunter blood still poisonous to them?"

Jason wouldn't meet my eyes, but he did nod, once. Interesting, I thought. I wondered if there was more to the legend about vampire hunter blood than they let on. Given how much of their order was shrouded in secrecy, I would have bet on it, but what, I wondered, made their blood so poisonous to a vampire that a sorcerer couldn't find an antidote?

Faith is a special kind of magic, he had said.

Pushing the speculation aside, I returned to the topic at hand. "This vampire could be anyone. We have a powerful, territorial vampire in town. Somehow, I doubt it was Luke."

"Me too," Jason said. "No offense, but you killed him too easily."

"None taken," I said, though that wasn't entirely true. "I fooled him into thinking I was under his spell, so he couldn't have been that bright, but I wonder if there's a way to find out if he turned Belinda?"

"There is, although my gut tells me no."

"Mine too. I think whoever she took to the cabin turned her."

"Interesting," Jason said, sitting forward. "That gives me something to think about, although I want to find out for sure whether Luke sired Belinda, before I jump to conclusions."

"Can I help you do that?"

"No, I just need to gather some potion ingredients. You should try to get some sleep tonight."

"I'll do my best."

21

The McClellan family rivaled the Hewitts in nastiness, and surpassed them in raw magical power. They liked to deal in curses, hexes, enchantments, and ancient dark objects. Sometimes, these ancient dark objects were not obtained through legitimate means.

One day, not long after I joined the force, a private investigator from New York came to pay us a visit. He represented an insurance company that was interested in tracking down a three million dollar sceptre, part of a private collection they insured. It had been stolen a month or so before, and his investigation had led him to Eagle Rock.

The investigator, Simon Wright, spoke to the sheriff the day he came to town to let him know what he was after, and why he thought it was in Eagle Rock. They were only in the sheriff's office for five minutes before Sheriff Adams called me in.

"Cassie, this is Simon Wright," Sheriff Adams said. "He's looking for something, and I thought you might be able to help him find it." He turned to Simon and said, "She knows most of the more interesting families in town."

Simon raised an eyebrow, but he didn't ask what the sheriff meant by interesting. He just told his story. "The sceptre was stolen from a private collection in upstate New York. The place was a fortress–video cameras, security guards, guard dogs, alarms–you name it. At 9:45 in the evening, the alarms went off, but the guards couldn't see anyone. The guard dogs might have seen someone, but they had fallen asleep and wouldn't wake. Then the video cameras shorted. At 9:50, the glass case with the sceptre inside shattered, but no one could see who had done it. An instant later, the sceptre disappeared into thin air."

Simon paused and studied my reaction, but my face was a calculated mask. I knew exactly what had happened, of course. It was a basic invisibility spell, one that did not fool dogs or cameras. A lot of people in Eagle Rock could have done it, but I had an idea which family might have been involved.

"This sceptre," I said, "did it have a reputation as a cursed object? Unexplained deaths, accidents, or bad luck?"

"Yes," Simon said. "It was first stolen from an ancient Egyptian tomb some fifty years ago, and it was said to bring death to anyone who touched it."

"Pleasant," I said. "So what brought you here?"

"An electrician," Simon said. "I found the man who shorted the cameras–don't ask how–and managed to track his payment to a bank here in Eagle Rock."

"Did you find out who owned the account?"

"Jasmine Hewitt."

I laughed.

"What's so funny?" Simon asked.

It was hard to explain why that was funny. Partly, it was because I couldn't see Jasmine Hewitt prowling an old mansion in search of a deadly sceptre. Partly, it was because I knew she didn't have the power or the money to pull it off. But mostly, it was because I knew of one family that would have loved to lay a false trail at her feet.

"It wasn't Jasmine Hewitt," I said. "I'm guessing it was a McClellan. They would be more than happy to cast false blame on the Hewitts. Plus, they deal in cursed objects."

"Well, if that's true, it makes my job harder," Simon said. "I don't have any evidence linking the McClellans to this robbery. I was rather hoping to just get a warrant, and have a look inside Jasmine Hewitt's house."

I shook my head. "Won't be there, and if you do that, it'll tip the McClellans off that you're around here, looking."

"I guess it's time to do a little stakeout, then," Simon said. "What's the address?"

ஐ

Several days passed before Simon came back to us with a taped conversation between David McClellan and his father, John. In the conversation, David mentioned the sceptre, and talked about a possible buyer.

It was enough for a warrant. I was excited. This was exactly why I had joined the force–to put people like the McClellans in their place. They couldn't get away with doing whatever they wanted, not when it hurt people or broke the law.

The judge issued the warrant, and I went with Simon to search the house.

When David McClellan answered the door, he had a sneer on his face, but it disappeared when he saw me. "What are you doing here?"

"We have a warrant to search the premises," I said, holding it out for him to see.

"Cassandra Scot?" David said. "You're a cop now?"

"Yes," I answered. I felt powerful. He had to let me in, and I guessed that he had not had time to get rid of the sceptre. He may try to make it invisible, but that was why I had brought a hand-held camcorder to look through. I had a badge, plenty of knowledge, and my parents' name to protect me.

The trouble was, Simon didn't have any of that, and sorcerers really don't think they should have to answer to any mere mortal authority.

David let us enter. We searched an informal living room, while he disappeared into a back bedroom. He came back out a few minutes later, a gloved hand carrying the sceptre quite openly. He offered it to Simon.

"Don't touch-" I started to say, but it was too late. Simon grabbed the sceptre with his bare hands.

He let out an ear-piercing scream and sank to the floor, clutching the arm that grasped the sceptre. It looked like he couldn't let go, and whatever curse was on that thing would eat him alive from the inside out. I could see his skin began to shiver and crawl.

"Can you undo the curse?" I asked David.

"Why would I want to?" he asked.

"It'll kill him." My heart was pounding now. I considered calling my parents, but wasn't sure what they could do. They had no particular expertise in cursed objects.

"You want him to live?" David asked.

"Of course."

"Fine, then, I'll make a trade. His life for mine. You pretend you didn't find the sceptre here and walk away." It was a magical deal he was offering me; completely binding.

I spluttered. "If he dies, I'll arrest you for murder!"

David shook his head. "What will you tell people the cause of death is, a magical sceptre?"

"Yes, and I bet people around here would believe me." I wasn't entirely sure, but it was a good possibility.

"You'll bet his life?" David asked. "Because I'm willing to."

Put that way, I really had no choice. I could see in his eyes that he would follow this through. "Undo it." I closed my eyes. "This never happened."

A few seconds later, Simon stopped screaming, though he continued to whimper for a few minutes. I just hung my head in defeat. Unfortunately, it would only turn out to be the first of many lessons about how the world really worked. In the end, it was why I left the force.

* * *

I spent another restless night tossing and turning beneath the sheets. Nothing had changed–there was still a vampire out there somewhere, I was still no closer to figuring out what had happened to Nancy and Belinda, and Mom was still pregnant. Yes, there had been a victory, but a small one.

I must have dozed off near dawn, because the sound of the doorbell ringing woke me from a nightmare that faded as soon as I saw the light streaming in through my window. Since the window faced the back, I couldn't see who had come to the door, so I quickly threw on some clean clothes and, without even running a brush through my hair, headed downstairs.

The entire family was gathered in the living room, including Jason, who looked like he had just come in from a long night. At first, I thought Jason had rung the doorbell, but then I saw Dad standing at the door, talking to someone on the other side.

"Who is it?" I asked.

"Go back upstairs," Dad told me, sharply.

"Cassie." It was Sheriff Adams, but for some reason, Dad wasn't letting him in.

"What's going on here?" I asked. "Dad, why don't you invite him inside?"

"I've got a warrant for your arrest," Sheriff Adams said.

"Huh?" I moved closer. There was Sheriff Adams, a fiercely determined expression on his face, waving a piece of paper around as if it were some kind of talisman. It reminded me of my visit to the McClellan's, almost a year before. Remembering how that nearly ended, I sucked in my breath. Not that this would be at all like that. My parents were not insane criminals like the McClellans.

"Cassandra," Dad said. "Go upstairs. I'll handle this."

"But-" I began.

"She's under arrest for the murder or Luke Foster," Sheriff Adams said.

My eyes went wide and I stared around the room at the grim faces of those present. Only the youngest three seemed immune to the ominous atmosphere. Elena, as usual, was caught in a far away place, Adam seemed frankly confused, and Christina was talking to a doll about fairies.

"Um, shouldn't I just go with him?" It had to be a simple misunderstanding, one we could easily work out without the drama and heavy-handed power plays.

"Yes," Sheriff Adams said.

"No," Dad said at the exact same time. His face was turned away from me, so I couldn't see it, but Sheriff Adams' eyes flickered in fear.

"We've always had respect for you," Dad said, "but I will not let you take my daughter to jail for a crime you and I both know she didn't commit."

"Technically, I did kill him," I muttered so that the sheriff couldn't hear.

Mom and Jason heard. The latter whispered, "Technically, he was already dead."

"You're not helping," I replied.

"I don't know what to think," Sheriff Adams said. "Last night, we got a report from a very good friend of hers that Cassie had killed her boyfriend. It looks bad."

"He was a vampire," I said.

Sheriff Adams focused on me, and when I actually took the time to study his face, I knew reasoning with him would not help. He was still on the love potion, and probably thought if I had staked Luke, then I had staked Belinda as well. I thought Evan had implemented a plan to take care of the problem, but it seemed to have failed. The only difference I could see was that the sheriff now had a full head of thick, brown hair.

"As fascinating as I'm sure this all is," Dad said, "I'm going to have to ask you to leave."

"Then I'll return with backup," Sheriff Adams shot back.

Better make it a full coven, I thought, ruefully. Dad did not sound at all inclined to let him in that door.

"I wouldn't recommend it." Dad slammed the door in the sheriff's face.

"Dad!" I tried to run to the door, but Dad stood in the way. So instead, I went to the window. Sheriff Adams was still standing on the doorstep, his face bright red, staring at the house as if he could work out a way to get inside if he thought long and hard enough. If I had needed further proof of how the mind-altering affects of the potion could harm a person, this was it. In his right mind, Sheriff Adams would know better than to consider breaking into a heavily warded house.

Jason joined me by the window a few seconds later, shaking his head.

"I have to go out there," I said. "I don't know what my parents think-"

"They think they're protecting you," Jason said. "Maybe you should trust them."

Suddenly, I heard an earth-shattering explosion from outside. I pressed my nose into the window, and stared in horror at the flames pouring out in all directions from what used to be the sheriff's car. A piece of shrapnel clanked against the window, and I quickly backed away, even knowing the wards would not let it in.

Sheriff Adams, meanwhile, had his arms over his face, trying to protect himself from flying debris.

"Dad," I said, "What are you doing?"

"It wasn't me," Dad said. "He tripped a ward."

"Someone's got to help him," I said.

I pushed past Dad, who by then was a bit more docile, possibly due to shock. He really didn't seem to have expected the ward to go off, and I know he hadn't wanted to hurt the sheriff. By the time I opened the door, however; Juliana had rushed past me and laid a hand on one of the sheriff's hands.

The sheriff didn't see her. He was curled up in a ball, facing the stone porch. By the time he looked up, she had slipped back inside, where Mom was scolding her for using her gift. For once, I didn't think she had done such a bad thing.

"Cassie, what the hell happened?" The sheriff's eyes looked blearily up at me, and to my surprise, I saw they no longer looked pink. Had I been mistaken in my earlier inspection, which had been from a greater distance, or had he suddenly broken free of the spell?

Before I had a chance to work it out, Dad pulled me back inside, then slammed the door in the sheriff's face. Again.

"Someone has to give him a ride back into town," I pointed out.

Dad, for once, was at a loss for words.

"I have to go into town anyway." Nicolas pushed past us and opened the door. "I'll be back before lunch." Then the door closed behind him.

"Mommy," Adam said, retreating to his little boy voice. "What's going on? Why's Cassie upset?"

"It's okay," Mom said. "Why don't you go play in your room for a while? In fact, it might be best if all of you go play in your rooms for a while."

It was a measure of how scared the kids were that even Isaac went without complaint. The only sound any of them made, as they retreated up the stairs, was Elena, who said, "Luke Foster's not very nice. He turned into a vampire on purpose." Then she shook her head and drifted away with the others.

That left Mom, Dad, Jason, and Juliana in the room with me. Mom gave Juliana a significant look, and she left as well.

"So," Jason said. "I need to brew a few potions. Mind if I use the lab upstairs?"

Mom and Dad both shook their heads, and he, too, retreated up the stairs.

"What happens now?" I asked.

"There's a debt I can collect on," Dad said. "By this afternoon, the town will suffer from selective amnesia."

I sucked in my breath, my mind reeling at the implications of what he had suggested. How many times had he warned me against the dangers of mind magic, and now he wanted to use it, quite blatantly, to protect me from a charge that probably wouldn't stick?

"Didn't you always tell me that mind magic was evil?" I asked.

"I told you that all magic is gray," Dad said. "I'm not letting you go to jail for killing a monster and I'd rather not get into a war with the locals."

"Couldn't we just hire a good lawyer?" I asked.

"There are no guarantees, and I don't want your name attached to a murder in anyone's mind."

"Does this sort of thing happen often?" I asked. "Amnesia, I mean?"

Dad shrugged, noncommittally.

I sighed. This sort of thing was exactly why I had quit the force. "I'm going up to help Jason."

22

THE LAB WAS ON THE SECOND FLOOR, BETWEEN THE LIBRARY AND THE largely abandoned gym. (Mom went through a health nut phase about ten years ago. When I think about it, I can still taste the rice cakes.) It was a windowless chamber that doubled as a storage room for complete potions, and in fact, that was its primary purpose. Most of the family preferred to brew potions in the kitchen, surrounded by light and company, but some potions require dark or privacy or both, so the lab was equipped with several Bunsen burners on a work table in the center. Around the edges were shelves reaching to the ceiling, filled with potion ingredients, tubes, jars, glasses, and a swirling vortex (don't ask me, I have no idea).

Jason had all three Bunsen burners going at the same time when I went in. As he appeared to be deep in concentration, I did not bother him, but only watched as he added something from a small silver flask into each, then took a drink before screwing the cap back on. Strange, since I couldn't imagine alcohol as an ingredient in the type of potion he was brewing.

He turned down the heat to a simmer and leaned back, startling when he saw me in the doorway. "Didn't see you there."

"I didn't want to bother you," I said.

He seemed to want to say something else, but he shook it off, making me wonder if I had walked in on something I shouldn't have seen.

"I got arrested once," Jason said, after a while. "Down in Arkansas, back when I was just getting started. I bagged this vamp in Russellville that used to be the mayor's son."

"How'd you get out of that?" I asked.

"Local sorcerer gave me a hand," Jason said.

"Mind magic?" I suspected the answer, even as I worked to accept one more aspect of the magical world I hadn't understood before.

"Yeah. Well, it's like your dad says–it's a gray area. He may avoid using it himself, but put his family in danger, and he'll rationalize it in a second."

I leaned against the door and closed my eyes, breathing in the garlic-scented vapors of the potions. I knew my father would do anything for the family, but the use of mind magic, especially on my behalf, bothered me more than I could say.

"Kind of makes me wonder," I said, "whether it's ever been used on me, and I forgot."

Jason didn't answer. He was staring intently at his potions, as if waiting for something. When he began chanting an incantation, I did not interrupt.

Most incantations are not in English, but that isn't because ancient languages work better or anything. In fact, they don't often use ancient languages at all. I've known sorcerers to make up their own languages, and once, when we were kids, I overheard Evan using Pig Latin. It's all about privacy and secrecy. They don't want anyone else to know what they're saying.

When Jason stopped chanting, he shook his head.

"What?" I asked, setting aside my concerns, for the moment, and snapping into investigation mode.

"Well, while I was out last night, I snuck into the morgue and grabbed a couple hairs from both Luke and Belinda. He definitely didn't sire her."

"Of course not, that would be too easy."

"Exactly my philosophy," Jason said. "So, do you want to hear an interesting theory?"

"Shoot." I walked properly into the room, finding a seat at one of the stools around the workbench.

"Rumor has it that Belinda was into love potions."

"Yeah."

"And last night, you suggested the vamp who turned her was whoever she took to that cabin with her."

"I'd definitely at least like to talk to the guy," I said.

"What do you suppose would happen if she gave a love potion to a vampire?"

I felt a chill run down my spine, even though this was something I had considered myself. "I don't think she'd do it on purpose."

"Me neither."

"Would a love potion work on a vampire?"

Jason stood, using the short length of the room to pace. "I've never seen it happen, but there's no reason to think it wouldn't work. What's a vampire, after all?"

I thought back to some of our family's least pleasant dinnertime conversations. "The dead, animated by a demonic presence. Their personalities are a combination of the host's and the demon's, but they are not human."

Jason nodded.

"Doesn't love destroy evil or something?" I asked.

He laughed. "You've been watching too many movies. Besides, Belinda's potions inspired false love–more akin to lust, adoration, admiration, and desire. Evil can feel all of those things, and so can vampires."

When I put it together with what we had discussed the night before, about a highly territorial sorcerer-vampire, I didn't like the resulting picture at all. "Sounds like the sort of thing that could lead to jealousy or rage."

"Exactly. I think the vampire might have desperately wanted to turn her into something like himself, to tie her to him forever."

"Why would he stake her, then?" I asked.

"I don't know that he did. Luke might have done it, in a fit of jealousy. It's hard to say. What I do think, with far more certainty, is she slipped a potion to the wrong man, and he turned her."

"I've been trying to figure out who she went to that cabin with since Tuesday, but I don't have any answers."

"Let's start with her current boyfriends," Jason said. "Any ideas who they are?"

I thought about the scrapbook with the missing pages, but shook off the image. It couldn't help me now.

"There's a hairdresser in town," I said, "and Dr. Shore, her gynecologist. The hairdresser isn't on the potion anymore; I know because I talked to him on Tuesday. Plus, he was able to touch my cross with no problem, so he's probably not a vampire."

"Who else?" Jason asked.

I hesitated, because I knew it was impossible, but I had to give him all the names I knew. "The sheriff."

His eyebrows shot up.

I shook my head. "No way. Don't you think I'd know if he was a vampire or a sorcerer, let alone both?"

"Whoever it is has been hiding in a community filled with practitioners for a long time. What do we all do best?"

"Secrets and lies," I said.

"Tell me about him."

I took a deep breath, and searched my mind for details. "I've known of him for ten years, ever since he moved to Eagle Rock and became sheriff."

"He's new to town?" Jason asked, and I didn't like his alert interest.

"Sort of. I mean, yeah. I've known him well for about a year, since I went to work for him. He's always trying to get me to go back."

"And today, he tried to arrest you."

"He was still under the influence of the love potion. It's been horrible, actually, because he's been acting crazy, and I haven't been able to confide in him about anything. In fact, when we were talking about who had killed Belinda, he kept talking about finding out who had staked her, rather than who had..." I trailed off, realizing what I had just implied. A vampire, especially one who had intentionally sired a mate, wouldn't take kindly to someone staking his intended bride.

I didn't want to accept it, especially since it would mean he had fooled me so completely, but I could no longer deny the possibility.

"I'll start checking things out tonight," Jason said. "The thing to do in the meantime is keep a low profile. If you can convince our guy that you think Luke was the answer, he might back off."

"Wouldn't that make him harder to spot?"

"I'll find him," Jason said, his voice sounding harsh for the first time. "I don't need to use you as bait."

"Oh." Put that way, it made sense, although I didn't relish the idea of ducking out of the investigation. It was still my responsibility, especially now that Jason suspected the sheriff.

23

Jason crashed around ten in the morning, and told me if I needed him, he'd be up in time for dinner. I wanted to go into town, but my parents weren't ready to let me out of the house, so I retreated to my fortress of solitude, where I decided to at least give more thought to the case, reexamining everything I knew in case I had missed something. No one would know, so it couldn't put me in any danger.

I had three suspects. I typed each of their names into my computer, then stared at them for a good fifteen minutes. A few hours ago, I would have dismissed all three of them because I had seen them in bright daylight. Now, that didn't seem certain. Nothing did.

I realized that Jason's revelation, or at least his intimation, had me deeply shaken. He seemed inclined to suspect the sheriff, an idea that twisted my insides in knots. I had worked closely with the sheriff for six months, and ever since then, he had continued to keep in contact with me, asking me to return to work for him.

What did I know about him, though? He had moved to Eagle Rock ten years ago, to take the position of sheriff when nobody else wanted it. He had no family nearby, but did being an outsider make him a good suspect?

I wrestled with circular thoughts for nearly an hour before they drove me crazy, and I had to escape. When I went downstairs, I discovered that everyone was either in their own bedroom or else in the library, so I tried to tiptoe out the front door without anyone noticing. The second I reached for the handle, though, a loud, disembodied voice shouted, "Don't even think about it."

I retracted my arm and sighed, throwing myself on the couch and staring at the black television.

After a while, I sifted through my purse for my cell phone, thinking I would make a few phone calls. As my hand closed around the phone, it brushed against one of the bottles of holy water I had been keeping in there. Changing course, I pulled it out of my purse and looked at it, my speculation of the night before flooding back into my mind. What might a vampire hunter do to make their blood poisonous to vampires? Jason had drunk something out of a flask that morning, something he also used in the potions. And he hadn't realized I was there.

The holy water looked just like plain water, but of course, it was the magic of faith that made it work. Would that same magic protect me or strike me down if I dared to drink it?

Nervously, I unscrewed the cap and brought it to my lips, then lowered it again. I repeated the process several times before I finally let the liquid spill into my mouth, swallowing quickly.

I'm not sure what I expected it to taste like, but holy water tastes precisely like regular water–if a bit stale. Perhaps I had been expecting an oilier texture. After I imbibed the liquid, I sat there for a few long minutes, waiting for lightening to strike, but it didn't. Perhaps it would come when I least expected it.

More to distract myself than anything else, I dove back through my purse for the cell phone and dialed Kaitlin's number. She picked up on the second ring, but sounded busy. I could hear dishes clattering in the background. "Cassie, I'd love to talk but the crazies are out in force and I've been swamped all morning. "

Strange, I thought, that she hadn't mentioned anything about me being wanted for murder. Surely word had spread, hadn't it? The Main Street Cafe was like grand central station for gossip. "I just thought I'd tell you I won't be there for lunch today."

"It's probably just as well," Kaitlin said. "There's this group of goth kids here hoping to find a vampire who will turn them."

"That's disgusting."

"I know. Say, Angie stopped by for breakfast and seemed pretty pissed at you, but she wouldn't say why...something about her boyfriend, but the police told her not to talk."

"Oh, that's nothing," I lied. I just put an arrow through her boyfriend's heart and was now wanted for his murder, even though he was a vicious blood-sucking monster who had put Angie under his spell. But it didn't matter, because apparently sometime in the next few hours, nobody would remember any of it. Or maybe no one did now.

"Okay," Kaitlin said. "But you'll tell me later, right?"

Maybe. If a powerful sorcerer-vampire didn't kill me first. "Right. I'll call you."

When I hung up, my gaze resettled on the black TV screen. I really wanted to talk to Angie, but I had no idea what to say to her to make her understand. She had never accepted magic, and our friendship had only ever worked so long as I hadn't pushed that button much. Maybe when whoever it was my parents had called for a favor worked their magic, she would forget about this, and we could go back to being friends again. Angie could go back to being blind and ignorant, and I could go back to letting her.

Before I was even aware of it, I had dialed her number. After five rings, it went to voice mail and I left a message. "Hi, Angie, it's Cassie. I hope you're not mad at me. Give me a call so we can talk." I intentionally kept my voice light and upbeat, and my message vague.

This time, when I hung up, I knew I needed to talk to the sheriff. It wasn't because Jason suspected him, and I wouldn't say anything to make him suspicious, but now that he was off the love potion, he would probably be suspicious if I didn't call him. Besides, I still couldn't quite bring myself to believe it was him.

My fingers found his phone number, almost before my brain caught up with them.

"Sheriff Adams," he said. At least his voice sounded calm and measured.

"It's Cassie." I held my breath.

"Yeah?"

Just then, the house phone rang. It echoed through the house twice before going silent.

"I wanted to apologize for this morning," I said.

"Strange thing about that," Sheriff Adams said, "is no one around here even seems to remember why I went out there in the first place."

"Do you?" I asked.

"When you've had my job long enough, you start to take notes and hide them in places no one else knows about."

That revelation took me by surprise and generated a million questions. When had his memory been manipulated in the past? How had he discovered this had happened? What made him decide to write down those notes today, and what made him check them later on?

Or was he somehow immune to mind magic?

Jason's warning came back to me then. Maybe I shouldn't have called.

"Um, look, I wanted to go with you, but-"

"But your family wouldn't let you," Sheriff Adams said. "I know it, and I'd even have been willing to forgive you if you hadn't cut me out of the kill. It's not like I didn't know Luke was a vampire."

"I didn't realize you wanted in," I said.

"How could you not? Until this morning, I thought I was in love with Belinda. I suppose you knew that, too?"

"Yeah," I said, relieved that he no longer felt compelled by her. "How did you figure it out?"

"I'm not sure. I just seemed to snap out of it, all of a sudden."

"So wait, if you knew Luke was the vampire who turned Belinda, then why did you come out to arrest me?" I intentionally let him think I believed the case was closed, just as Jason had warned me to do.

"I don't know," Sheriff Adams said. "I assume someone forced my hand, but I didn't write down who that was. It might have been Luke's parents."

"What do they think now?" I asked.

"The official record of Luke's death is accident. I assume they believe that."

We exchanged a few more words, but I had learned everything I needed, and the sheriff was busy, as always. A few minutes later, I hung up, closed my eyes, and took a few deep breaths to center myself. When I opened my eyes again, Elena stood there, staring at me expectantly. She looked oddly present in the real world.

"What?" I asked her.

"Mom and Dad want to talk to you."

"All right." I started to stand up, but Elena shook her head.

"Nana says they're being stupid. She told me to tell them that."

"Um-did you?"

Elena nodded. "But they told me I was only nine and didn't know what I was talking about. So I told them Nana's like a hundred,"

"Sixty-five," I corrected. "She was sixty-five when she died."

Elena just gave me a blank look. Maybe sixty-five and a hundred just aren't that different to a nine-year-old.

"Sorry," I said. "Did she say what they were being stupid about?"

Elena shrugged, vaguely, which was annoyingly in character.

"All right, then, I'll see you in a bit. I'm staying home for lunch today."

Elena shook her head. "Nana says you're not."

"Right." Sometimes, it's better not to ask.

24

My parents waited for me in the library, which had been cleared of the other children. The large table in the center of the seating group was overflowing with books, star charts, and pages of half-finished homemade incantations. Mom sat with her back to me, writing furiously. After a moment, she scratched out whatever she had been working on, and started again.

"Hello, Cassandra," Dad said, with a stiff formality I was unaccustomed to. He sat by the fire, causing the flames to leap and dance in interesting patterns. He did that for amusement sometimes. Or because he was anxious. I suspected the latter.

"What's up?" I asked.

"You don't have to worry about the murder charge," Dad said. "The Blairs say this more than makes up for the favor they owed me, but at least it's taken care of."

I had gathered as much from my conversation with Sheriff Adams. "That's great. I guess I can leave the house now?"

Dad looked significantly at Mom, who hadn't said a word yet. She looked on the verge of tears, and I suddenly got that odd prickly feeling you get right before someone tells you someone died.

"What's going on?" I asked.

"Sit down," Dad said.

I chose a chair a little away from both of them, and stared at the mass of star charts and calculations. I had never really learned how to do any of that, so I had no clue what they were working on.

"Apparently, Nana says you're being stupid," I said.

Mom bit her lip. "Cassandra, you know we love you, right?"

There wasn't anything good that was going to follow those words, but I nodded, mutely.

"We'll always do anything for you, no matter what," Mom continued.

"But?" I said. Whatever this was, I didn't want to draw out the anticipation.

"Well," Mom said, "the thing is that we feel it's time you found a life for yourself, away from sorcery. We've watched you torturing yourself for years, but you're a naturally independent woman, and you've proven you can take care of yourself.

"And we're very proud of you," Dad added. "Even the way you handled the vampire."

"Yes, yes, exactly," Mom said. "We just think it might be best if you moved out on your own. You know, there's no better way to really learn to take care of yourself."

I tilted my head to the side a bit. This conversation wasn't adding up. I had already told them that I was thinking of moving to Chicago with Braden at the end of the summer. If they wanted me to leave in the next few months no matter what, then they could have found a less ominous way to say so.

I wondered if this had anything to do with the new baby. Technically, they could turn the guest bedroom into a room for the baby, but they might not want to give up the guest room, in which case, they would need my room.

"Well, I said I might go to Chicago with Braden. I guess if I decide not to, I could find my own place around here."

I searched their faces for a reaction, but they continued to look rather grim.

"Look, you're probably right," I said. "Maybe I should have moved out last year, after I left junior college and started at the sheriff's department. I guess I just didn't want to give up your cooking."

I smiled, but Mom didn't smile back.

"So, it's settled," I said. "I'll either move out with Braden, or I'll find my own place. Either way, I'll be out by August."

"Tonight," Dad said.

"Tonight what?" I asked.

"You have to move out by tonight," Dad said.

"We've run the calculations a dozen times," Mom cut in. "It has to be tonight."

I closed my eyes, but resisted the urge to pinch myself. When I opened them again, I was still in the library, my parents still looked as if someone had just died, and the bazillions of star charts still spelled disaster.

"Um, you're kicking me out?" I said. "Just like that? You couldn't have given me like two minutes notice?"

"Well, you see, we weren't sure-" Mom licked her lips. "It's just that we didn't think-"

"This has something to do with a spell you're doing tonight, doesn't it?"I asked. "What is the spell for?"

"It's a disownment spell," Dad said.

The words hung there for a long time. I'm not sure if Mom and Dad were each hoping the other would speak, or if they thought I should. I'm pretty sure my mouth wouldn't have worked just then, so if they were waiting for me, they were in for a long, uncomfortable silence.

Twenty-one years of self doubt crashed down around me. How was I supposed to feel, I wondered? Angry? Scared? Sad? Hurt? Confused topped my list.

I remembered the conversations I had heard through the vent, the uncertainty about whether or not I counted as one of their seven children. I had supposed, when they got pregnant again, that they had decided I didn't count, but obviously, they still weren't sure, and they wanted to make sure.

"We've been staying up all night since I found out I was pregnant," Mom said. "We're making calculations, reading tarot cards, trying to scry into the future..."

"We consulted a seer," Dad added. "She told us the family would face unprecedented danger in the next year."

"We thought we'd have until the baby was born to decide," Mom said, "but earlier this week, we found out the only time in the next year the planets line up right for this spell is tonight. So we had to decide quickly."

"Decide to disown me?" I said. Or maybe I just mouthed it. I'm still not sure my voice was working right.

"Since this baby would make seven magical children," Mom said, "it's possible there's no need, but we're just not sure enough."

"And we are sure you'll do great," Dad said. "You're strong, smart, and independent."

"And it's just in name," Mom said. "You'll have to move out, of course, but we'll help you get started, and of course, we'll always protect you."

"And I talked to my brother, too," Dad said. "He'll help protect you as well. He even said you could stay with his family for a while."

Dad sifted through the pile of calculations on the table until he found an envelope. He tried to give it to me, but my hands remained firmly planted in my lap, so he set it down on the table in front of me. "There's always more, if you need it."

The envelope was partially open, and I could see a thick pile of hundred dollar bills inside. I did not take it.

"They just built those new apartments on the edge of town," Mom said. "We talked to the landlord this morning, and he said you could get in right away. You just need to go over there and fill out the paperwork this afternoon. Or you could stay with your Uncle John for a while, like your dad said."

This was crazy. They were kicking me out, *disowning* me, and trying to hook me up with a nice new place?

"Cassandra," Mom said.

"My name," I told her, "is Cassie."

I'm not sure why saying that became so important to me at that moment, but I felt I had to reclaim some dignity. It might have been the only thing I had left.

Somehow, my legs found purchase, and I stood. For a minute or two, I just studied the flames licking the walls of the fireplace, then I scanned the room, memorizing it. There was the scroll work in the mantle piece, the scratches in the wooden bookshelves lining the room, and the gleam of the golden floor lamps.

In the middle of the room, there were the nine high-backed armchairs set in a square around the low table where star charts tried to forecast my destiny. Nine chairs. Three by three. Seven children. No, I no longer had any part in that formula.

I bent low over the table, but I didn't take the envelope of money. Instead, I grabbed a fine tip pen, pulled off the cap, and turned to bury it in the upholstery of the chair I had just vacated. It sank satisfyingly deep into the cushiony back of the chair. I yanked downward, spilling its guts.

It didn't make me feel any better, so I grabbed one of the books on the table and threw it into the fire.

"Cassandra!" Mom said. "Are you throwing a temper tantrum?"

"Why not?" I shouted the words, my voice hoarse and almost painful. "I'm apparently not too old to need your assurance that the baby isn't going to replace me. Remember? We covered that when I was two and you were pregnant with Nicolas."

With one last flourish, I picked up the envelope of money, took out the wad of bills, and ripped them in half. I flung the tattered halves at my parents before racing from the room, so they wouldn't see my tears.

25

I fled from my home—no, my parents' home, for it no longer had anything to do with me. All I took with me were my purse and the clothes on my back. I left behind me books, clothes, electronics, and a lifetime of memories.

For some reason, I was finding it difficult to breathe. When I reached the large circular driveway, I stood in indecision, gasping and nearly choking on a huge lump in my throat. I couldn't find my car. Or was it mine? It suddenly occurred to me that I had nothing but what my parents had bought for me over the years. They had seemed willing enough to give me whatever I liked on the way out the door, but what did they think they were doing? Trying to buy my forgiveness? My acceptance?

There was Nicolas's car, parked behind an old Ford Taurus. Where was my Jaguar? Oh yes, I remembered. It had landed at the bottom of a ditch, smack against a tree, and was now being totaled.

"Cassie?" I heard Nicolas coming out of the house, and approaching from behind.

I froze, every muscle in my body tense. Did he know? Had my parents told everyone, or were they planning a disownment celebration tonight after dinner?

"What's wrong?" he asked.

So he didn't know. Well, I wouldn't be the one to tell him. "Leave me alone," I managed to say. The words came out like a gasp. Then I flew to the ugly green Taurus and threw myself inside.

I couldn't see. Tears blurred my vision as I tried five times to shove the key in the ignition. Finally, I found the right angle and turned the engine.

"Cassie," Nicolas said, coming up beside the driver's side door. "Wait! What's going on?"

I shook my head. I didn't think I could speak, and even if I could, Nicolas was not the person I wanted to speak to. He was the eldest child now, the powerful one. Eighteen years of sibling rivalry and yes, jealousy, came bubbling into my throat and I tasted bile.

I pressed my foot to the gas pedal and tore away from him, not looking back, but barely able to look ahead. It was a good thing I knew the driveway and the forested roads beyond so well, for my vision nearly failed me. All I could make out, beyond the haze of tears, was a blur of green and gray.

A few hundred yards down the road, I pulled over before I missed a turn or an oncoming car. I leaned my head against the steering wheel and took a few deep breaths, trying to still my racing heart. It didn't help. I kept reliving the moment my parents had decided I wasn't good enough to be their daughter anymore.

My cell phone sounded Nicolas's ring tone. I ignored it, wondering all the while who I could talk to. Kaitlin would be too busy, even if she could understand. Evan's face popped instantly into my mind, but I had no way to get in touch with him. He would understand, as much as anyone could, but it seemed strange that I thought of him before thinking of Braden.

Braden. I dialed his number, wondering if he would speak to me after my indecisive response to his marriage proposal. He had tried to understand my reluctance, but I could tell he hadn't really, and that I had hurt him.

He didn't answer, and I didn't leave a message. I knew I needed to get a grip, so I fished inside my purse for a package of tissues. There wasn't one. Of all the days not to have a package of tissues! Though I suspect I would have gone through a small pack in about thirty seconds, and still had problems. This wasn't even my car, so there wasn't the usual towel and blanket I kept in the trunk.

Great. I wiped my eyes with the backs of my hands, and dried them on the cloth of the passenger seat, then I shifted the car into gear and headed for town. There weren't many places that Braden could be, and since it was lunchtime, I had a pretty good idea he would be at Kaitlin's diner. Still, I called the law offices of Lloyd and Lyons to rule out that possibility, even managing not to sob into the receiver when a paralegal answered, and reported that Braden had, indeed, gone to lunch.

Kaitlin's Diner was full to overflowing when I arrived. I managed to find a parking space, most likely thanks to the number of patrons who would have walked from downtown businesses. That's what I would normally have done.

I passed by a long row of windows on my way to the front door, but I drew up short before I got there. There was Braden, sitting in a booth by the window, deep in conversation with a blonde woman I recognized as his girlfriend, Charlotte. Supposedly, his ex-girlfriend, but you wouldn't know it from their posture, and the way they looked at one another. Had he called her seconds after leaving me on Tuesday night?

He didn't see me immediately, but I must have stood there in frozen disbelief for a full minute, maybe two. Sooner or later, he would have to glance my way and see me. He waved, as if there were nothing wrong with meeting his ex-girlfriend for lunch two days after proposing to me.

I turned my back on him and took a look around the busy street, trying to decide what to do. My heart beat a little faster when I spotted a blue Prius parked a block or so away. I scanned the street until I saw Evan, heading from the direction of Lloyd and Lyons. He had spotted me and waved, but I didn't wave back.

I'm not sure how much time passed, but before long, Braden was coming out the door, waving at me. "Charlotte's grandmother died. She was upset, so I took her to lunch to talk. It's not–we're not seeing one another again. She's just upset."

"I'm upset," I said.

Braden tilted his head to the side. "We can talk tonight, all right? I get off at five."

Tonight? It seemed like an eternity away. "You had time for her."

"Yeah, her grandmother died," Braden said, as if I were a slow child. "Look, I'm sorry it got you upset but-"

"That's why you think I'm upset?" I could feel another lump forming in my throat. A few feet away, I could see Evan, pausing just outside the door of the diner, trying to look like he wasn't listening.

"If it's not about her, then what is it?" Braden asked.

"My parents," I managed to say.

"Are they all right?"

"They kicked me out."

"Oh. Why don't we talk tonight after I get off work?" He glanced at his watch. The gesture, however small, was more than I could handle at that moment. I knew things were rocky between us, and I knew I wasn't being fair to him, but I needed someone more than I ever had before, and he had become emotionally unavailable.

I swept past him, not even glancing over my shoulder as I approached Evan, still standing just outside the door to the diner. He took a step backward at my approach, but I didn't stop. I sailed right up to him, pressed my body fully against his, lifted myself on tiptoes, and pressed my lips into his in what I meant to be a defiant kiss.

After that, the world turned upside down.

It's difficult to describe how I felt in that moment. There was a sort of explosion from somewhere deep inside of me, somewhere private and heretofore unknown. My heartbeat doubled in the space of a second. Warmth rushed to every part of my body and I trembled, unable to rein in the things I felt. Dampness spread between my legs and I began to throb with a need I hadn't realized was there.

I gasped. All thoughts of Braden, Charlotte, and especially my parents were gone from my mind. The only thing that remained was this aching need. I pushed myself closer, tasting him, drinking in his scent.

For a moment, all was right with the world, and then it wasn't. Evan was gone, leaving me there with the need and the echo of Braden's angry shout.

I stood on the curb and looked both ways, temporarily dumbfounded by his sudden disappearance. Then I heard a car door open, and I spotted his Prius a few yards away. Before I could move, the door slammed shut again, moved by some invisible force, and it roared to life. I ran after it, but it tore down the street before I reached the place it had been.

My brain wasn't working the way it normally did. It felt as if a cloud had settled in and obscured everything but the memory of that kiss. My hand flew to my lips, feeling the lingering warmth.

I couldn't just stand there, I had to find him, but my car wasn't there. It took me a minute to remember that the rental car parked just down the street would have to suffice.

Evan's car was long gone by the time I was ready to go after him, but it didn't matter, I knew where I needed to go to find him. With any luck, I could find the small, unremarkable dirt path that led to Henry Wolf's house without Evan to help. If Evan wasn't there, I would simply wait until he returned.

It should have been a twenty minute drive, but I made the trip in ten, somehow managing not to kill anyone as I sped through the winding forest roads. I passed the dirt path at first, but realized it a few yards later. Backing the car up, I made the turn down the unpaved road.

No one was home when I knocked on the door. I pounded on it until my knuckles bled, and then collapsed against it, allowing the odd numbness to completely fill my body and brain. I would wait. Sooner or later, he would come back. At least, for the moment, my brain was utterly distracted from my more serious problems.

Time passed quickly in my lust-filled haze. I didn't look at my watch. I didn't even think, except about Evan. In truth, there wasn't anything else I wanted to think about. Everything else hurt too much.

Some time later (I don't know how long), I began feeling uncomfortable. My pulse slowed, taking the throbbing with it. The ache subsided. My brain began trying to process what had happened. It didn't get far, but it tried.

When Evan sat down beside me on the porch, I barely flinched.

"Feeling better?" Evan asked.

"What the hell was that?" I managed.

For a long time, he didn't say anything, and I risked a look at his dark profile. His hair fell in casual waves to his shoulders. It was longer than mine since I had cut my hair, but on him it somehow emphasized his masculinity. He had started wearing it that way in high school, right around the time I had first developed my crush.

My eyes settled on his lips, full and slightly parted, and a flush of embarrassment made me look away. I didn't need him to tell me what that was; he had already done that. Madison had also tried to tell me, but I had dismissed her as casually as all the silly girls who thought he hypnotized them with his eyes. Madison may have been shy, and she may have been afraid of Evan, but she wasn't stupid. In fact, she had the sort of intelligence that caused some people to keep their distance.

"Master Wolf calls it the kiss of death," Evan said after a small eternity had passed.

"I'm not dead," I said without thinking.

"It's not literal."

My already red cheeks grew redder. What had I been thinking to throw myself at Evan like that? Well, I knew what I had been thinking. My parents had hurt me so deeply I couldn't think straight, and irrationally, I had sought comfort from him. I couldn't even pretend it had anything to do with Braden, because despite his marriage proposal, he hadn't been the first person I had thought of.

No, I had almost been glad of the excuse to fling myself at Evan, relying on our history of friendship to soften the blow should he reject my advance. Mindless grief had lowered my inhibitions, giving me leave to do precisely what I had wanted to do since Monday afternoon, when he had strolled back into my life.

On some level, I had known that getting involved with Evan would be playing with fire, even if I didn't know the specifics. Maybe that's why I had maintained a careful distance in high school, despite my attraction–or because of it. Maybe that's why I had ended up dating Braden, a man with a lot of the same attributes–a desire to help people, and a certain lust for power–but who I could ultimately handle.

I could never handle Evan. If I hadn't understood that before, that kiss had made sure my eyes were wide open now.

"It's a gift," Evan said, interrupting my thoughts, "but not one I have much control over."

"I don't know anyone else who has two gifts." I knew it was theoretically possible, but very rare.

"Dual gifts run in my family, actually." Evan's face drew blank, telling me that's all he would say on the matter.

"Does *this* gift run in your family?" I asked.

"Not that I know of." Evan ran his fingers through his hair in a characteristically anxious gesture. "I'm sorry."

My brain couldn't immediately process his apology, not when I had spent the past few minutes blaming myself, but gradually, I began to see his role in all of this.

"So that happens every time you kiss a girl?" I asked.

"Sort of. You kind of caught me off guard today and got a full dose. I can tone it down. Plus, not everyone reacts exactly the same way..." He seemed at a loss to finish his explanation, and we again lapsed into silence.

"Wait a minute," I said, thinking back, "I kissed you once before. When we were eight."

"I remember," Evan said. "I think it started when I hit puberty."

"You lied to me." In fact, he had lied more than once. He had lied when I asked him, point-blank, if he was putting love spells on the girls, and he had lied to me the other day, by telling me the truth in a way he knew I wouldn't believe.

"I'm sorry, although technically, I did tell you the other day."

Something inside me snapped. I stood, and whirled to challenge him head on. "That was as much a lie as the time I asked you straight up if you were putting love spells on girls. You knew I wouldn't believe you. What did you think you were doing? Keeping your secret safe in such a way that you could throw it back in my face later on, if I ever found out for sure?"

He stood, using his height and presence to full advantage, in a pose meant to intimidate. Around us, the wind stirred, and I had the eerie sense that it wasn't natural. It occurred to me that Evan probably wasn't used to direct challenges, at least, not anymore. He had done a good job making people fear him, or at least be in awe of him.

"Why should I have answered your questions?" Evan demanded. "You know perfectly well how much of magic is shrouded in secrecy. I never told any of the other girls who've kissed me, either before or after. I just let them think what they would, and spread enough wild rumors that the whole thing would get hopelessly confused."

The wind stirred more restlessly around us. Oh yes, I had played with fire, and if I got burned, I no longer had access to the wonders of magical healing. But despite his attempts to intimidate me through words and actions, I knew I had to stand my ground.

"So what, am I supposed to feel grateful?" I asked.

"You did kiss me."

"I kissed *you?*" It was true, but still all wrong. "You're half a foot taller than me. I couldn't even reach you if you didn't meet me halfway, and don't tell me you couldn't have held me off, because you did it pretty easily when I spilled the lust potion."

"You're making an awfully big deal out of this. A lot of girls actually like it."

"You really are full of yourself. You dated half the girls in our class, and you probably kissed them all. Even Madison, and she's scared to death of you."

He flinched when I said that, and I could see I had finally put a chink in his armor. "I admit, that was a bad idea."

"Just that one? Come on, Evan, what were you thinking? Did it make you feel powerful or something?"

Around us, the wind began to die, and Evan stared over my shoulder at something in the distance that only he could see. "Yes."

The blunt honesty sideswiped me, making me take a step back. "I see."

He ran his fingers through his hair again. "Sorry to ruin your perfect image of me."

"Trust me, I didn't have one." But his brutal honesty dulled my anger, and reminded me that I hadn't been innocent in this encounter, either. Besides, I wasn't there to judge him for all his past sins.

"I am sorry you found out that way. It's not what I wanted. I've made mistakes in the past, but I would have told you first, if things had gone differently."

A shiver ran down my spine as I recognized the significance of what he had said. It sounded as if he had made plans for me, and I had walked right into them. Only now, I didn't want any part of him or his plans.

"Why did you do it, anyway?" Evan asked, gentling his voice. "I know it wasn't that girl Braden was with. I heard you say something about your parents."

The kiss and the argument had been therapeutic, because I had managed to shove my more serious issues to the back of my mind, but now they came flooding back. I didn't know if I could talk to Evan about it anymore, not if I wanted to assure some distance between us, but I already felt the sting of tears threatening to fall once again.

"I gotta go." I spun on my heels before he could see my eyes glistening.

"Wait," Evan said when I was halfway to my car.

I picked up the pace. The sting had dulled, and I thought if I could get in my car and away, I could find someplace to cry in peace. Maybe my office. Which my parents had paid for.

"Stop," Evan said as I reached the car door. He started after me, but he didn't leave overtaking me to chance. My body froze in place, my hand just touching the handle. Seconds later, he was there, releasing the magical hold on my body at the same time he put his arms around me from behind, drawing me against his chest.

The human contact felt so good. I wanted to be angry with him for his show of force, or wary at the reminder that I had played with fire, but I couldn't. I needed someone strong to hold me while I broke down, and the moment he made contact, the tears began to spill forth, washing away the desire to leave.

"Sh, Cassie, it's okay." He stroked my hair. "Come back to the porch and tell me about it."

I let him lead me back to the porch, where we sat together on the swing, his arm around me, and his body pressed right up against mine. I turned my face into his chest and cried out all the pain, telling him, in broken syllables, what my parents had done.

"They disowned you?" Evan's voice was full of disbelief. "I know you said you felt like they were pushing you out, but I never imagined anything like this."

"Me neither."

"I've never even heard of a disownment spell." This he said almost to himself.

"I always knew they were disappointed in me." I sniffed and tried to wipe some of the tears from my face. "But I thought they loved me anyway."

"Who's protecting you?" Evan asked.

"Um-" I wasn't sure I understood the question. "I am an adult."

He narrowed his eyes. "I'm talking about magical protection."

"I don't know. They kept talking about always being there to protect me. Or my Uncle John. I don't want their protection, though, not if they don't want me as a daughter anymore."

Beside me, Evan tensed, but he didn't say anything. Part of me wondered what had him so on edge, but most of me just wanted to shut my brain off for a while.

"I just want to go to sleep and wake up in a year," I said.

I suddenly felt feather light. Evan had me in his arms, and he walked into the old cabin. Taking a right past some rustic hunting lodge décor, he opened a door to a bedroom, and laid me down on a soft, full sized bed.

"It's the middle of the afternoon," I mumbled, as he slipped off my shoes and pulled the covers over me. "I'm not tired."

"You need rest." Evan began lighting candles and muttering an incantation. "In the morning, we'll figure something out."

"What are you going to do?" I asked. "Knock me out with magic?"

"I prefer to call it an enchanted sleep," he said. "It's very relaxing. Close your eyes."

I wanted to argue with him, but no words occurred to me. When he finished muttering his incantation, he sat on the bed beside me and ran a hand through my hair again. He seemed to like doing that, but my sleep-fogged brain welcomed the touch, oblivious to all the reasons I needed to keep my distance. Just for one night, I could lean on him. Like a friend. We had been friends once. Surely, we could be again.

26

I WOKE THE NEXT MORNING TO THE SOUND OF BIRDS SINGING, THE SIGHT OF sunlight streaming in through an open window, and the feel of a heavy body spooned around mine, an arm draped possessively over my waist. I stiffened, wondering exactly what Evan thought was happening between us.

Pushing the arm aside, I scrambled out of bed, turning to see Evan, still asleep, fling his arm to the side and roll over onto his stomach. He had slept in his clothes, blue jeans and a now wrinkled blue t-shirt, but that didn't settle the unease I felt at waking with his body wrapped around mine.

He looked peaceful in sleep, even harmless, but I couldn't let illusion cloud my image of him again. He belonged to the same world as my parents, the one they had kicked me out of the day before.

My heart gave a pitiful little twang when I realized they must have cast the spell by now. Yes, they had well and truly cast me out, and I needed to take the hint by separating myself from magic. My mom had been right about one thing–I didn't belong in their world.

When I had opened my normal detective agency, I had made the distinction for the benefit of those who would want me to cast spells or investigate haunted houses. Under my parents' roof and their protection, I never intended to live a life completely separate from magic. I was Marilyn Munster, different but accepted, normal among the abnormal.

Maybe they had recognized something that I hadn't wanted to accept–that I just plain didn't belong. There were things I would never understand, and living in their world put me at risk, either by accident or design. My family had enemies, the Blackwoods chief among them.

I considered Braden's proposal again, more seriously this time, though I wondered how he would feel about it after I had flung myself at Evan the day before. Leaving town had been the last thing I'd wanted to do when he had asked. Leave behind my family? My friends? Now I wondered if I should find someplace to carve out a chunk of normal for myself.

Evan stirred, bringing me back to the present. I scanned the wooden floor of his bedroom, searching for my sandals, but I couldn't find them. Aside from the bed, he had an old-fashioned roll-top desk, the kind they used to make before the advent of computers, and a large cedar wardrobe. Not sure where else to look, I opened the door of the wardrobe. To my relief, I spotted my sandals on the floor, alongside several pairs of his shoes.

I took them out and closed the door, but there would be no quiet escape. Evan sat upright in bed, sleep-ruffled in a way that still left him looking good.

"Good morning," he said. "How do you feel?"

"Better, thanks. I guess that sleep spell was just what I needed." I paused, wondering if I had incurred a debt by allowing him to cast it. I probably had, although not a big one.

"Were you planning to sneak out?" Evan asked, nodding at the shoes clutched in my hand.

"Oh, um, no, I just didn't want to wake you. And, well, I have things to do. I've got to find a place to stay, and there's still a vampire out there, somewhere, and did I mention he might be able to go out in the sunlight?" I knew I was rambling, but I couldn't help it.

"Slow down. Why are you so jumpy?"

I looked at the bed, but couldn't bring myself to mention the intimate position I had found us in when I woke.

Evan seemed to take my meaning, anyway. "Was I supposed to sleep on the floor? We were both fully clothed and I stayed on my side."

"Hmm."

He frowned. "Didn't I?"

I shrugged. "It's okay." At least he hadn't meant to do it. That was something.

"And what's this about a vampire walking around in sunlight?" Evan asked.

"Oh, that's something I learned from my cousin, Jason. He apparently had our back the other night, when I shot Luke through the heart." Briefly, I summarized what Jason had told me about the vampire, and what we had conjectured, including the possibility that the vampire was on a love potion.

"A vampire that can walk in the daylight," Evan said, shaking his head. "This is too dangerous."

"Don't," I said.

"Don't what?"

"Don't tell me you want me off the case. It's all I have right now."

"I didn't hire you to put yourself in danger. You've already been attacked once."

"Do you really think I'll be safe as long as this thing is alive?" I asked. "Luke came after me, and I think whoever turned him sent him to kill me."

"Maybe he'll leave you alone if I fire you."

"Maybe, but it won't stop me from trying to find him. It's personal."

He didn't say anything for a long time, and then, finally, he stood and walked to his desk. In a top drawer, he withdrew a small, pink crystal, which he placed in my hand.

"What's this?" I asked.

"If you need me, hold this in the palm of your hand and think of me. It's not quite as useful as a cell phone, but it's all I have. I worked on it yesterday afternoon while you were sleeping."

I stared at it, knowing I couldn't use it, and wondering if he realized it as well. If I did call him for help, I might incur a debt, and I had nothing in the world to trade against a magical debt at the moment. "Jason's in town, you know. I didn't exactly plan to fight a vampire myself, just help Jason identify him."

"Good. Then use that when you figure it out, to let me know."

That, I could do. I shoved the crystal into my pocket. "One more thing. The sheriff came by to arrest me yesterday morning, and he still seemed to be under the influence of the love potion. Then, suddenly, he wasn't."

"I was hoping it would have faded on its own," Evan said. "I worked a spell to regrow his hair, so he wouldn't have to use whatever potion she gave him anymore. I thought it would be easier than breaking into his house and finding it."

"Then why did it suddenly stop?"

"What happened right before it did?"

I thought back. "He tripped a ward, and his car exploded."

Evan nodded, as if that explained everything. "A good, sharp shock can sometimes work wonders."

"Look, I should go. I've intruded long enough, and I need to figure out what to do." I set my sandals on the floor and slid my feet into them.

"Please, don't go yet."

The please got to me, and I paused long enough to search his face for some hint of his intentions, my cheeks heating up slightly when I focused on his lips. I wanted to put some distance between us, but the day before he had been a friend when I desperately needed one, and I couldn't turn my back on that.

"Why?" I asked.

"There are some things I'd like to tell you before you go. Yesterday, you were upset and angry, and I probably made things worse."

"No." Well, sort of. There had been anger and misunderstandings, but none of it seemed important now. "I needed a friend, and you stepped up."

"I could use one today."

He had the look of someone who wanted to unburden himself, and unfortunately, that kind of look never fails to get a response out of me. He knew it, too. Ignoring the warning bells ringing through my head, I sat down on the only horizontal surface that wasn't a floor—the bed. I perched on the edge, putting distance between Evan and myself, but he moved to sit beside me, feet planted on the ground, bare inches between us. I could feel the heat of his body, and I glanced nervously at his lips.

I wanted to kiss him again, I realized with a jolt. What was wrong with me? Even knowing what would happen, knowing I would completely lose control, I wanted another taste. It must be like a drug, creating some kind of dependency. Either that, or the effects hadn't quite worn off.

"We used to talk all the time," Evan said. "Back when I let people push me around. Then, one day, you asked me if I was casting love spells and I couldn't stand to tell you the truth because I hadn't admitted it to myself. I'd kissed two girls by then—well, post-adolescence—and I couldn't figure out why they acted so strangely."

I bit my lip, remembering how I had accused him of lying, and regretting it now. I guess he had lied to some degree, but it hadn't occurred to me that he might also have been scared and confused.

"It took me another half a year to work up the nerve to ask my father about it," Evan said.

"Right around the time you started talking to me again."

He gave me a rueful smile. "Yeah. Of course, things were never quite the same after that, and I never told you. But I wanted you to understand what happened."

"I blamed myself." Maybe that's why I had been so reluctant to believe the rumors, even when someone as reliable as Madison confirmed them.

"Sorry." He frowned and tossed me a sideways glance. "I seem to be saying that a lot lately."

I smiled and tried to make light of the situation. "You better watch it, or people won't be properly afraid of you anymore."

"You never were." He lay his hand on top of mine, linking our hands in a simple touch that nevertheless awakened my senses.

I pulled my hand away from his. It still tingled where he had touched me. Yes, I was definitely still under the influence of that kiss, and I needed to get away before I did something I would regret.

"Anyway," Evan said, "When Master Wolf found out about it, he told me no girls while I was apprenticed to him."

"Oh." I put another couple of inches between us. "So does he know I'm here?"

"No. Last night was the new moon. He was out doing a spell all night."

The thought that I might have gotten Evan in trouble because of my actions made me realize that I hadn't apologized for my role in all this, and I cleared my throat to do so. "Evan, I'm sorry I threw myself at you yesterday. I hope I don't get you in any trouble."

He reached out and took my hand again, pulling it and me closer to him. "I hope I don't get in trouble, too, but if I do, it'll be worth it."

A shiver ran down my spine, but whether of dread or anticipation, I had no idea. I couldn't deny the attraction between us, but my reservations remained intact, especially since I suspected the attraction, at least in intensity, was the lingering result of the kiss. I also realized that he hadn't really explained how it worked.

"So, um, what, exactly, does that gift of yours do?" I asked.

"It depends upon the intensity, and the girl." He looked away as he spoke. "It's mostly intensely arousing, and I think it kind of makes it hard to think. A full dose has been known to induce an instant climax."

I nodded, grateful he had been completely honest, even if the facts made me feel awkward. "How long do the affects of the kiss last?"

"It depends. If I tone it down, only a few minutes. Never more than an hour."

I choked on a laugh. "There's no way it only lasts an hour."

That was a mistake. I had to stop talking without thinking, especially around Evan, who was not at all slow on the uptake. He turned my face to look at him, and his eyes sparkled with amusement.

"It really does," he said. "I'm told it's addictive, though."

With that, he leaned down and captured my mouth in a kiss that drove me, quite literally, senseless. It didn't take me straight over the edge, the way it had the day before, but drove me crazy with wanting, with needing. Reason walked out the door, leaving behind raw pleasure that went on and on.

Unlike the day before, he didn't leave me aching and empty. He stayed to kiss and touch, torturing me with teasing caresses. He had one hand on my back, the other on my leg, moving slowly up to the hem of my shorts.

At one point, I cried out. I wanted to touch every part of him I could reach–his back, his chest, his shoulders–but when my hand strayed lower, he captured it and drew it upward.

"Please," I whispered.

"We need to stop."

At that moment, I couldn't imagine why we would want to do such a thing, but he took control, drawing me against his chest while he stroked my back in gentle, soothing circles.

Suddenly, his bedroom door banged open, and Evan drew away from me as if I were on fire, jumping clear of the bed to stand by our intruder. Earlier, I must have cried out a little too loudly, because Henry Wolf stood framed in the doorway, not looking a day over sixty, though no one was fooled. I didn't know how old he was, but something in his eyes said he'd seen things no one else had.

"What the hell do you think you're doing?" Mr. Wolf asked.

Evan, who stood at least six feet two inches and towered over his smaller master, had the look of the boy I remembered from grade school. "Well, you see, Cassie's in some trouble and she came to me for help–"

"Cassie?" Mr Wolf interrupted. His eyes found me for the first time. "Cassandra Scot? Isn't there enough bad blood between your families?"

"Yes, but the thing is, she needed some help–"

"And you thought she needed seducing?"

If any lingering affects of the kiss remained, they disappeared at that point. I sat up straight, red-faced, as the truth of his words sunk in. Of course, I wasn't blameless, but Evan had lured me in with his casual touches and his air of vulnerability. I believed it was genuine, but perhaps, well played.

"I'm sorry," Evan said.

"Don't apologize to me," Mr. Wolf said. "You do your apologizing to her parents."

"No," I said, uncertainty disappearing. "Mr. Wolf, this was my fault. And I don't have any parents."

"What the hell are you talking about?," Mr. Wolf asked. "I've known your family for fifty years."

"Yes, and last night, they cast a spell to disown me."

The room went silent as Mr. Wolf let the news sink in. "Heh. I don't know what the hell they think they're doing, but you can't break a bond of love. And your parents love you."

I wanted to argue, but you just don't argue with someone like Henry Wolf. "Maybe, but they still disowned me, so there's no point–"

"I'll decide if there's a point," Mr. Wolf said. "Evan, you make sure Cassie is settled somewhere safely, then you go talk to her parents like I said."

"Yes, sir," Evan said.

Henry Wolf shook his head and started muttering. "Damn young fools. I tell them to talk to me before they do something stupid and they don't listen, so now I'm going to have to clean up their mess." He left the room, but he continued to mutter to himself all the way to his own room.

"What was that about?" I asked.

Evan shrugged. "Come on, let's drive into town. Is there anyplace you can go?"

"Kaitlin's Diner," I said. "I'm sure Kaitlin will let me stay with her."

27

Leaving Evan's house felt like coming out of a fog bank. I could no longer pretend like my problems did not exist, although it seemed more possible to manage them now that I'd had some time to get over the initial shock and turmoil.

There were fifty-two messages on my phone when I left Evan's place, most of them from Jason, Nicolas, and Juliana. Even Isaac had left me three messages, and I hadn't even been sure he knew my number. I didn't listen to any of them.

The first thing to do, my rested, somewhat more rational mind decided, was find a place to stay. I could worry about vampires, my siblings, and finding a source of income better once I knew I had a threshold to return to that night. So I steered my car over to Kaitlin's Diner, where I hoped to get a private word with Kaitlin.

My timing was good. At ten o'clock in the morning there were only four customers in the diner, one of whom was about three month old and, apparently, not happy about it. Aside from the baby and his parents, the only other customer was a tall man in a business suit, sipping a cup of coffee at the bar.

There was no sign of Kaitlin, so I strode up to the bar, where Mrs. Meyer was pouring coffee for the lone man seated there, flashing him a flirtatious smile highly reminiscent of Kaitlin's.

"Is Kaitlin here?" I asked.

"Hi Cassie," Mrs. Meyer said, tucking a strand of dyed blond hair behind her ear. Dark roots were showing at the top. She didn't look much like Kaitlin, who seemed to favor her absent father in looks, but Kaitlin had learned how to smile and flirt from her mother. "Good timing. I just sent Kaitlin on break. She's just getting breakfast."

At the mention of breakfast, my stomach gave me a sharp reminder that I hadn't eaten in a while. I grabbed a menu and ran a finger down the options. I was trying to decide between French toast and pancakes when I noticed something that I had never paid much attention to before–the prices. Setting the menu down, I opened my purse, took out my wallet, and checked the contents.

I had never owned a credit card and, as far as I knew, neither had my parents. They had very superstitious ideas about getting into any sort of debt, even when backed by legal contracts and repayment agreements. They had at least half a dozen books on the topic of magical debt, which they tried to get me to read, but I never did. I asked Nicolas for a brief summary, which was enough to get me through several dinnertime quizzes, but not enough for me to really feel as if I understood my parents' reluctance to so much as own a credit card.

I did have a debit card, which tied me into an empty bank account. I had managed to save some money while working at the sheriff's department, but I had blown through all of it and more during my attempt to start a business.

Earlier in the week, I'd had a couple hundred dollars in cash, but half of it had been destroyed, and I had blown through the rest replacing the contents of my purse. All that remained was five dollars and some change.

Sighing, I placed the wallet back in my purse, and set the menu in its holder.

"Can I get you something?" Mrs. Meyer asked.

"I'm not hungry," I lied. Not wanting to meet her eyes, I glanced at the patron seated three stools down. With a jolt of recognition, I saw that it was Frank Lloyd, and that he was studying me.

"Good morning," he said.

"Morning." I searched for something clever to add, but came up with nothing. Earlier in the week, when life had seemed so simple, he had hired me to do a job that should have been easy. I had never finished the job, and now life was far more complicated.

"Don't worry about Belinda," Frank said. "That was hardly your fault."

"Thanks," I managed, weakly.

"If you're available, I may have some more work for you," he continued.

I smiled. "Thanks. I'm working with Evan a bit this week, but I should still be able to take on more work." I emphasized the work I now had, hoping that I sounded valuable and sought after, rather than too busy.

Frank gave me a curt nod. Then he tossed a bill onto the counter and left the diner.

Just then, Kaitlin came out of the kitchen, balancing a glass of orange juice and a plate of pancakes. When she saw me, she flashed me a brilliant smile, and nodded me over to a booth in the corner.

"Sit, sit," Kaitlin said. "I've been trying to call you since yesterday. What's going on? Say, are you hungry? Can I have my mom get you something?" She said all this in a rush and it was hard to know what to answer first.

"I'm not hungry," I said. My stomach growled loudly in protest, and Kaitlin arched an eyebrow at me.

"What's going on?" Kaitlin gave me a thorough appraisal, starting with my newly shortened hair, and working her way down to my dusty sandals. "You look like you slept in your clothes, and I've never seen your hair quite so frightening before."

Self consciously, I tried to smooth down the hair I hadn't even had a chance to run a brush through. "It's been a rough week."

Kaitlin didn't answer. She just looked at me, expectantly.

"First, there was a vampire," I said. I started rattling off the details of my story with a more practiced fluidity to it, since I had already told Evan all about it the day before. I left out a couple of magical details when recounting it to Kaitlin, especially omitting the part about the anti-venom potion and the sorcerer-vampire, but she didn't seem to notice. When I told her about my parents abandoning me, she stopped eating and stared at me in wide-eyed horror.

"Oh God, Cassie! Why didn't you come to me yesterday? Do you even have a place to stay? Or money?"

"Things got confusing yesterday." I decided not to get into the part with Braden and Evan, since I still hadn't sorted it out in my mind. "My parents tried to give me some money, but I was too angry to take it."

"Could you take it today?" Kaitlin asked.

I opened my mouth to answer, then closed it and shook my head.

"Figures. You don't know how much money is even worth. How much do you have?"

"Five dollars," I said.

Kaitlin turned around and called over her shoulder in a loud, carrying voice, "Hey Mom!"

Mrs. Meyer walked over to the table. "What do you need?"

"Cassie needs breakfast," Kaitlin said.

"Oh no, it's fine-" I started to say.

Mrs. Meyer shot me an odd look. "Absolutely. How do you like your eggs?"

I started to refuse again, but Kaitlin cut me off. "Over easy."

Mrs. Meyer nodded and walked away, her hips swaying slightly as she disappeared into the kitchen.

"And you're staying with me," Kaitlin said. "I haven't had a roommate since my last one slept with my boyfriend. I assume you won't do that?"

"Thanks, Kaitlin."

"You'd do the same for me."

"Yes."

There was an awkward silence for a minute or two before Kaitlin asked. "So where did you stay last night?"

"Um..." I began, not sure how to tell her that part of the story.

"Not with Braden?" Kaitlin's eyes widened. "Oh, Cassie, I forgot to ask how your date went. He was in here yesterday with some girl who was in tears half the time. He seemed kind of annoyed with her, to tell you the truth."

"He-he did?" I said, feeling confused. I hadn't really given a lot of thought to Braden yesterday, but a wave of guilt washed over me as I considered how it must have looked to him, me kissing Evan and then tearing off after him like a madwoman.

"Yeah," Kaitlin said. "I wanted to ask him how things went with you but with her there...So, what happened?"

"Well, he asked me to go to Chicago with him in the fall," I said.

"He asked you to marry him?" Kaitlin's face brightened. "I knew it. So what did you tell him?"

I hated to disappoint her, but there was no getting around it. "I said maybe."

"What? Are you crazy? He's perfect for you."

I didn't think he was. In fact, I hadn't given his proposal much thought, which told me a lot. Granted, I had been busy, but if he was what I really wanted in life, wouldn't my heart have said something by then?

"And then," I said, "yesterday, when I came to talk to him about what happened, he was in here with Charlotte."

"Oh, no," Kaitlin said. "Did you break up?"

"I don't know. We never really said."

Mrs. Meyer approached with a plate of pancakes, eggs, and a glass of orange juice. She set them down in front of me with a small smile and walked away.

I ate in silence for a minute, trying to organize my jumbled thoughts and emotions.

"So, Cassie, who were you with last night?"

I nearly choked on my orange juice.

Kaitlin observed me with bemused interest while I coughed. When I finished, she repeated, mercilessly. "Who was it?"

I remembered the way she had been flirting with Evan the other day, and tried to work out how she would react to the news that I had slept with Evan the night before. Not that we had *slept* together, although it had been disconcerting to wake up in his arms, even fully clothed. The truth was, it hadn't been entirely innocent, either. There had been the kiss. And then the other one.

"Evan was there when I got angry with Braden, and I ended up going with him."

Kaitlin's eyebrows flew up.

"Nothing happened," I lied.

"Right," Kaitlin said. "I saw the way he was looking at you the other day."

"You did?" I managed not to ask her how she had noticed when she was so busy flirting with him.

"Madison, Angie, and I all saw it," Kaitlin said with a sigh. "Did he kiss you?"

I nodded.

"He's put a love spell on you, hasn't he? Everyone said he does that, but you never believed them."

"He doesn't," I protested, although far more weakly than I would usually have done.

"In that case, are you going to make up with Braden?"

"I don't know if I want to."

She groaned. "Cassie, you have to see what's happening here."

I didn't. Sure, I could still feel his lips on mine if I thought about it, but that didn't mean anything. He'd admitted it was a powerful gift, and I'd gone and given myself a full jolt of it–twice.

"You were supposed to get together with Braden," Kaitlin whined. "I had my bridesmaid dress all picked out!"

I laughed. "I know you want to live vicariously through my fairy tale romance, but I'm afraid it's not working out very well right now."

"Yeah, well, you know who Evan is in that fairy tale, right?" Kaitlin asked.

I shook my head.

"The evil sorcerer."

ꕥ

A bouquet of red roses waited for me outside my office door, and I felt a moment of shame for what I had done to Braden. Apparently, I had even led him to believe the fault lay with him and that girl he'd been with, but I knew better. Maybe if he'd had a moment to spare for me, things would have gone differently, but they hadn't, and now I needed to face up to what I had done.

As I brought the roses into my office, I found the attached note, short and to the point: *I'm sorry.* But the signature wasn't Braden's, it was Evan's.

I nearly stumbled into my desk, hurrying to set the roses down as if they were on fire. From Braden, the roses would have been sweet, if not entirely deserved, but from Evan, they meant something else entirely.

The magical world is full of symbols, many of them culturally conceived, but powerful nonetheless. Colors had meanings. Each type of flower had meanings. Together, the red and the roses meant passion, romantic love, and even fertility. The note may have read *I'm sorry,* but the roses said, *oh, and by the way, I'm interested in sex and babies.*

A sorcerer didn't bring red roses on a casual first date.

My head spun, trying to figure out if I had sealed some kind of spell by taking the roses into my office, in effect, accepting them. Why did it have to be so complicated? And why was Evan suddenly coming on so strongly?

"Knock, knock."

My head flew up to see Braden framed in the open doorway, his eyes fixed on the roses.

"Braden." I didn't need this confrontation right now, with everything so confused in my mind. He would need explanations, and I would need to give them to him, and I hadn't even figured out whether or not I wanted to marry him.

Or had I? After three years, if I couldn't decide whether or not I loved him, was it really that tough a question? I wanted to love him, but the only reason I could think to marry him was to escape, and using a person like that has nothing to do with love. I had nothing to offer in return. Not that I wouldn't try, but I had to stand on my own two feet before I could be what he deserved.

"Who are those from?" Braden nodded towards the flowers.

"Evan."

A dark shadow spread across his face. "I see. I take it you two are together now."

"No!" The word exploded from my lips, carrying the force of desperate denial. No, I couldn't be with Evan, and somehow I would have to convince Evan of that fact, when he could so easily manipulate me. *He's put a love spell on you,* Kaitlin had said.

Not that I loved Evan, but it would have been convenient at that moment if I could bring myself to love Braden. And there was my second bad reason to marry Braden: to use him as a shield against Evan.

"Cassie," Braden said, "you've told me before that red roses are a symbol of romantic love and fertility."

"I didn't realize you were paying attention."

"I always pay attention to what you say. That's why I never brought you red roses before Tuesday night."

"Oh." Somehow, I had always assumed that I was more into the relationship than he was, because I never dated anyone else, despite our non-exclusivity agreement. He had, and I had never begrudged him that fact, but I still thought it had meant more to me than to him. Now, I realized, it was the other way around.

"So, is it over?" Braden asked. "Are you choosing him?"

"No, I mean, yes." I closed my eyes and took a deep breath. "Braden, I don't think we should get married, but it has nothing to do with Evan. He was just a friend when I needed one yesterday."

"A friend?" Braden lifted a finger and jabbed it at the roses. "He doesn't think so."

"No, I don't think he does."

"I know I screwed up yesterday."

"No, Braden, you–"

"Let me finish," he interrupted. "I did screw up. You were upset, and I didn't realize how much. I pushed you away. I don't suppose you'd tell me what happened?"

I hesitated, but I figured the whole town would know about it soon enough. "My parents disowned me."

"Oh, wow." His hand twitched, like he wanted to touch me but he had to strain to keep his distance.

"Exactly, so please don't blame yourself. You had no way of knowing what was going on and I think I already knew I didn't love you enough to marry you. Besides, you need someone with her act together, not someone who needs a convenient escape."

"Can't I be the judge of what I need?"

"It's over, Braden," I said, as gently as I could, but there's no way to say those words gently.

"I see." He started for the door, but paused and looked back, still staring at the roses. "You said your parents kicked you out. Where did you stay last night?"

Swallowing nervously, I said, "Evan's."

"And now he's sent you red roses." Braden had the look of someone trying to work something out in his mind, but I had a feeling he was jumping to all the wrong conclusions. "He's done something to you, hasn't he?"

"Not exactly."

"I should have seen it yesterday when you went tearing off after him." He took a few steps closer to me. "He's put a spell on you."

"No," I said. "I told you, we're not together, and I have no plans to get together with him."

"What are his plans? How easy do you think it's going to be to say no to him?"

Since I had wondered the same thing, I forced myself to keep my mouth shut.

"It's not over between us," Braden said.

"What?"

He held up his hands to fend off further comment. "Look, I think we're good together, but even if I'm wrong, I think you need someone to stand between you and him."

"That sounds like an awfully dangerous place to stand."

"If you think it's so dangerous, you definitely need me there."

I didn't know how to respond.

"Don't marry me," he said. "Just come to Chicago with me in the fall. Maybe I can change your mind, and maybe I can't, but at least in the meantime, you won't be alone."

"I can't just use you like that."

"Sure you can. I volunteered." With that, he strode out the door, leaving me gaping at his retreating back.

28

THE REST OF THE DAY OFFERED ME NO RESPITE. SHORTLY AFTER BRADEN left, the sheriff called, and he didn't sound happy.

"I called you at least five times yesterday. Where were you?"

"I had problems." I decided not to get into them. "Why did you call?"

"Because, as soon as we got off the phone yesterday, I realized you were holding out on me."

"Oh?" I held my breath.

"Belinda was turned into a vampire at that cabin, and she went there with a man. She signed him in as Mr. Hewitt. So, either this unidentified man was also attacked, and we've seen no evidence of a second victim, or the man in question was the vampire who hurt her. I don't think it was Luke, and neither do you."

I had no idea what to do with a direct challenge, so I kept my mouth shut.

"I've tried to talk to the other two men I was sure she was seeing, but neither of them is answering their phone. There seems to be a rash of that."

"Sheriff, I'm working on it," I said.

"Then why are you lying to me? I might have understood, when I was under that witch's spell, but not now."

"This case is dangerous," I said. "I just don't want the vampire to suspect anything."

"Or you think it's me."

"No," I said, a little too quickly.

"Interesting. That suggests daylight may not be the problem you said it was."

The sheriff had always struck me as a man with more than a little intuition, and just then, I hated it. "I can't talk about this."

"Fine," he said, "but I've still got duties, so if there's anything you think I should know, anything that might save my life, I'd appreciate you telling me."

"Just, be careful, and get behind a threshold. If I can tell you anything else, I promise I will."

I was still feeling unsettled by the conversation with the sheriff when I received another call, from Frank Loyd, but this time, with good news. He had a small snoop job for me, and I desperately needed the money. All I had to do was follow the husband of one of his clients and get some pictures to prove his infidelity. It was simple enough, and it came with a two hundred dollar advance.

Of course, I reasoned as I followed Arthur Jenkins home from work and waited just across the street for him to make his next move, I could probably ease my financial difficulties by going back to my parents' house to get my clothes. The only thing forcing me to start my new independent life without so much as a toothbrush was me. My parents had even offered me a fistful of money–probably several thousand dollars–that I had thrown back in their faces.

What was I trying to prove, anyway? That I didn't need them? Probably. The hurt and betrayal had overwhelmed me, and all I could think at the time was: If they don't want me, then I don't need them or anything they might give me.

How could I go back to them now and ask for my clothes? They hadn't just asked me to leave; they had disowned me. I was no longer their daughter. If I went back, it would be as a beggar asking for handouts.

Well, I didn't need handouts. I had two hundred dollars from Frank, and two hundred more when I finished. Evan wasn't paying me for that investigation, thanks to our deal, but there would be more work. Kaitlin hadn't asked for any rent money, but I intended to help her pay for the apartment and for groceries. I could get new clothes somewhere, too. They didn't have to be as expensive as my old clothes; I could ask Kaitlin where she got hers. Or would that sound insulting?

I bit my lip, and looked at the Jenkins' house with its flower beds and white picket fence. It wasn't exactly out of *Better Homes and Gardens*–some of the paint was peeling and there was a crack in the front upstairs window–but it had that aura of home. There was a tricycle in the driveway, and a couple soccer balls in the front yard, yet Arthur Jenkins had chosen to turn his back on it.

If Mrs. Jenkins had hired Frank Lloyd, then she was ready to push him out and try to raise however many children she had all by herself. At least I didn't have children to worry about. With my luck, maybe I would be better off if I never did. I couldn't help but remember my mom's suggestion that despite my lack of talent, the magic might skip a generation and settle in my children.

I waited in the hot rental car for two hours, trying to read a book, but mostly worrying about money. The cost of the rental was currently on Evan's credit card, but that wouldn't last forever, and then I would have to find a way to get a car. I wondered what I would be able to find for two hundred dollars. Nothing flashy, I was sure. I would have to hit up the used car lots but even then, I was pretty sure that two hundred dollars wouldn't be enough. Hadn't Kaitlin said she spent a thousand dollars on her beat-up 1996 Ford pickup truck? And it kept breaking down.

Well then, I would have to walk. Kaitlin only lived a mile or so from my office. It would make snoop jobs like this almost impossible, but maybe I could borrow Kaitlin's truck until I could afford my own.

By the time this was all over, I would owe her big time. Good thing she wasn't a sorcerer.

Finally, at around seven thirty, the garage door groaned open and Arthur's car backed into the street. He didn't even glance at me.

I followed him for about ten blocks before he stopped in front of a house not entirely unlike his own–though without the tricycles and soccer balls. A dumpy, red-haired woman met him on the porch, and they spent a minute or so posing for the camera. Luckily, I had kept a digital camera in my office, in case I ever needed it for a job.

When they finally went inside, I shook my head, and muttered an unflattering curse at Arthur and his dumpy mistress. I had what I needed, and it hadn't taken nearly as much time as I had feared. If I hurried, I could even get to Kaitlin's apartment before the sun set. Not that it mattered, now that I knew the vampire could get me day or night.

I had just put my car into drive when my phone rang, and I recognized Frank Lloyd's number on the caller ID. I flipped it open. "Hello?"

"How are things going?" Frank asked.

"What an idiot," I said. "He was making out with his girlfriend on the front porch. I've got lots of great shots. I'll get them to you in the morning."

"Can't you send them to me tonight?" Frank asked.

My laptop was back at my office, which meant there was no way I would be able to get behind a threshold by sundown, but I needed Frank's businesses. Besides, day or night, I wasn't safe. "All right, I'll swing by my office and e-mail them to you. You should have them in half an hour or so."

I hung up, then dialed Jason's number to let him know I was still out. Hey, I'm not completely stupid.

29

THE SUN HAD DIPPED BELOW THE HORIZON BY THE TIME I REACHED MY office building. If only I had thought to bring my laptop with me, I wouldn't have had to go back. Or maybe Kaitlin had a computer I could use. Why hadn't I thought of that before? I'm sure it had to do with my independent streak, and my feelings of guilt for taking advantage of her hospitality.

It didn't matter. I was at the office, and I just needed fifteen vampire-free minutes to upload the pictures to the computer. Then I could escape behind a threshold until sunup when, apparently, I would be no safer.

Stop that, I berated myself. There was no sense getting worked up. What would happen, would happen.

There was someone waiting for me when I opened the stairwell door and stepped into the hallway, but it wasn't a vampire. From the look on Nicolas's face, though, this confrontation wouldn't be much better.

"Cassie, where the hell have you been? Do you have any idea how worried I've been? I must have called you a million times. Why did you turn off your phone? You better have been unconscious somewhere. No, wait, you'd better not have been. Where the hell were you?"

His eyes were flashing, which was a bad sign for the wooden structure of the building. He usually had his gift under control, but a powerful rage had even been known to set Dad off.

"Calm down before you set the building on fire." Or me, I added silently, thinking of Mom setting my purse on fire the other day.

"Calm down?" Sparks shot out of his eyes, and with a tiny yip of surprise, I flattened myself against the wall while he continued to lay into me. "There are vampires running around out there and where are you? In an unprotected building with no threshold."

"Mom and Dad kicked me out," I said, a little defensively.

"Don't you have friends?" Nicolas demanded. "What about Kaitlin? She would have taken you in."

I couldn't argue with that. "Um, do we have to have this confrontation, I mean conversation, in the hall?"

"I'd prefer to have it behind a threshold," Nicolas said, "but I guess your office will have to do."

Shaking a bit, I turned the key in the lock and let us into my office. I had just wanted to upload the pictures and leave, but now it looked like I would be there for a while longer, dealing with Nicolas's hurt feelings. I didn't think he was nearly as angry with me not being behind a threshold as he was that I hadn't called him back.

"Where were you last night?" Nicolas asked.

"With Braden," I said, the lie springing easily to my lips.

"Don't lie to me." He put on a haughty, arrogant look that told me he knew something I didn't.

"Well, if you know the answer then why are you asking? Why don't you tell me where I was?"

I didn't actually expect him to know the answer, but he did, in quite a bit more detail than I would have preferred.

"You were with Evan Blackwood. Apparently, he put some kind of love spell on you."

"That's not exactly what happened."

"He admitted it. He came by this morning to apologize to Mom and Dad for any harm he may have done to you."

I had forgotten that Master Wolf told him to do that. My face burned scarlet, thinking about it, but then I shook my head, standing my ground. "They're not my mom and dad anymore. I don't care what they think, and I don't care what you think."

He glared at me, his eyes still sparking. I glared right back, silently praying he didn't burn down the building. His fists tightened and released, and for the first time, it struck me how very much he reminded me of Dad. It wasn't a comparison I relished at that moment.

"I didn't disown you," Nicolas said, finally. "I've been trying to find you for two days to tell you that."

My voice failed me, so I nodded. In my heart, I had known that's what the calls were about, I was just afraid to hear it. It was easy enough for him, he had always been Dad's favorite–his eldest son, the one who shared his gift. His place in the family had always been assured, and so he had never felt the least bit threatened by any of our brothers or sisters. Even as a small child, he had not had the normal amount of sibling jealousy.

"When Mom and Dad told me what they were going to do, I blew up the garage. They both need new cars now."

I almost smiled, picturing that, but I couldn't make my face form the expression. There was still a question weighing too heavily on my heart. "I guess they actually went through with it?" I held my breath.

"Yeah."

"I figured."

"So, about you and Evan-" Nicolas said.

I threw my arms up in frustration. "How can you possibly be angry with me for that if you think he put a spell on me?"

He grunted. "You're right. I'm not angry with you, I'm angry with him. And at you for not calling me back. Did he tell you not to call me back?"

"No, of course not, and I'm not under a spell. Look at my eyes."

I held still and let him lock gazes with me for a few long, seconds. He kept staring, even past the point when he should have recognized that there was no pink tinge, probably because he couldn't believe it.

"Well, you shouldn't trust him, anyway," Nicolas said. "I've never heard a less sincere apology in my life. He looked way too pleased with himself, and when Dad told him to stay away from you..."

"What? You can't just stop there."

Nicolas took a deep breath. "He laid into them, told them they'd abandoned you, and they had no power to either control or protect you."

"That's all true."

"It was the way he said it," Nicolas said. "I don't trust him."

I opened my mouth, prepared to defend Evan, even if I had my own private doubts, but I never got the chance. At that moment, my office door crashed open with such force the glass shattered, and a vampire rushed inside–the walking corpse of Dr. Shore.

30

At least, I assumed it was Dr. Shore, or had been at one time. I had never met the man, not having spent much time around mundane medical providers, but he looked like a doctor–complete with blue scrubs and a white lab coat. The coat was caked in dirt, making it look as if he had just risen as a vampire, which, given the insanity shining in his feral yellow eyes, was just possible. No one would mistake this creature for a powerful sorcerer-vampire who had lived among us in secret for countless years. This was one of the unfortunate victims of fate whose transformation had gone badly wrong, either because the original personality was unstable, the demon who chose the body was insane, or some combination of the two.

None of which mattered at that moment. Insane or not, unstable or not, he remained strong and deadly. He grunted in a way that made me wonder if he could speak, his eyes dancing past Nicolas as if he were invisible, but settling irrevocably on me.

No academy award-winning performance would work against this thing. He didn't have foreplay on his mind, or what was left of his mind, only death and destruction.

I saw all that in his eyes the instant before he lunged at me, one hand going around my throat in a strangle hold I thought would break my neck. He lifted me off the ground, letting my feet dangle helplessly as he cut off the oxygen supply to my brain.

I couldn't breathe, but unlike my plunge into a dark pool, this time I wouldn't be able to kick my way to the surface. My mind flashed back to the other incident, making me live the two together, back and forth, like bits of my life flashing before my eyes. I kicked, but to no avail. My hands tore uselessly at the iron noose around my neck until my vision began to blur, and stars danced before my eyes.

When a burst of scalding heat surrounded me, I was sure I had died and gone to hell, but to my surprise, the vampire dropped me, and I could breathe again. Gasping for breath, I looked up to see the vampire's clothes on fire, his face twisted in pain and rage as he bellowed some wordless oath.

There are times in your life when instinct takes over, because there simply isn't enough time to think or reason. With a fiery vampire dancing around my office, likely to set his sights on me again at any time, now with new and improved flame-throwing ability, I didn't hesitate. I couldn't make it out the door with a vampire in the way, but I made it to the window, forcing it open with enough raw panic to shatter the glass, and jumped.

My office was on the third story, and I didn't exactly have a lot of practice jumping from such a height, nor a conveniently soft place to land, so when I hit the pavement, I hit it hard. My legs slipped, I fell to my knees, scraping them raw, and for the second time in less than a week, I was sure I had done something to my ankle.

But I didn't have time to lie there and feel sorry for myself. I had to get up and run, or a bad ankle would be the least of my complaints.

Above me, a stream of fire rushed out my office window, and realization flooded into my soul. I had fled, but my brother remained in that office, fighting for his life with a weapon that couldn't kill a vampire, only make it angry.

I couldn't leave him. I couldn't help him, but something in me, the same something that wouldn't let me leave Angie to Luke's questionable mercy, refused to let me run away now. My earlier feelings of jealousy no longer mattered, nothing mattered except the battle. I probably couldn't outrun the vampire anyway, but I could go down fighting.

My car, parked half a block away, might as well have been on the moon, but I hobbled to it, found the keys in my pocket, and remotely popped open the trunk, which still held my bow and arrows. Halfway there, an ear-piercing scream rent the air. Whirling, I saw a fireball fall from my office window, landing gracelessly on the pavement below.

The vampire, oblivious to the pain of the fire or the fall, cried out again, and started running in my direction. I stood there, keys held limply at my side, a lifetime of distance between me and the arrows that were my only weapon, learning firsthand what people meant by frozen in terror.

The fireball never reached me. One second, I felt the hot tendrils of death reaching out for me, and the next, a sonic boom flew out of the night to knock the vampire off his target.

Jason had arrived, though I couldn't see him clearly. He looked to me like a force of nature, a whirlwind of strength and speed bent on destroying the evil creature threatening my existence.

I had never seen a vampire hunter fight, and I hope I never have to see it again. They moved together in a sinister dance, impossibly fast, destroying everything in their paths. At one point the sidewalk cracked, several shop windows shattered, a lamppost crashed to the ground, and a mailbox exploded, sending letters fluttering into the night.

The vampire lost his fiery edge quickly, the speed of his movements finally snuffing the flames, so I couldn't tell friend from foe, and had no way of knowing who would win this fight.

Suddenly, a hand closed around my arm, causing my heart to miss several beats before I realized the hand belonged to Nicolas, and he was okay. Well, mostly okay. His clothes were charred, his face sooty, and he bled from multiple cuts, but he would live.

"Why aren't you gone?" Nicolas had to shout to be heard over the sounds of the deadly fight.

I wanted to explain about my inability to leave him in danger, but it no longer sounded in any way rational, not even to myself.

"Let's go," I said instead, leading him toward my car.

No sooner had the words escaped my lips, then something flew overhead, landing hard on the green rental car that had been mine for the past three days. The car alarm chirped once, feebly, then died, as the vehicle flattened beneath the onslaught.

"This way." Nicolas steered me back the way we had come, to his car, parked thankfully a few places away. I flung open the passenger door, sliding inside seconds before Nicolas joined me on the other side.

"Shouldn't we wait for Jason?" I asked, looking anxiously around, but not spying the combatants.

"If he wins, he'll find us. If he loses, we don't want to be here."

It was infinitely sensible, and the exact logic I should have used when fleeing the vampire and Nicolas, but it left my heart empty.

Nicolas turned the key in the ignition, but before he had a chance to pull into the street, the back door flew open, and something fast and heavy fell into the backseat.

I screamed. The sound echoed through the car, or at least, that's what I thought at first. Then I realized Nicolas was screaming too.

"He's dead," Jason said, panting.

My racing heart remained unconvinced, so I shifted in my seat to make sure it really was Jason back there. It basically looked like my cousin, but with a lot more cuts and bruises than the last time I had seen him.

"I'll be okay," Jason said. "I heal quickly. Let's just get to a threshold before we run into more of them."

"Do you know where Kaitlin lives?" I asked Nicolas.

He shook his head.

"Then I'll guide you."

31

If I hadn't already been sure how good a friend Kaitlin was, I would have been sure when I showed up at her door with bruises around my neck, blood trickling down my leg, a bloody younger brother, and a slightly worn vampire hunter. She didn't even say anything. She just stood aside for us to come in. I noticed she did not specifically invite us, though. That was smart–a vampire wouldn't have been able to come through the door without the invitation.

She also wore a gold cross around her neck–one of those I had given to the entire cheerleading squad back in tenth grade.

Kaitlin lived in a small apartment with a combined living/dining area, a small kitchenette, and three closed doors which led to two bedrooms and a bathroom.

The furniture in the living room was old, mismatched, and free. I headed straight for the orange armchair, Jason landed hard on the plaid love seat, and Nicolas took a more tentative seat on the purple couch.

"Anyone want a soda?" Kaitlin asked.

Nicolas and I nodded, but Jason shook his head as he took a swig from the flask at his hip. He grinned at her, and she gave him an uncertain smile in response.

"What happened tonight?" I asked. "That guy came out of nowhere, and he specifically wanted to kill me."

Nicolas nodded his agreement. "He didn't even notice I was in the room when I set him on fire."

"What have you been doing since yesterday morning?" I asked Jason. "Did someone find out you were poking around?"

"I paid a visit to our three suspects," Jason said. "I saw Dr. Shore first, and he wasn't a vampire yesterday evening. Since it takes twenty-four hours for a vamp to turn, someone got to him right after I left."

My face paled. "What about the other two?"

"Robert, the hairdresser, was clean. I couldn't get to the sheriff." Jason gave me a significant look. "Did you tell him about Luke?"

"No, but he figured it out. He tried to call me yesterday, but we didn't talk until today, and that's when he told me Luke couldn't have been our vamp."

From somewhere in the kitchen, Kaitlin fumbled a tray of ice, and the contents spilled to the ground. I couldn't imagine what she thought of our conversation. It was one thing to know sorcerers were real and lived in the community, another to have them sitting in your living room, casually discussing vampires.

"What I want to know," I said, slowly, "is whether our guy sent Dr. Shore after me to kill me, or to try to convince me he was our guy. Surely, he didn't think I was that stupid."

Jason seemed to consider the question for a long time. "There are a couple of possibilities. He may have been getting desperate, because he thinks we're too close to him, which is likely, but also, Dr. Shore didn't turn well. It may have been an accident that he went tearing after you like that."

There was a tense silent for a minute, while I tried to figure out if I would ever be safe again. Too close...too close...the only person we were close to suspecting at this point was the sheriff, but I hated the idea.

"We should find out for sure how long Dr. Shore was a vampire," Jason said, finally. "There's always a chance he found a way to fool me."

"How do we do that?" I asked.

"I need to brew a potion."

"What do you need?" Kaitlin asked from the kitchen, sounding remarkably composed.

"Most of it I have on me," Jason said, "but I don't suppose you have some garlic?"

"In a jar in the fridge," Kaitlin said. "It's not fresh."

"Doesn't matter," Jason said. "Nicolas, want to give me a hand?"

The two men went into the kitchen, took out a saucepan, and started warming up the ingredients for their potion, while I limped into the bathroom with Kaitlin by my side. She dug out a first aid kit, helping me clean my hands and knees.

"That's your cousin?" she asked in a low voice.

I nodded.

"You never said he was good looking," Kaitlin said.

I shrugged. "He wasn't that impressive the last time I saw him."

"He is now."

"Yes." I gave her a wary look. "Kaitlin, what's going on with you and Curtis? First you were flirting with Evan, and now you're asking me about my cousin..."

She looked away.

"Kaitlin?"

"I'm not going to tell you. You'll just say you told me so."

"No, I won't. Am I really that mean?"

"No," she said, "but I'd deserve it. You did tell me so."

I didn't say anything, didn't push. I assumed he had cheated on her again, but if she didn't want to say it out loud, that was her prerogative.

"Oh, stop being so understanding all the time," Kaitlin said. "So I'm looking for a way to get back at him, all right? I admit it."

"And you think sleeping with someone else will help?"

"No."

"Okay," I said.

"So, is he seeing anyone?" Kaitlin asked.

For a moment, I had no idea who she was talking about. Then I put it together. "Jason? Not that I know of, but you don't want to get involved with him. He never stays in the same place long, and he's in a high mortality profession."

That seemed to be exactly the wrong thing to say, because Kaitlin's eyes grew suddenly dreamy.

"Snap out of it." I finished putting a large band aid on my knee, then limped back into the living room to join Jason and Nicolas. My ankle didn't feel sprained, only twisted, but without magic, I had no idea how long it would take to heal.

"What did you find out?" I asked, lowering myself to the couch.

"Someone turned him last night." Jason gave me a significant look, and I knew when he said someone, he meant the sheriff.

"How can it be him? I've known him for a long time. He's a good person. He keeps asking me to go back to work for him."

"Some vampires are very good at putting on an act to blend in with society. I've known vampires to take wives and adopt children. The smart ones. When a cunning demon merges with an intelligent personality, they come up with all kinds of disguises. Some go crazy, like Dr. Shore seemed to have done, but they don't all do that."

I shook my head. "But he's not a sorcerer."

"As far as you know," Jason said. "Do you think you know every practitioner in town?"

I hesitated. I did, actually, think I had a good idea who every magic user was, but, I supposed, I could have been wrong. Some liked their privacy, and worked hard to attain it.

"It all fits," Jason said.

"Nothing fits. If it was him, then why would he be pushing me so hard to find the real vampire?"

"Because he knew you'd do it anyway," Jason said. "Because he wanted to be there when you figured it out."

It wasn't proof. It was all circumstantial, and it didn't feel right. "We're missing something."

"What?" Jason asked, his voice a challenge.

I closed my eyes, trying to shut out the noise of the world. "Monday night," I said, "he came to Hodge Mill. He expected Belinda to be there, too."

"It could have been an act."

"If so, he's doing a lot of acting," I said. "And I know he was on a love potion then, I saw it in his eyes. The love potion might have driven a vampire to torture Belinda until she agreed to turn into one, but then, why stake her afterward?"

No one spoke, but I didn't open my eyes to see their reactions.

"We've been assuming," I said, "that Belinda only had the three lovers we know about from town gossip and rumors. But none of the latest conquests were in her scrapbook..." I trailed off. In fact, I had already supposed that someone deliberately removed those pages. Who said it was one of the three people we knew she had been involved with? If someone had removed pages from the scrapbook, he had removed all the pages, not just his own. There would have been little point in removing all of the pages, except that Belinda often cross-referenced her simultaneous conquests. So who else might she have enthralled? Who, that no one else knew about? It would have had to be a recent conquest, since word tended to spread quickly.

"I need to think. And sleep." I often thought better after a good night's sleep. Since I knew the spare bedroom was empty, even of a bed, I looked meaningfully at the couch.

"Fine," Nicolas said, "I'm going home."

"Good night," I said, fighting back the lump in my throat that formed when I thought of home.

"Jason?" Nicolas said. "Coming?"

"Oh, maybe not," Jason said. He shot Kaitlin a big smile and she melted into shy giggles.

You've got to be kidding me, I thought.

"Good night, then." Nicolas gave Jason a conspiratorial wink, then let himself out.

"There are blankets and pillows in the closet in the second bedroom," Kaitlin said, "but there's no bed in there. You'll have to sleep on the couch."

Not wanting to see them flirt or disappear into Kaitlin's bedroom together, I eagerly took the hint. I took my time in the second bedroom, choosing more blankets than I needed, and by the time I returned to the living room, they were gone.

When I laid down on the couch, I had every intention of pretending I didn't know they were in Kaitlin's bedroom together, but then the giggling started. Luckily, I spotted Kaitlin's MP3 player lying on the end table and, setting the headphones firmly over my ears, I attempted to drown the noises in music.

It didn't work. After a few minutes' effort, I started looking for something to do to take my mind off the two of them, and what they were undoubtedly doing in the other room.

It's not like it should have bothered me all that much, since they were both adults and Kaitlin wasn't exactly innocent, but I knew that however much she would try to pretend this was a meaningless fling, she would get hurt. In a week or a month, when she knew Jason had blown through town, with or without saying good-bye, she would need a shoulder to cry on. And I would offer her mine, even though I could have told her what would happen, even though I did try to tell her. I had done it before, only this time it was my cousin on the other side of that tryst. He had saved my life, probably countless people's lives, and yet I would have to be angry with him because that's what best friends do.

I turned off the MP3 player and took off the headphones, because it wasn't doing anything except filling my head with more noise. What Kaitlin did wasn't any of my business, I reminded myself, and I had far bigger things to worry about, like the identity of a vampire, and how to earn enough money for groceries.

Which reminded me, I had forgotten to e-mail those pictures to Frank. And, thanks to the vampire, I had left my purse and camera at my office. I tried to remember when I had dropped the purse, and thought I might have done it while talking to Nicolas, before the vampire arrived, but that didn't tell me whether or not the purse had been burned in the fight–along with the work of an evening.

Worse, if it had been burned, I had no idea how to replace any of it. Kaitlin might have a camera she could loan me for a while, but I couldn't take advantage of her forever.

One problem at a time, I told myself. Somehow, I had to explain to Frank why I hadn't delivered the pictures, and that they might have been destroyed. Just an average, everyday vampire attack. No big deal. He would understand. They happened all the time, at least to me. At least, lately.

Suddenly, I sat bolt upright, my eyes popping with realization. I knew who the vampire was.

32

When Frank had walked into my office earlier that week, I had thought he was crazy for filing a lawsuit against Belinda. The old witch would curse him, surely, but then, I reasoned, he had some ace up his sleeve. Perhaps he did. A bigger one than I could have imagined at the time. But the real flaw in my thinking was that Belinda would curse him. Whatever she was, Belinda wasn't her mother, and her preferred poison came in the form of love potions. How could he dare to sue her, if he believed he loved her?

Well, he had gone through with the lawsuit, which complicated things. And he had asked me to serve a subpoena to Belinda on Monday. So had she been alive on Monday? I started second guessing my theory, until I remembered how difficult it was to pin down the time of death for a vampire. Jason might have been able to do it, with trade secrets, but he hadn't gotten access to her body.

But tonight, Frank had wanted me to send him those pictures. Why? He couldn't file anything in court over the weekend. It just didn't strike me as that urgent, but he had asked, and I had told him I would swing by my office to e-mail them.

A few minutes later, another vampire had attacked, heading straight for me. He had barely noticed Nicolas when my brother set him on fire. He had come for me, and, somehow, known exactly where I would be. It wasn't as if I could normally be found in my office on a Friday night.

Was there another explanation for his actions? Someone else who knew where I would be? A mad coincidence? I didn't know, but my instincts told me I had it right, even if I didn't understand all the details. I remembered Evan's assertion that I had a touch of intuition, and for once, instead of denying the possibility out of hand, I prayed he was right.

With trembling fingers, I found Kaitlin's phone (the state of my cell phone being as dubious as that of my camera), and dialed Frank's number. He answered on the first ring.

"Frank Lloyd here."

"Hi, it's Cassie."

"Cassie, I was expecting those pictures an hour ago. I tried to call you, but you didn't answer your phone."

"I'm sorry, but there was some trouble at my office when I got there. A, um, vampire attacked me."

"Another one? You've been having a hard week." He sounded so sincere, so sympathetic, and so human. But he wasn't. Even Angie didn't remember my other vampire attack that week, and she had been there.

"That's an understatement," I said, hoping my fear didn't sound in my voice. "Also, there was a fire, so I'm not even sure if my camera is still okay."

"Is the fire out? Can you go check?"

"It's kind of late, and like I said, there was a vampire. I'd like to stay safe until morning." I hoped that would throw him off, thinking I didn't know of his special abilities, or, indeed, about him, but something felt wrong. I don't know if it was him or me, but the tenor of the conversation had changed, and all I wanted to do was get off that phone as quickly as possible.

"I suppose it can wait until morning," Frank said.

"That's great, So I'll see you tomorrow morning, first thing."

"First thing after you check on your camera," Frank reminded me.

"Right. Second thing, then."

"Good-bye, Cassie."

"Bye." I hit the off button but didn't otherwise move. I simply sat there, with the phone in my lap, staring at it, and wondering if, in an attempt to uncover the truth about Frank, I had let him in on my discovery as well. I hoped not. I hadn't said anything to give it away. Quickly, I reviewed the conversation in my mind, replaying it over and over again, trying to find anything I might have said wrong. I couldn't, but the feeling wouldn't go away. Not that it meant anything, since I had no gift, intuition or otherwise. I would know if I did, right?

Kaitlin's bedroom door squeaked open and I jerked my head around so fast I nearly got whiplash. Jason stepped out, quietly at first, but when he saw me awake and staring, he abandoned the pretense.

"What's wrong?" he asked.

"The vampire we're looking for is Frank Lloyd."

He sat next to me on the couch while I quickly ran through what I knew, what I suspected, and most importantly, our recent phone conversation.

"I didn't give anything away, did I?" I asked.

"Probably not," Jason said, "but I need to move on this tonight. You should be safe here, behind a threshold."

"What are you going to do?" I asked. "You weren't planning to go up against him alone?"

Jason shook his head. "I'm not crazy. I came in alone to do the ID because we're stretched thin, but there are two other hunters no more than three hours from here."

With that, Jason took his cell phone from his pocket and started making calls. When he disappeared into the kitchen for a little privacy, I noticed Kaitlin, wearing a bathrobe, framed in her doorway. Her cheeks were flushed, her eyes sparkling, and a tiny smile played at the corner of her mouth.

"Are you stocked up on crosses and holy water?" I asked.

"I only have the one cross," Kaitlin said, fingering the one around her neck, "but I've got a five-gallon drum of holy water in the pantry."

"You do?"

Kaitlin's smile widened. "Of course I do. You told me there were vampires, so I bought a big thing of water and stopped by the Catholic Church on the way home to have Father Owens bless it."

"That was smart," I said.

"I have my moments."

"So, have any water guns to go with them?"

Her smile faltered. "I should have thought of that."

"We'll make do."

"The team's on its way," Jason said, shoving his phone back into his pocket as he strode into the living room. "Now, I just need to do some prep work. I'm low on holy water-"

"Kaitlin has a five-gallon drum of it in the pantry," I said.

"Really?" Jason arched an eyebrow at Kaitlin and winked. "Great. And I don't suppose there's something to eat around here? I missed breakfast this evening."

"This evening?" Kaitlin asked.

"I usually wake up around five p.m."

"All right, eggs and pancakes it is. Cassie, you want any?"

I remembered the only meal I'd had that day—also eggs and pancakes—and my stomach gave a loud growl. "Sounds great."

While Kaitlin worked, Jason ran to his car and returned with a gym bag full of water guns ranging from pistols to super soakers. Quickly, he began filling them with the holy water, his back to us, but at one point, I could have sworn I saw him fill his own flask from the jug.

"Does holy water kill a vampire?" Kaitlin asked as she cracked eggs into a frying pan.

"Mostly it does surface damage," Jason said. "If you drench them in the stuff, you may be able to cause lethal damage. More likely, though, you'll just cause enough agony that they can't attack you while you stake them. The water burns them, but it evaporates."

"What if they drink it?" I asked.

Jason quirked an eyebrow. "Now, that's an interesting question. It's even more interesting to watch happen."

"I don't think I'd want to watch it," Kaitlin said.

He shrugged. "When enough vampires try to kill you, you start enjoying watching them writhe in agony a bit."

For the first time since I had tried the holy water, I gave serious thought to trying it again. I was afraid, because my parents had disowned me right after I had taken the sacrilegious drink, but my parents had been planning that for days, so the events couldn't have been related?

Mustering my courage, I took an empty glass from a pantry shelf and filled it from the jug. Jason saw, but didn't comment, either to encourage me or discourage me, which I took as a good sign. Closing my eyes, I chugged the glass of water in a matter of seconds, before I could change my mind.

A few minutes later, Kaitlin served eggs, pancakes, and peaches while we talked about mundane things. I think we were all a bit afraid, and trying, in some small way, to push the feelings aside. Kaitlin and Jason did most of the talking.

It was a little disgusting to watch Kaitlin exaggerate and lie to try to impress Jason. It's not like I went out on dates with her, but if she hid her true nature like that with other men, then it was no wonder she never had any luck in her relationships.

When Kaitlin told Jason she planned to return to school when she had enough money, so she could become a nurse, I excused myself and sauntered into the living room. I didn't think I would be able to sleep, so I didn't bother to try, but I did lie down on my side and stare at the blank television screen.

Something in my pocket kept jabbing me in the side. Sitting up, I pulled the crystal Evan had given me from my pocket and clutched it in my hand. I had promised to let him know when I figured things out, and somehow, despite everything, a part of me wanted the comfort of his presence on what I expected to be a very, very long night.

"Evan," I whispered, holding the crystal in my hand. I didn't know if speech was necessary, since he had said all I needed to do was think of him, but I didn't think it could hurt. As I spoke, the crystal grew warm, almost hot, and I smiled in satisfaction before putting it back in my pocket.

That's when the building's fire alarms went off.

Jason stood bolt upright, knocking aside the wooden chair with such force it splintered. Without apologizing, or even seeming to notice, he made a mad dash for the kitchen window and looked out.

"Oh shit," he said.

I stared out the window, though I couldn't see anything from the couch, as the implications slowly settled in. I think it took a while because fire was somewhat normal in my life. My father and brother were both fire starters and, apparently, my newest brother or sister would be as well. Accidental fires were fairly normal, and the house was always fully stocked with burn ointment and flame resistance potions. The walls themselves had woven protections against fire, and we normally had either Dad or Nicolas on hand before things got out of control. Fires were just not a big deal in my life, or hadn't been.

Who's protecting you? Evan had asked. *Magical protection.*

We had to leave the building, or we would burn alive, but if we left, I had no doubt that a powerful sorcerer-vampire awaited us. It was too convenient to be anything else. Too much of a coincidence.

When Jason turned from the window, I knew he saw the truth as well.

"What do we do?" Kaitlin asked, pale-faced and trembling, twisting the belt of her robe around her finger in a tight knot.

Jason and I made a move for the pile of super soakers and water guns at the same time. We each grabbed a super soaker, Jason throwing his at Kaitlin. Then, he pocketed several smaller guns.

"Kaitlin," I said, lifting my voice to be heard over the shriek of the fire alarm, "doesn't your mom live a few blocks from here?"

"Yes."

"Then keep that cross around your neck and run for it," I said.

She started for the door, pausing to slip her feet into a pair of sandals but otherwise taking nothing from the apartment. Beneath us, I felt the floor begin to grow warm.

"Kaitlin," I added as she moved out.

"What?" She threw a glance over her shoulder.

"Don't wait for me, and don't look back." I had a feeling she would be okay, as long as no one associated her with me. I hoped.

She swallowed, hard, and nodded. Then, wordlessly, she fled through the door.

33

There were eight apartments in Kaitlin's building, four on the ground floor, four on top. I raced down the stairs, away from Kaitlin's second floor corner apartment, my eyes flying left and right to see the evacuation of the other apartments well underway. Smoke billowed up from directly beneath us, and as I flew down the rickety outside stairs to the ground, I saw flames dancing and licking their way up the outside of the building.

I spotted a woman carrying a screaming toddler from a downstairs apartment, and my heart lurched, wondering if everyone had gotten out. It had all begun so quickly, and spread so quickly. A faint smell of gasoline lingered in the air, confirming my suspicion that this was not at all natural.

"Go with Kaitlin," Jason called from just behind me.

I hesitated, wondering if doing so might put Kaitlin in more danger, but here I would probably just get in Jason's way as he hunted the vampire, so I nodded and sprinted after her retreating form. It had been a few years since I had visited Kaitlin at her mother's place, but I thought I still remembered where to find it, so I stayed a few yards back, letting her get a head start, so that no one who saw us would necessarily think we were together.

Ahead of me, a scream rent the air, shrill and piercing. Kaitlin's scream. She slid to a stop, but I couldn't immediately see what had frozen her in place. Then, Frank Lloyd stepped from between two buildings.

"I take that to mean you do know what I am," Frank said, smoothly, stalking toward Kaitlin's quivering form like a hunter scenting prey.

"Leave her alone," I said, hoping I sounded braver than I felt. My knees quaked, and my breath came out in shallow pants.

"Cassandra, how nice to see you."

I strode forward, super soaker in hand, aiming it at him. "She's got a cross, and this is loaded with holy water. Too many people know what you are now, so you may as well leave town while you can."

"I will," Frank said, "but I wanted to thank this town properly for uncovering me."

"I uncovered you. Leave the rest of the town out of it."

He laughed. "Wow, barely a tremor of fear in your voice, although your legs are a bit wobbly. You know I'm going to kill you, right?"

"I had a feeling." But if I kept him talking, Jason might get there in time.

"Go," Frank said to Kaitlin, "before I change my mind."

Kaitlin turned back to look at me, her eyes wide and staring, and I saw in them the reluctance to leave me behind.

"Go," I urged her. "Please. There's nothing you can do."

She hesitated for a few more seconds, and I saw tears glistening in her eyes before she nodded, stiffly, and fled the scene. Maybe she could get help. At least she could get away.

"I am armed," I said, waving my super soaker in his direction. He seemed supremely unconcerned, and an instant later, I knew why. He moved, faster than thought, grabbing the feeble weapon from me before I had a chance to pull the trigger, and tossing it harmlessly aside. Then, in a single, smooth motion, he hoisted me over his shoulder and took off.

At those speeds, the wind cut into me, biting me with its intensity, and I couldn't see a thing. If there was a blur of colors, I couldn't even see it, because I had my eyes closed against the wind. I'm not sure how long he ran, seconds or minutes, but they were the most terrifying moments of my life, including the moments I spent in the pool with Luke. Then, at least, I had hope. Now, I had nothing. Maybe the holy water I had drunk would poison him and maybe not, but either way, I wouldn't live to find out. He'd tear me apart first. The best I could hope for was to take him down with me.

When I blinked open my eyes, we stood in the last place I expected–the burnt out shell of my office. The larger furniture, like the desk and filing cabinets, had more or less survived, though they were blackened husks. The floor, ceiling, and walls were blackened as well, reminding me a little of my fortress of solitude, painted all in black. Strangely, it gave me renewed courage.

"What are we doing here?" I asked.

"I figured this would be about the last place anyone would look for us." Frank took a step away from me, reaching his hand deep into the pocket of his suit coat. "I have a proposition for you."

He withdrew a clear glass vial, containing some blue liquid that sparkled in the moonlight streaming through the broken window.

"P-proposition?"

"If I bite you now, you'll die," Frank said. "If you drink this first, you won't."

My stomach twisted. "Is that the same stuff you forced Belinda to drink?"

"You guessed that, did you? Yes, for a couple of unsettling days, I couldn't bear the thought of life–such as it is–without her. It wore off quickly. By Monday morning, I could think straight again. It must have been in the chocolates. I don't usually eat, but at the time, it seemed useful to maintain a pretense."

"Why did you kill her?" I asked.

"She wasn't stable. I don't think she ever was. When I found out she'd killed the Hastings girl, I knew I had to end it, but by then it was too late. I've hidden in this town long enough to know which lines not to cross. Somehow, she had never figured it out. That, or the bloodlust overwhelmed her. First kill and all."

I took a step back, bumping against the desk. "Why do you want me to take that stuff?"

He lifted the potion, studying its contents, letting them swirl a bit, almost hypnotically. "Belinda made me think a companion would be nice, but not someone like her. Someone more stable. Someone I can control."

I swallowed, hard.

"I've been watching you all week. You're clever and determined, and I like that. Plus, I like the fact that turning you would be a parting shot to nearly everyone in town. They're not as strong as they think they are."

"I won't take the potion," I said, softly.

"Won't you? You'll be strong and fast and powerful. You never again have to feel weak or helpless in a society full of sorcerers."

I closed my eyes. He knew my heart better than I had given him credit for, but I still would never do it.

"Look at me," he said.

I knew better than that. With the power of hypnosis, he might be able to make me drink the potion against my will, and I knew, despite the temptation, despite the fact that he had spoken to my deepest, darkest desires, that the one thing I could not do was drink that potion.

"Do you want to die a meaningless death?" he asked.

Maybe not meaningless. There was still the holy water I had consumed. Jason had never really said one way or the other if it would work, but I tried to have faith, because in the end, it was the faith that mattered more than anything else. It was the faith that had kept us all safe on that terrible day in high school when a bus had collided with a semi. It was faith that had burned a cross into my palm and saved me from Luke's hypnotic gaze.

Faith, have faith. My blood will poison him. He'll burn up from the inside.

"I should warn you that I don't have quite as long to torture you as I had with Belinda. I won't count on us remaining undiscovered here for long, but I can try to tempt you with a few nibbles. Let's see...the upper arm is a nice place to start." He drew up my short sleeve and lowered his head, very slowly. I could feel hot, wet tears on my face, and I choked back a sob. Have faith, I kept repeating, have faith.

But what if it didn't work? I needed to have faith in myself. Faith that I would not give in as Belinda had, and allow myself to turn into a monster. Faith that whatever wrongs may have been done to me, I loved my family enough to suffer this pain to the last.

Think of Christina, I told myself. I forced her angelic, three-year-old face into my mind and stared at it with my heart. She would be the one to suffer if I failed.

Razor-sharp teeth pressed into the soft flesh of my upper arm. Then with a rapid slash like that of a knife, they cut their way through skin and muscle as he drank.

My eyes squeezed shut, but even though I could have, I didn't scream. Something like a hoarse whimper might have escaped my throat, but I kept my focus on the pictures in my mind. Christina's face had been replaced by Adam's, and again I told myself to be strong for him.

Frank lifted his head, and I held my breath, unwilling to move or open my eyes.

"There's blood trickling down your arm," Frank whispered. My heart plummeted. He didn't even sound like he was in pain. "What a waste. The potion would help. There would be no more pain, and you could live forever. Powerfully."

It wasn't going to work. How could I have even let myself hope it would be so easy? A vampire hunter would know more than a few tricks to make their blood poisonous to vampires, and I had let myself believe that it was a simple matter of drinking holy water.

"Where shall I bite next?" Frank asked.

It didn't even occur to me not to answer, because I had a suggestion all ready for him. Mutely, I pointed at my throat. Get it over with, I was telling him.

He chuckled, a sound that ended rather abruptly. "Maybe the wrist."

He lifted my hand to his, razor sharp teeth pressing against the smooth flesh, but he did not bite. Instead, he dropped my arm and fell backward a step.

That's when I dared to open my eyes again. His face was twisted in pain and rage. "What have you done?"

I didn't let my face give anything away. I had no idea how the poison would effect him, how serious it would be, how long it would last, or if it would kill him, but if I broke into a run, then maybe, just maybe, I could survive this encounter. If only I didn't have the twisted ankle to contend with, but I would simply have to ignore it.

My feet began moving before my brain caught up with them, but when I paused to fling open the office door, Frank caught me by the heel and dragged me back.

That's when I screamed.

"What did you do?" Frank demanded again. This time, when he spoke, smoke drifted out of his mouth, and he began to gag. He let go of my heel and put his hands around his throat in the universal sign for choking. Blood trailed out of the corner of his mouth.

I scrambled to my feet and flung myself at the door, but once again, Frank stopped me before I could get there. He was weakening, but still much stronger than me. This time, he closed his fist around my ankle until I heard bone crack.

Once again, I screamed, and fresh tears spilled from my eyes. I'm not sure whether a broken bone hurts more or less than a vampire's teeth tearing into your flesh. Suffice to say, I would avoid them both if you can.

Frank could no longer speak, but he wasn't done fighting. His eyes told me if he was going to die, then he would at least take me with him. He could barely breathe, blood flowed freely from his mouth, and there was a new wound forming on his stomach, as if something was eating him from the inside out. His clean white shirt was stained with blood.

He dragged me toward him, clawing with both hands while I tried to resist with my mere human strength, further encumbered by a broken ankle.

I could tell when his strength continued to wane. He had nearly dragged me close enough to rip out my throat when I was suddenly able to slip away a bit. Crawling on my back, both hands clawing at the scorched carpet for extra purchase, I slipped away.

He roared, a sound like that of a dying animal. For a brief, shining moment I thought I might make it out of the room alive, if not unscathed.

Then, with one last burst of energy, he lifted my shirt and sank his teeth into my belly, the only thing he could reach. He didn't drink, he tore, his goal clearly to do as much damage as possible.

I'm not sure when he died. By the time he did, the pain had become too much for me, and I lost consciousness.

34

THE VAMPIRE MUST HAVE KILLED ME, BUT AS I SLOWLY BLINKED BACK INTO awareness, I was struck by how painful death felt. People always described it as a release from pain, an end to normal, human suffering, and yet there I lay, weak, nauseated, and with a throbbing in my head that made it difficult to think.

Sensations slowly penetrated, but they seemed too loud, or bright, or real. The light from a dozen candles illuminated an otherwise dark room, tearing into my eyes like shafts of brightest sunlight. Heat enveloped me, surrounding my body in satiny fire that constricted my lungs. Somewhere nearby, a low voice rumbled, but the deafening volume neither helped me identify its owner, nor make sense of the sounds.

I started tossing my head back and forth, kicking at the constricting folds of heat I later identified as sheets. Then I felt a hand pressing me down, and something cold touched my lips. Liquid spilled into my mouth, bitter and oddly gritty, but though I tried, I couldn't seem to spit it out.

The pain eased. I risked opening my eyes, but saw little more than the outline of a stark bedroom before I shut them again. The low rumble of sound became coherent, and familiar.

"Evan?" I said.

"I'm here. How do you feel?"

"Hot." I kicked the covers further away, but when cool air hit bare skin, the fact of my nakedness penetrated my foggy mind. I scrambled to retrieve the covers, but Evan beat me to it, tucking a sheet around my shoulders.

Once again, I tried opening my eyes, and Evan swam into view. He looked exhausted and unkempt, several days' worth of stubble shadowing his face, his eyes bloodshot.

"Am I alive?" I asked, my voice creaking.

"Yes."

"Why?"

"Because I saved you."

That didn't answer much, but as sensations returned to my body, so did the realization that Evan was beyond exhausted–he was drained. Magical exhaustion, or draining, can happen when a sorcerer overextends himself, and it can lead to serious complications.

"Are you okay?" I asked.

"I will be, when I get some sleep. I wanted to make sure you would be okay first."

"Will I?" The pain was slowly easing, but I still felt weak.

"Yes. Now, go back to sleep."

I didn't want to go to sleep, I wanted to ask questions, but no sooner had he made the suggestion, then sleep seemed all I was capable of doing.

ꕥ

I woke several times over the next few days, just long enough to drink a few potions Evan forced down my throat before falling back into exhausted sleep. Each time I woke, the angle of the sunlight slanting through the drapes told me some time had passed, though I never knew how much. The sparsely furnished room didn't even have an alarm clock, just a bed and next to it, a padded rocking chair. Evan often sat in the chair when I woke, and at first, his eyes were full of fear and exhaustion. Gradually, he began to look better–less drained. As he recovered from his magical overexertion, his appearance improved as well, his shirts becoming less wrinkled, his hair brushed, and finally, his face cleanly shaved.

The day he came to me, clean shaven, I asked him not to drug me back to sleep again.

"I haven't been," Evan said, "at least, not after the first couple of nights. You're just that exhausted."

"How long have I been here?"

"About a week."

"A week!" I nearly sat up, before remembering my naked state, and sliding back under the covers. "Where are my clothes?"

"They didn't make it," Evan said, "but I went into town yesterday and got you some new ones. Hope I got the right sizes."

I rubbed my fists into my eyes, trying to blink away sleep. Honestly, if the clothes covered me, I didn't care what size they were. I felt awkward and vulnerable this way, especially when I considered that he must have looked. Frank had torn into my guts, and when I gently explored my abdomen with my fingers, it still felt tender there. It had probably been easier for him to work on me without clothes, I reasoned, but still, I couldn't help but remember the kisses...and the roses.

"Kaitlin," I said, suddenly remembering the fire. "Is she okay? Did everyone get out?"

Evan leaned forward, stilling the motion of the rocking chair. "Everyone's fine. I think Frank just wanted to smoke you out. But the apartment complex was a total loss."

"Poor Kaitlin." How was she going to replace all her things? I suddenly understood what she'd meant when she'd said she wished I had taken my parents' money. If only pride hadn't gotten in the way. If only it still wasn't getting in the way. "Do you know where she's living now? Is she staying with her mom?"

"The whole town has been pitching in to help them out. Most of them are staying at this new apartment complex at the edge of town. It's more expensive, but someone made a rather large anonymous cash donation."

"You?" I asked.

"I've been busy."

"I see." Using the sheet to cover myself, I slowly sat upright, scanning the plain white walls of the rather large bedroom. A master bedroom, probably. A set of double doors led into an elegant bathroom suite, drapes hung over a large bay window, and a ceiling fan spun from the vaulted ceiling. Otherwise, the place was a blank slate.

"Where am I?" I asked.

"My new place. Master Wolf kicked me out–his version of a graduation ceremony–just after I apologized to your parents. I've had this place waiting for months, but as you can see, it's not decorated."

"I don't think my family bought the apology," I said, vaguely, remembering Nicolas's rampage.

"I didn't really mean it." He smiled, and his eyes sparkled.

Inside, I felt a growing sense of unease. My pain and sleep-muddled mind was missing something, I knew, something important.

"The clothes I got you are in the bathroom." Evan gestured towards the double doors. "Why don't you get cleaned and dressed, and we can talk after? I'll make some sandwiches."

"I'm not hungry."

"You need food." His tone told me he wouldn't take no for an answer, but I didn't protest. After taking two seconds to think about it, I remembered that magical healing often saps a person's appetite along with their strength, but the food was no less necessary.

As soon as he left, I made my way into the luxurious bathroom, complete with whirlpool tub, large shower with multiple shower heads, and a two-person sink. To my relief, the shower also contained a bench, which I eagerly used to help fend off the waves of dizziness that attacked.

The warm water felt good, as if it were washing away the aches and pains. I reveled in it, washing my hair twice with the shampoo I found, before stepping out and wrapping a large, soft towel around myself.

When I looked in the mirror, I saw that a week without food had taken its toll on my body. My face appeared gaunt, and dark circles rimmed my eyes. The clothes Evan bought for me, including, somewhat to my embarrassment, plain white underwear and a bra, were indeed in the correct size, except they hung loosely on my sickened body. That, more than anything else, told me how close to death I had been. No normal doctor could have repaired me. Most sorcerers wouldn't have been able to heal me, for that matter. I even thought, though I hated to consider the implications, that Juliana would have had trouble.

When I emerged from the bathroom, dressed and freshly clean, Evan sat on a metal folding chair that hadn't been there before. Another folding chair sat across from him, a card table set up in between, along with two plates of sandwiches. Beside the table, the drapes had been pulled back, letting bright afternoon sunlight spill into the room.

He looked up at me and smiled, gesturing to the plates. "My pantry isn't fully stocked yet, but since you haven't eaten in a week, I'd rather not challenge your body right now."

I remained frozen in the bathroom doorway, staring at him, and wondering. Images began to flash through my mind, chief among them that of Evan, crushing a large tree into splinters. That had been the closest he'd come to showing me how powerful he really was. No one knew for sure, not that sorcerers typically advertised. That would be like telling an enemy nation exactly how much firepower you had. Yet he had given me a glimpse the other day, for no better reason than to talk me out of wanting to fight a vampire. And then, this week, he had reached into the very core of his power to bring me back from the brink of death.

"Cassie?" Evan frowned.

"How strong are you?" The words escaped me before I could stop them and properly consider the affront.

Indeed, his face hardened, taking on that mask he had perfected, and that cracked for only a few people. "Strong enough."

I supposed that was all that really mattered, and I wished desperately that I hadn't asked. I didn't really want to know, anyway. It wasn't as if I planned to have anything to do with magic any longer, and I didn't want to step away from that world fearing someone who had been so good to me. Or was it too late? My heart raced, but in response to fear, nerves, anxiety, sickness, or lingering physical attraction? Magically induced physical attraction, I mentally corrected myself.

"Does anyone know I'm here?" I asked when I had dutifully finished my sandwich.

"No. I didn't have a phone until I went to the store yesterday." He dug a cell phone out of his pocket and handed it to me. "Call whoever you like to let them know you're okay."

I reached for the phone automatically, but when I held it, I didn't know who to call. It served my former parents right if they thought

I was dead. I didn't feel the same way about my brothers and sisters, of course, but if I called Nicolas and told him where I was, he would go ballistic. He had eagerly inherited his father's dislike of the Blackwoods.

I should call Kaitlin, and find out if she still had room at her place for me. If that didn't work...well, I didn't want to think about it. I would probably have to go to my Uncle John.

"I'll give you some privacy," Evan said, after a tense silence. "I'll be downstairs if you need me. First door to the right at the bottom of the stairs is the den, and the only room I've really furnished."

"Thanks."

As soon as he'd gone, I dialed Nicolas's number, then I held my breath as I waited for him to answer.

"Hello?" he said.

"It's Cassie."

"Cassie! Oh, thank God!" He let out a loud whoosh of breath. "I really thought you were dead. God, where have you been? Why didn't you call?"

"I'm sorry, I've been unconscious or asleep. It was bad."

He sucked in a breath. "We found a lot of blood in your office, and a pile of dust Jason said was Frank. He was pretty old."

"At least he's dead."

"Where are you?" Nicolas asked again. "How did you survive?"

"Evan saved me. He's been nursing me back to health all week."

Not unexpectedly, Nicolas sucked in another deep breath. "Evan?"

"I'm fine."

"You're fine?" To my surprise, Nicolas began to laugh. "Fine? That's what you think you are? Do you have any idea how much you owe him?"

I could feel the blood run from my face. Of course I owed him. It was the most obvious thing in the world. Hadn't I realized, if I used the crystal, that I might end up indebted to him? Either I still needed a lot of sleep, or I had been intentionally refusing to acknowledge the truth.

"Cassie," Nicolas said, his voice a bare whisper, "he owns you."

The phone fell from my numb fingers to land with a thud on the table. Distantly, I heard Nicolas shouting something, but he may as well have been on the moon.

He owns you, Nicolas had said. The words pierced my soul and twisted my heart. *He owns you.* They echoed through my mind as if bouncing off the walls of an immense canyon.

"Cassie!" The one, clear word broke through my mental fog and I picked up the phone.

"I love you, Nicolas. Tell the kids I love them." With that, I hung up.

Stay strong, I tried to tell myself. It's Evan. He's a friend. He wouldn't hurt you. At least not physically. Or intentionally.

Outside the large picture window, the world moved on, blissfully unaware of my dilemma. I could see all the way to the lake, through a cluster of trees, and I watched as several boats raced by.

Life goes on, I told myself, *and at least you are alive.*

ꟳ

Somehow, I managed to take a nap. When I woke, the scent of baking bread filled the house, and my stomach gave a pitiful little growl. A good sign, I decided.

Knowing I couldn't avoid Evan forever, I slipped from bed, ran a brush through my hair, brushed my teeth, and headed out the door. I was in a second floor hallway, lined with closed doors that probably led to other bedrooms, but I didn't take the time to explore. Instead, I found the long, curved staircase that would take me to the first floor and to that delicious smell.

Evan wasn't in his den, but I found him by following my nose, passing through several unfurnished rooms that I supposed would become a formal living and dining room, before reaching the kitchen. Evan flashed me a quick greeting as he pulled a sheet of rolls from the oven, and slid them into a napkin-lined wicker basket.

"How do you feel?" he asked.

"I'm-" I stopped, because I suddenly saw, there in the breakfast nook, something that forcibly reminded me of Nicolas's proclamation: The table was set for two, lit only by romantic candlelight cast by two flickering white candles. A vase of red roses stood proudly off to the side.

Evan followed the direction of my gaze. "Dinner is almost ready. You can have a seat."

Mutely, I moved to one of the two chairs. What was it my father had said the other day? *If Evan decides he wants her, how would she even resist?* I might have tried to pretend or explain away the signs before, but now I knew for certain: He did want me. The debt only made it a hundred times worse.

"Did you make the calls you needed to make?" Evan asked.

"Yes." I set his phone down on the table. "Kaitlin only has a one-bedroom place now, but she still insists I stay with her. She says we can spend the next month looking for someplace else to stay."

"Did you call your brother?" Evan asked.

"Yes."

"And?" Evan set the basket of rolls in the middle of the table, then pulled two salads out of the refrigerator, setting one in front of me before taking his own seat.

"You mean he didn't come by and try to burn your house down?" I tried to make the question sound light.

"Not yet. I thought maybe he'd be glad I managed to save you."

A wave of shame washed over me, and I busied myself buttering a roll so he wouldn't see.

"When I gave you the stone," Evan said, "I wasn't sure you'd use it."

"Thank you. For the stone and for, you know, saving me." Debt or no debt, I was glad to be alive.

"You're welcome."

We ate without speaking for a few minutes. When he cleared away the salad plates and replaced them with dishes of pasta, he broke the silence. "You're not usually so quiet."

I wasn't. I usually tried to fill uncomfortable silences. "A lot has happened to me lately. Maybe it's all finally catching up with me."

"Cassie," Evan said, reaching across the table to lay his warm hand on mine, "You know I'd never hurt you."

"Yes."

"What did Nicolas say?" Evan asked.

"Oh, you know, he was worried, he's glad I'm alive, that sort of thing."

Evan arched an eyebrow. "And?"

I closed my eyes. "He said you own me."

"Oh."

"It's true, isn't it?" I opened my eyes a crack, but his face was a mask.

"I wouldn't have put it that way."

"How would you have put it?"

His mask remained firmly in place, but he played with his pasta. "There is an easy way to void the debt. Not only that, but it would keep you protected."

I looked at the red roses, and instantly understood. He was talking about marriage. That kind of family bond made magical debt irrelevant.

"I don't need protection," I said, hoping to steer the conversation away from the more dangerous path.

"Your parents disowned you. They may have claimed to offer you protection, but if they're serious about cutting you out, they can't."

I had already worked that much out, not that I wanted their help. "There's my Uncle John-"

"Interesting thing about your uncle," Evan said. "I went to see him a couple of days ago, just to feel him out. He is of the opinion that the best way to protect you would be to marry you off to a powerful local sorcerer."

"What?"

"Don't worry, he won't step aside for just anyone. They have to promise to treat you well, and they have to have enough money. He didn't think I was a good candidate, though, despite my money."

My face drained of color. "That's insane." I couldn't even imagine why any of the local sorcerers would want to marry me, but I didn't ask.

"Your brother will probably give protecting you a good try, but he's young, and still not fully trained."

I nodded, acknowledging the truth of that. "So what are you saying? I'm in danger and there's nothing I can do about it?"

"No, that's not what I'm saying. You're under my protection."

"I can't be under your protection. I already owe you more than I can possibly repay."

He reached across the table, and put his warm hand over mine, stroking gently. His eyes bore into mine, and I felt oddly captivated by them.

"So marry me," he said.

I froze, every cell in my body seeming to react at once. My fingers and toes tingled, my heart thudded painfully, my guts twisted, and my head spun. I couldn't breathe. My lungs began to burn painfully, but I couldn't take in any air.

I had to tell him no. I had to tell him that the other day, when I'd flung myself at him, had been a mistake. I'd just been upset and hadn't meant to imply anything between us. I couldn't be with him. I couldn't be with a sorcerer. How would I survive in a relationship like that, always the lesser partner?

No, my mind screamed. *No! The answer is no!*

I sucked in air, opened my mouth, and said, "Yeah, okay."

"You look a little off," Evan said. "Do you need to go back to bed?"

Somehow, I didn't think sleep would fix a thing this time. I kept trying to open my mouth to speak, to refute the words that had, despite my best efforts, emerged from my mouth, but nothing happened.

"Cassie?" Evan was by my side in the next instant, his hand on my forehead, as if checking for fever.

Nononononononono!

"Let's get you back upstairs." Evan pulled back my chair and effortlessly swung me into his arms. I didn't protest. I couldn't protest.

So marry me, he had said. And I, bound by magic beyond my control, could say nothing but yes.

I stared at his chest as he carried me up the stairs, unwilling to look him in the eyes and see what the rest of my life was going to become. I continued to refuse to meet his eyes until he laid me back in bed–his bed, I felt certain–and made the demand.

"Look at me," he said.

I looked.

"Where does it hurt?" he asked.

He didn't get it. He thought I was having some kind of relapse. It wasn't funny, but I laughed.

"Cassie?" Evan said.

Gradually, my body began to relax, until I no longer felt quite so strongly that I was going to explode. It took me a minute to figure out why, until I realized I was no longer trying to tell him no, to deny his will. As long as I didn't try to mention my feelings about the marriage, it seemed, I could say what I wanted.

"Cassie, please, tell me what's wrong."

"You wouldn't put it quite like that?" I said.

"What are you talking about?"

"You own me, but you said you wouldn't put it quite like that."

He took a step back, away from the bed. "No, I wouldn't."

"Then tell me to jump on one leg. Go ahead, I dare you. Or...or jump out the window."

I saw the moment understanding struck him. He took another step backward, and his face hardened, betraying nothing.

"You don't want to marry me."

I didn't even try to answer, though still, my head spun.

"Why not?" From the tone of his voice, he might have been asking me why my favorite color wasn't green.

My head spun a bit more, and my stomach began to feel dangerously as if it wanted to eject dinner.

"You don't have to marry me if you don't want to," Evan said, finally.

The nausea eased. My head stopped spinning, and I took a deep, steadying breath. I would like to have said I felt relieved, but didn't, not even a little bit. I had felt what he could do, and that was something I would never forget.

"Why not?" he asked again.

"Why do you think?"

"I spoke carelessly," he said. "I didn't realize how powerful the compulsion would be."

"It doesn't matter. I'm done with it. The whole thing. Your whole world. I'm done." I rolled over and shoved my face in a pillow.

"You think you can just walk away?"

I nodded against the pillow, thinking once again of that move to Chicago. I couldn't marry Braden, of course, but maybe I could take that job lead.

"You can't just walk away. You have the Scot name without the protection. Your Uncle John has had a few offers already, from people who would love the alliance. Not to mention-"

When he didn't finish his thought, I prompted him. "What?"

"Never mind. Look, Cassie, you're on your own, without any money or a place of your own to stay. I can take care of you."

It was exactly the wrong thing to say. Gritting my teeth, I said, "I don't want to be taken care of."

"I didn't mean it like that," Evan said.

Yes, he had. He had meant it exactly like that.

"I'd like to move in with Kaitlin tomorrow."

He took so long to answer that I almost thought he had left the room. I risked a peak from beneath the pillow, and saw his expressionless face, his defenses set against the world.

"Fine, you can move in with her, but I'm setting wards around the place."

"I think I owe you enough, don't I?"

"So much, this will barely make a dent." He began to stalk from the room, but paused in the doorway, turning to face me. "For the record, I'm not giving up on you."

I wasn't sure I liked the sound of that, but I had no idea what to say.

He stalked through the door, but I distinctly heard him say, in a muttering voice, "You do, at least, owe me a chance."

Epilogue

Evan Blackwood sat on the steps outside Kaitlin Meyer's new second floor apartment, having just finished laying the wards he insisted be in place before Cassie could move in. He felt exhausted. Not drained, as he had been a few days before, but certainly more tired than he should have felt. He hadn't slept in two days, ever since he and Cassie had argued, but he still didn't know if he felt angrier at her or at himself.

Maybe he had moved too fast or pushed too hard, but she had seemed willing enough when she'd flung herself at him the week before. Nothing had worked like he had planned it, but in that moment, he thought it might all be much, much easier. Then again, he'd thought they'd had a silent understanding for years, but then she'd said things were "serious" with Braden.

Now, here he was, trying to protect her from a distance, with wards built on a flimsy temporary threshold, and she didn't even understand the danger she was in. Her parents should have told her. Arguably, he should have told her, when he'd realized she didn't know, but she was already afraid of him.

As if that wasn't bad enough, her brother, Nicolas, had been one spark away from setting the building on fire. That kid needed someone like Henry Wolf to take him in hand, even more than Evan had. He would have loved to hate Nicolas, especially since Nicolas hated him, but he had too much respect for loyalty. It reminded him of why he had always wanted a brother or sister.

Evan was so lost in his thoughts that he didn't notice anyone emerge from Kaitlin's apartment. When the person tapped him on the shoulder, his first thought was of Nicolas, and he lashed out, instinctively, the potentially lethal force he manipulated as easily as air through his lungs throwing the intruder to the ground.

The high, feminine shriek alerted him to his mistake, and when he turned, he didn't see Nicolas pinned to the hallway floor, but Madison. Cursing inwardly, and wondering if the day would get any worse, he let her up.

"Are you okay?" Evan asked.

Madison took a deep, shaky breath, and nodded once, sharply.

"If you ever decide to talk to me again," Evan said, guessing she probably wouldn't, "you should remember that sneaking up on me is a bad idea."

She nodded again, scooting across the carpet to lean against the wall.

"I thought you were Nicolas." Evan didn't know why he felt the need to continue explaining. He would have liked to have one of Cassie's friends or relatives on his side, but Madison seemed the least likely prospect. "So, what did you want?"

"Just..." She glanced back at the doorway to apartment #4, where she had been helping Cassie unpack the boxes of clothes her brother had brought. "I was wrong about you. I'm not sure why everyone's mad at you, but I thought I'd tell you at least one of us is glad you saved her."

"Thanks." Now that he had the support of one of her friends, he didn't know what to do with it, but he appreciated it, anyway. What was it Cassie had said about her? She was lonely, and didn't trust easily. Evan could have described himself the same way, so he understood the effort she was making.

"I was also going to say you're not half as scary as everyone thinks, but then I changed my mind." To his surprise, she was smiling.

"It's safer that way," Evan said, returning the smile.

"Probably." Madison suddenly sobered, and she looked down at her hands. "But not for Cassie. I'm guessing she already knows better than to sneak up on you, and besides, you're in love with her."

Evan didn't confirm or deny the charge, because he wasn't ready for Cassie to hear it yet. Coming on the heels of everything else he had said to her, he thought adding that revelation would drive her further away from him.

The trouble was, her fears weren't entirely groundless. The life debt she owed him made it impossible for her to refuse anything he asked of her, and difficult for her to refuse anything she knew he wanted, whether he asked for it or not. All of which left him wondering, far more than whether or not she would fall in love with him, how he would know if it was real.

To complicate matters, there were greater threats out there than she realized, and the best way he knew to protect her was to stake his claim. She didn't know it yet, but he had done far more than ward her new apartment. He had warded her; he only hoped she never had cause to find out.

The door to #4 opened again, and this time Nicolas did appear in the hallway, though Evan did not react.

"We need to talk." Nicolas shot a meaningful look at Madison, who leaped to her feet and hurried back inside the apartment.

"What?" Evan asked.

Nicolas took a few steps closer, and lowered his voice, though his words were no softer. "I want to buy her debt."

Evan gaped at him, understanding the words, but unable to believe he was hearing them. "Are you crazy? Do you have any idea what I could do to you?"

"Yes, which is why I don't want you to have that kind of power over Cassie."

Evan revised his opinion of Nicolas to loyal, but stupid.

"No," Evan said.

"Look." Nicolas lowered his voice further. "I can offer an equivalent service. I can pay it off."

"Oh?" Evan was interested, despite himself.

"I can give you access to a true healer, anytime you need it. It could save your life."

Evan had suspected Cassie had a healer in her family, after the way she had healed from her attack in the swimming pool. And there was no question that it was a tempting offer, one that made Evan realize he had underestimated Nicolas's intelligence.

"It might not be a good idea," Evan said, half to himself. "Cassie's debt puts her under my protection, and she needs that right now."

"She's under my protection," Nicolas said, in an arrogant manner that highlighted his youth.

"What are you going to do? Half the single men in town are about to realize she doesn't have her parents to protect her any longer, and decide she'd be a great marriage prospect, whether she's willing or not."

Nicolas's face turned red. "That's ridiculous. She's a throwback."

Evan cringed inwardly at the offensive term, but barreled on. "If you say so, but I've never heard of a throwback in a family like yours, and there are rumors going around that might put her in danger."

"What kind of rumors?" Nicolas asked.

"That she's repressed, burnt out, or drained." Evan didn't expand further. There was no need. They both knew the value some men would put on a potentially powerful young woman with no active magic–that of a wife who could not threaten their own power but who could, nevertheless, help produce strong children.

"That's not true," Nicolas said. "Is that what you think? Is that what you want?"

"No." Evan practically growled the word. Although actually, he had toyed with the possibility that she might be burnt out, he couldn't imagine any scenario that would have left her drained or repressed, not in a family like hers. "Not that it matters. Even as a...throwback... she's got value. Odds are still good she'll breed true, and it's a hell of a lot more respectable than buying a drained woman off the slave market. Plus, let's not forget, she has access to many of your secrets. Such as, apparently, a healer in your family."

"I can protect her," Nicolas said. "And so can my parents. The disownment was in name only."

"If you say so. Luckily for Cassie, it's my decision now."

Nicolas clenched and unclenched his fists several times. "How are you better than any of the others? If you make her marry you, she'll hate you forever."

"As bad as you think I am, I'm surprised you'd think I care."

"You do though, don't you?"

Evan shrugged, unwilling to acknowledge the truth that, in the wrong hands, could be perceived as a weakness.

"You'll be better off letting her go. You can still protect her, if you really think you have to, and she won't feel so threatened."

"Maybe," he said, more to end the conversation, than to suggest his willingness to bargain.

"Why don't I just give you a few days to think about it?" Nicolas turned, and strode back into the apartment.

Evan didn't need to think, though, despite his reservations about how the debt complicated everything. If he were a better person, he would take the deal, leaving Cassie more room to refuse him, but, he realized, he wasn't that good a person. He wanted her, and while he didn't have her heart, yet, now that he had this much of her, he had no intention of letting her go.

End

About the author

Christine Amsden has been writing science fiction and fantasy for as long as she can remember. She loves to write and it is her dream that others will be inspired by this love and by her stories. Speculative fiction is fun, magical, and imaginative but great speculative fiction is about real people defining themselves through extraordinary situations. Christine writes primarily about people and it is in this way that she strives to make science fiction and fantasy meaningful for everyone.

At the age of 16, Christine was diagnosed with Stargardt's Disease, a condition that affects the retina and causes a loss of central vision. She is now legally blind, but has not let this slow her down or get in the way of her dreams.

Christine currently lives in the Kansas City area with her husband, Austin, who has been her biggest fan and the key to her success. They have two beautiful children, Drake and Celeste.

http://www.christineamsden.com

Don't miss any of these
other exciting SF/F books

➢ *Angelos*
(1-933353-60-0, $16.95 US)

➢ *Gaea*
(1-60619-183-7, $18.95)

➢ *Griffin Rising*
(1-60619-210-8, $15.95 US)

➢ *Griffin's Fire*
(1-60619-212-4, $15.95 US)

➢ *Shadows of Kings*
(1-60619-223-x, $17.95 US)

➢ *The Coal Elf*
(1-60619-216-7, $16.95 US)

➢ *The Immortality Virus*
(1-60619-003-2, $18.95 US)

➢ *The Nameless Prince*
(1-60619-243-6, $16.95 US)

➢ *Touch of Fate*
(1-931210-97-8, $18.95)

Twilight Times Books
Kingsport, Tennessee

Order Form

If not available from your local bookstore or favorite online bookstore, send this coupon and a check or money order for the retail price plus $3.50 s&h to Twilight Times Books, Dept. LS513 POB 3340 Kingsport TN 37664. Delivery may take up to two weeks.

Name: ______________________________

Address: ____________________________

____

Email: ______________________________

I have enclosed a check or money order in the amount of

$__________

for ______________________________________ .

If you enjoyed this book, please post a review
at your favorite online bookstore.

Twilight Times Books
P O Box 3340
Kingsport, TN 37664
Phone/Fax: 423-323-0183
www.twilighttimesbooks.com/

CPSIA information can be obtained at www.ICGtesting.com
Printed in the USA
LVOW08s1439211113

362271LV00002B/355/P